CW01559070

FUNNY BETWEEN

...the lines...the wines...the crimes

Karen Jay

*For the Easter Egg Hunters, the
bedrock of my life.*

CHAPTER 1

It started badly. Dulcie Staples struggled to yank the last piece of luggage from the back seat of her cab as rain fell in torrents, soaking her and all of her worldly goods. Dragging her suitcase out of the gutter caused rainwater to splash across the tottering tote bag, which rolled into a puddle in protest. The clouds above, having cheerfully dumped their payload, scudded across the sky in search of their next victim.

Brixton was filled with the smell of fried onions and damp leaves. 'Welcome home,' she thought.

Squinting up at the tall red-brick house on Minet Road, Dulcie took a long, deep breath and let out a sigh that fogged her glasses. Struggling to make out the shapes around her, she made her way to the stone steps at the front of the house. Years of feet and frost had hollowed out the centre of each tread, and the worn edges snagged at her suitcase as she heaved it towards the door. She paused halfway up when a memory surfaced: her as a child, sitting in this very spot with a lime and chocolate ice lolly melting down her arms, pooling into the creases in her elbows. Back then, the house had buzzed with voices, laughter, and the comforting hum of other people's lives. This time it wasn't a place to visit, but a place to stay. Great Uncle Les called it a 'temporary arrangement,' but no timeline was set.

The solid, story-book, suburban house had once belonged to Les's parents, and now stood as a patchwork of lives: the upper floors converted into rentals, while he kept the garden flat for himself. It was a place full of corners and quirks, but the real charm lay in the yard, where a large, timeworn outbuilding hunched in the garden like a sleeping giant. Dulcie had visions of coaxing it awake, turning it into a bustling workshop where she could hammer, tinker, and paint to her heart's content. That dream, among others, had persuaded her to become a resident of Flat 1, 67 Minet Road. Another reason was that her widowed uncle, always generous and thoughtful, had offered to let her stay rent-free while she found her footing.

With no fingers available, she pressed the doorbell with her elbow. Nothing. She waited a moment, shifted the bag teetering on her knee, then tried again. Inside, hurried footsteps clattered down the stairs, followed by a thump, a crash, and an inventive string of swear words.

The solid front door swung open. A young man, clearly not Uncle Les, stood in the doorway with a tea towel slung over one shoulder. He had an open, likeable face with a straight nose, deep blue eyes, and a broad mouth. His lips pursed together as he took in her appearance.

"You're not the curry," he stated.

"No," Dulcie replied, her coat gently steaming. "I'm Dulcie. Les's great-niece."

The man's eyes flicked to the bags. "Ah. Yes, he mentioned you. You're moving in."

There was a pause filled with the silence of two people trying to find their social footing. Dulcie extended her palm, which was awkward, given that her sleeve was sticking to her wrist. He accepted her hand and shook it quickly before stepping aside to let her pass. "Come in before you mildew," he said. "I'm Owen, from the second-floor flat," he added, nodding towards the stairs. He studied his new housemate. She wiped the rain from her cheeks with the heel of her hand, and he guessed that she was about his age, which was late twenties, perhaps a year or two younger. Her clothes clung to her slender frame, and her copper-coloured hair hung in damp, loose waves around her face. Dripping on the doorstep, she looked both annoyed and bewildered by her misfortune; an attractive redhead caught in a very British welcome.

"Les is in the lounge, probably napping through 'Bargains in the Attic' or some such. He'll have the subtitles on, but it's so loud, it's like being heckled by antiques." Owen stepped back to let her in.

Together, they entered a narrow hallway, painted in cheerful colours and showing signs of wear. The magnolia walls bore scuffs from passing bags and the bustle of activity. At the end of the corridor, a dark green door featured a well-used brass knocker, dulled with age. To the left, a staircase with a wooden handrail, once painted white but now faded to ivory, curved steeply upwards. The base

3

was marked by a newel post, its top smooth and polished by the hands of generations.

Almost immediately, the door to Flat 1 flew open, spilling the booming noise of a television from somewhere deep inside. Great Uncle Les stepped into the hall, looking exactly as Dulcie remembered. Short and round, he had the shape of a man well-acquainted with pies, siestas, and the comfort of a good chair. What little hair was left on his head clung in wispy grey tufts above his ears. With twinkling eyes and pink cheeks, a large nose dominated his face, its bulbous tip flushed purple with broken veins. He looked at them with an expression of happy anticipation.

"Is that you, Dulcie?" asked Les. "London's least likely to succeed?" His arms were folded across his chest, a mug of tea balanced on one elbow like a trained budgie. He studied her from top to toe. "You look like something rescued from the canal. I take it you got caught in the downpour?"

"I'll let you settle in." Owen helped her wrestle the suitcase across the hall, then straightened up, looking at her with a friendly smile. "Shout if you need anything. Like towels. Or naan bread."

"Thanks." She brushed damp strands away from her forehead. "And… sorry for not being the curry."

He grinned. "Still holding out hope."

Owen skipped up the staircase, and Les reached out to take one of Dulcie's bags.

"Thank you so much for letting me stay," she said, setting the other bag down and pulling the suitcase painfully over her shins. "I'll keep out of the way."

"Don't be daft. You can keep in the way. Long as you like."

4

Les squinted at her untidy auburn hair. "What have you done to your face? It looks different."

"I treated myself to a fringe, a different haircut, to celebrate the beginning of my new career. What do you think?"

Les looked thoughtful. "Well, I suppose it will be all right when it's finished." He squinted at her wet coat, gesturing toward the rooms behind him. "You should come inside before one of those modelling agencies catches sight of you and puts you on the front page."

As Dulcie stepped into her new home, she inhaled a familiar mixture of furniture polish, laundry detergent, and lavender soap. Once upon a time, Great-Aunt Margaret's L'Aimant perfume had been part of that comforting blend. Three years had passed, but her presence still lingered, like the fading scent of a cooling campfire.

Les had vacuumed the carpets twice that morning. Not because they were especially dirty, although he had discovered a surprising amount of vintage fluff, but because it felt like the sort of thing Margaret would have wanted. He dusted the photo frames on the mantelpiece, carefully lined up the coasters, and opened the back windows to let in some fresh air. A tea towel was neatly draped over the draining board, precisely as she had always left it. These small acts were his way of honouring her memory. And, honestly, they gave him something to do while he awaited Dulcie's arrival.

"Right then," he slapped his hands together like a man about to assemble a cabinet without instructions. "First things first. You look like you need to dry off. The spare room's still at the end of the hall. Remember the little step; it's one of the quirks of the place."

5

Dragging the reluctant suitcase and balancing both bags, Dulcie made her way to the room and immediately tripped over the step.

"Bit of a rite of passage, if you'll excuse the pun," Les called cheerfully. "I don't know why the hallway isn't level, but these old houses are full of mystery. And woodworm. And draughts from the windows, but you'll find that out for yourself soon enough."

The spare room possessed an old-fashioned charm. Faded floral wallpaper, curling at the edges, patterned in shades of rose and cream. Along one wall stood a heavy oak wardrobe, its mirror dulled with age. The bed, framed by a high wooden headboard and dressed in a striped duvet, gave a protesting creak as Dulcie heaved her suitcase onto it. It was the sort of room that seemed quietly considerate, unwilling to impose too much personality on its guest.

Off came the damp coat, which she hung on the hook behind the door, leaving it to drip silently onto the carpet. She pulled a thick, cheerful jumper splashed with bright colours and a pair of soft leggings from the suitcase. A towel, neatly folded at the foot of the bed, was used to rub the rain from her hair. Speckled with droplets, her glasses were placed on the bedside shelf before she carefully prepared her contact lenses and slipped them in. As the room came into focus, the chaos of the day started to loosen its grip.

Physically, she was feeling so much better—no more tingling fingers or complaining toes. But deep down, something still felt a bit off. Weeks of careful planning had gone into this move, and she kept telling herself it was the

6

fresh start she needed. Yet now, with everything in place, the excitement had fizzled out, and reality was weighing on her, a feeling of discomfort below her ribs.

The house felt both reassuringly familiar and oddly strange. It had been a place visited during the holidays, when it smelled of roast dinners, pine needles, or sun cream, depending on the season. She had never imagined living here, yet there she was, standing on the brink of a future she hadn't expected, in a house she had always thought she would merely pass through.

Catching her reflection in the mirror, she gave a firm nod. "It's time to pull the big-girl knickers on and get started," she said aloud to herself. With a deep breath, she turned from the mirror and stepped out of the room.

In the lounge, the television blared at full volume, shaking the windows with the drama of a soapbox race. Uncle Les sat hunched forward in his armchair, elbows resting on his knees, trying to influence the outcome with the power of thought. Eyes fixed on the screen, he watched as a blur of go-karts thundered toward the finish line, chased verbally by a breathless commentator.

Dulcie walked in and paused by the arm of the sofa. Les didn't look up. He shouted at a competitor dressed as a hot dog, who was bringing up the rear. "*Avoid* the haybale, don't head for it!" With wild abandon, the go-kart driver gripped the sausage-shaped steering wheel and veered into the safety zone, sending plastic bread buns flying. Uncle Les looked at her, then pointed the remote at the television and switched it off.

"Never bet on a racing team called 'Bangers and Smash," he

advised, sadly. "Turns out, it's not a double bluff. Are you all dried off?" When she nodded, he picked up the remote and switched off the television. The sudden silence was startling. "Right," he said, standing up with a slight grunt. "Come along. Let's get some lunch."

They headed into the cosy kitchen, a bright and inviting space where sunlight streamed through a ripple-effect window, casting playful patterns on the spotless surfaces. Beneath the cabinet, a row of mismatched mugs hung next to a cheerful Toby jug. Blue-and-white checked curtains stretched across the sink's base instead of cupboard doors, which was Aunty Margaret's resourceful solution to the lack of space. The room smelled both sweet and sour, as if something had been pickled there. Possibly an urban gherkin. Possibly Les.

On the wall above the drainer was a small wooden plaque, which read, *Today is the tomorrow that you worried about yesterday... and all is well."* Once, the words had seemed meaningless. Now, they felt prophetic.

Lunch was served with a fanfare usually reserved for weddings: tuna sandwiches, ham, bread rolls, half a family packet of cheese and onion crisps, and a hearty jam tart.

"Wow, this all looks very... filling," Dulcie remarked, eyeing the buffet as she sat at the wooden table, which had seen better days. Dark brown and sturdy, its glossy surface has dulled over time, marked by pale, milky rings made by countless hot cups. Faint scratches crisscrossed the top, indentations from Aunty Margaret's shopping lists. Les handed her the cutlery from the drawer before settling into his chair with a contented sigh.

"I want to say how pleased I am to have you here." He offered her a plate. "Truly. It means a great deal to me." Each word had been carefully chosen. "This old house has great charm," he continued, glancing around the room, "but it will be better with you in it. The tenants here are decent folks, and they're already looking forward to meeting you." He chuckled softly, tapping the side of his nose. "I may have let slip once or twice that my great-niece was coming to stay."

Lifting a slice of ham onto his roll, he started spreading mustard as if it owed him money. Leaning forward, elbows on the table, he looked at her earnestly. "Dulcie," he said, keen to show his grasp of the subject and the breadth of his vocabulary, "you becoming a millennial recycling entrepreneur is a fantastic idea. I want you to know, I support your ambitions."

"I really appreciate that, Uncle Les. This is such a big change for both of us, but I'll do everything I can to fit in." Her eyes twinkled. "Mum has given me lots of instructions on how to behave, and if we ignore *all* of those, I think we can make it work."

"You're probably right," he grinned. "I think we will get along fine." He took another bite of his roll, the mustard hitting the back of his throat like a boxer landing a punch. "You've got a keen eye and an enterprising spirit running in your veins," Les declared. "We've always been a family that can turn our hands to anything. 'Make do and mend' has been our motto." Glancing up from his empty plate, he added, "If there's anything you need, I'm your man. I even have a plan for how your business can operate. You can start by collecting plastic from around the streets here. Things like bottles, containers, garden gnomes, if they're hollow."

"Gnomes?" Dulcie raised her eyebrows.

"If they're discarded," Les added quickly. "Then, take all of it to the big workshop in the garden. My old pigeon shed, as was."

"Mum said that shed hasn't seen a pigeon since 1998."

"Exactly! Loads of room. We can convert it into a mini-processing plant." Les was undeterred. "Wash the plastic in buckets, melt it down with a heat gun or something. I'm still figuring out that part. Then, it can be moulded into new items, like plastic coasters in the shape of local landmarks. Sustainable, unique, and perfect to sell at the Sunday market.

Dulcie took another bite of her sandwich. Chewed. Swallowed. "Let me get this straight. You think I should melt bits of plastic with a heat gun, in a timber-framed building?"

"Temporarily, he agreed, undaunted. "I'm sure we can sort something out," Les crunched on a handful of crisps, his thoughts racing. For the first time in a long while, his mind was full of possibilities. "I've even got a name for your business," he announced proudly.

"Alright. What were you thinking?"

Uncle Les leaned back in his chair, a gleam in his eye. "*Shed Happens: Plastic Reborn.*"

"Brilliant," she declared. "The perfect name for a recycling centre with highly flammable headquarters." Laughing merrily, she added. "Even though blowing up your garden does sound like the most tremendous fun, Uncle Les, we might have to rethink." She hurried on, hoping not to discourage him, "My idea focuses on upcycling rather than recycling. I'm trained in refurbishment, French polishing, and fine finishes. The plan is to transform furniture that would otherwise be thrown away," she continued, "there's good money to be made, if you know what you're doing."

"One of those 'starts-in-a-shed-made-millions' type ventures?"

"Exactly! Retro furniture, all upcycled. Think Paris flea market meets Peckham Rye."

"I'm not sure about that. My shed mostly meets dry rot and cobwebs."

"Perfect. Exactly the atmosphere I'm hoping for," Dulcie gave him a thumbs up.

"Oh well, sounds very 'green', I suppose." Les poked the last bit of bread roll into his mouth with a stubby finger. "A modern Rag 'n' Bone operation. Once, it was horse-drawn carts, men ringing bells, and calling out as they went. You'd throw any old stuff you had on the back, and they took it away. Not that you could do that now. The buses would get in the way for a start…"

Lost in nostalgia, he absentmindedly chased crumbs around the plate before reaching for a glass pudding bowl etched with leaf patterns around the rim. Using a fish slice, he cut into the jam tart and served himself a generous wedge. With deliberate care, he sprinkled a fine layer of granulated sugar over the top.

"Does it need sugar?" enquired a surprised Dulcie.

"Certainly, it does," Les ladled a second spoonful over the crust. "If there is one thing I've learned in life, it's that everything tastes better with a bit of 'scrunch' on the top." He studied his cup, looking at the surface it rested on. "Could you maybe have a go at this table?" His hand lovingly stroked the veneer. "It was once Margaret's pride and joy, and I'd like to see it restored to its former glory."

"I'd be delighted. It's a lovely piece," she said, genuinely pleased. "My tools are arriving tomorrow, and I could get straight on to it." During her training, she'd upcycled a similar table, sanding it down and painting it with a bright, eggshell finish. Eyeing the formidable heirloom in front of her, she pictured it in soft pastel swirls. Elegant, yes. Fresh, certainly. But would Uncle Les judge the result as if she'd glued rhinestones to a church pew?

"Hold your horses," Les held up his hand. 'You can't start yet; what would we have our dinner on? It'll take a bit of thinking about. But if you want to make yourself useful, there's a job you can take on for me." Les had been pondering how to steer the conversation towards the errand he had, in truth, delegated to her before she arrived.

"Name it."

"Go and say hello to Big Maccie in the basement," Les pointed at the floor. "He'll sniff you out otherwise."

"Big Maccie?" Dulcie hadn't heard the name before.

"Aye," Les now adopted a flaky Scottish accent. "Detective Sergeant Duncan McCallie from over the Borders," he said, rolling his 'r's. "He's an ex-copper, retired allegedly. But I've seen him inspecting vans that have overstayed their welcome. He's going to hospital for a couple of days tomorrow; nothing serious. The thing is, I've agreed to feed his cat while he's away." He reached the heart of the matter.

"To be honest, I think I'm allergic. Cats always make me sneeze. I wondered if you could take it on? It would be easier for you to go up and down the stairs with your young legs," he continued. "I've told him you'll be around. Why don't you pop down now and introduce yourself?" He sat back, with the air of a man who had gift-wrapped a chore and called it a favour.

Dulcie narrowed her eyes, unconvinced. "Cat?"

"Yes," Les was offhand. "Enormous tabby thing. Bit temperamental, but I've heard she only scratches if you look at her too long."

Dulcie opened her mouth, then shut it again. "Right," she narrowed her eyes. "And... how will I know if she's in a scratching mood?"

"You'll know." He tapped his spoon on the side of his plate for emphasis. "She never leaves room for doubt, and Maccie has the scars to prove it."

"I suppose I'm not really in a position to say no, am I?"

"Nope," Les patted her cheerfully on the shoulder. "Go on, pop down and say hello. Tell Maccie you've accepted the role of cat caterer. He'll be thrilled, though the cat might have a different opinion." Les made a 'cheers' motion with his mug and winked at her, shuffling back in his chair like a man delighted with the world and everyone in it.

CHAPTER 2

Leaving Les to do the washing up, Dulcie grabbed her coat from the hooks by the stairs and opened the front door. The latch clicked reluctantly, as if the house disapproved of any comings and goings. Big Maccie's flat sat separate from the main house, tucked away in the basement; a remnant from the days when tradespeople used the back entrance and households relied on coal. Back then, every house on the street boasted a practical lower level, perfect for storing firewood, tin baths, and disillusioned servants.

Stepping outside, she saw Owen struggling with an overloaded bicycle, trying to push it up the stone steps one wheel at a time. Tall and lean, he had narrow shoulders and long arms, suggesting he could lift a chest of drawers, but would likely regret it. A mop of chestnut-brown hair fell over a face that was turning red from exertion, as the uphill bike-wrangling continued.

"You've got your work cut out there," she called to him, "but I'm rooting for you."

Owen looked up, recognised her, and explained: "The chain has come off the damn thing. One way or another, I'm going to have to carry it up." He wriggled the handlebars in frustration. "Why do all the houses around here have staircases, inside and out? And why did I choose a second-floor flat? Not exactly ideal for a cyclist."

"Masochist," Dulcie agreed instantly, then realised she had called a total stranger a masochist. "I mean, structurally. Architecturally, masochistic," she stammered.

"Right," Owen's eyes were dancing. He pulled the front wheel higher, and it repaid his efforts by locking into a forty-five-degree angle.

"Here, let me help with that," Dulcie offered, stepping toward the bike. She tried to lift it gracefully, as if she were accustomed to shifting heavy, mechanical things. Instead, she only succeeded in tilting it to one side, and with the flair of a magician's trick, the left pannier sprang open in response. A cascade of books, pens, and notebooks spilled down the steps. They both stared at the untidy heap.

"Well," Owen mused, "that's one way to unpack."

Dulcie fell to the floor, fumbling with paperbacks and files. "I'm so sorry, I didn't realise this thing was booby-trapped."

"You've triggered the Literature Defence System," he said, crouching beside her and snatching up a copy of 'Best Beloved' before it could fall into the gutter. "You're lucky it wasn't the poetry satchel. Those are hardcovers."

She glanced up at him. A streak of bike grease marked his cheek, and his eyes twinkled as she fished a soggy notebook out of a puddle. Unfazed by the chaos, he collected the remaining books and slipped them into the leather bags attached to either side of the bicycle.

"Is this the part," she asked, "where I offer to carry your things upstairs to make amends for my mistake?"

"Only if you promise not to dislodge any more vital documents," he said, zipping the last of the scattered books back into place.

"I make no such promises, but I'll do my best." She grabbed the front of the bike, steering the handlebars as if born to guide rusty relics into tight stairwells.

Together, they heaved the bicycle and its heavy saddlebags over the threshold and staggered up to the second floor. Owen stood on the landing, breathless, not just from hauling his bike up two flights of stairs, but also from the unexpected company.

"Well," she said, brushing a strand of hair from her cheek, "I feel like I just signed up for the weirdest gym in town. It may surprise you to know that I don't often manhandle bicycles on weekdays."

"Really? You did it so well." Owen teased back. He shrugged as he unlocked his flat. "It's a vintage model bicycle and I've had it for years," he added. "I'm too fond of the old workhorse to part with it, but if I pedal extra fast, the chain flies off in protest."

"It's charming," Dulcie said. "Ideal transport for a man about town – an antique with attitude."

She was funny. Owen felt the familiar tightness in his chest, the one that whispered, Oh no, not this. He'd sworn off complications, hadn't swiped right in months, and definitely wasn't open to new prospects. But Dulcie had that deadly mix of dry wit and bright eyes which always sidestepped his defences. He could feel himself leaning towards the inevitable, and couldn't decide whether that was exhilarating or deeply unwise.

"Thanks for the help," he said, parking the bike against a coat-covered hatstand that tilted in protest. "Can I offer you a cup of tea, or is that too predictably British?"

She hesitated. Tea was still sloshing around in her system, but she felt it would be rude to refuse, and her new acquaintance was shaping up to be good company. "A quick cup would be lovely. I was on my way out to run an errand, but I can stop for a swift drink and precisely one awkward attempt at small talk."

"Oh, I can deliver at least two awkward attempts," Owen said, gesturing her inside. "I'm a part-time lecturer. It's practically a core skill."

Flat 2 resembled the one Les lived in but was brighter, featuring modern furniture and contemporary art posters on the walls. Owen opened the door with a flourish, wheeled the slightly traumatised bicycle inside, and made a grand gesture towards the rooms.

"Welcome to my domain," he said. "Please ignore the stacked boxes, stuffed shelves and general clutter."

"Smells like cinnamon," she sniffed as she stepped further inside.

"Ah. That would be the candle I lit to mask the smell of our chip-shop supper last night. It was like living inside a fish finger."

Her eyes swept over his cluttered flat and noticed

clothes strewn in a pile, plates that needed washing, and an embroidered pillow that declared, 'Busy making other plans' in fluorescent orange. Across the room, a tall bookshelf was crammed into a narrow alcove, overflowing with a jumble of colourful hardbacks, battered vintage volumes, and paperbacks stacked in every direction.

"Literature or folklore?" she asked, pointing at the book spines.

"Both," he said. "I teach a course on mythical tricksters and the tragedies of their poor dating choices. It's eerily autobiographical."

"Sounds like a riot," she smiled, plopping down onto the couch. The sofa, oversized for the small room, had a metal frame and futon-style padding. Dulcie settled into the cushions and glanced around. Every corner was filled with more books. A small corkboard on the wall displayed handwritten notes and yellow Post-it notes, half of which read things like "buy light bulbs" and "never trust a lettuce".

She pointed. "Should I ask about the lettuce thing?"

Owen looked at her gravely. "You ever bought lettuce with the full intention of using it and then watched it decay into green slime, while you lie to yourself for six days straight?"

"Every, single, time." Dulcie agreed. "So, have you lived in this flat long?" She asked

"A couple of years." He delivered the freshly brewed tea and settled into the armchair by the bookcase. "I moved here when I started at the university. My specialism is fairytales," he grinned. "I tell people it's a choice made to balance my excessively macho mindset."

"Interesting. That would also explain the ten-ton, boys-only bicycle," she smiled back. "My specialism is pretending to work from home. Well, I will be working from home," she corrected herself. "Here. Soon. I'm setting up a new business."

"Perfect. You're the kind of modern antihero I teach my students to analyse. Someone who follows their dreams and goes against the normal constructs of society. I may have to make you into a case study."

"Oh good," she said. "Please assign me a tragic backstory. I've always wanted to be haunted, but I never found the time." She was enjoying their back-and-forth chat.

"I'll get to work on it," he promised. Owen sat in the armchair, nearly eye to eye with Dulcie. She was half-turned towards him, with sunlight streaming through the window above, casting her in a golden glow. Her fingers, slender and precise, bore the marks of manual labour, with reddened knuckles and scuffed nails; a Venus with mortal hands.

"This was worth climbing the stairs for," Dulcie commented brightly. "Your place is nice. Who needs clean lines and minimalist furniture?"

"Yeah, I guess you could say that it's… lived in." Owen scratched the back of his neck.

"Lived in by both of us, as it happens," said a new voice. A Greek god strode out of the bathroom with a towel across his shoulders, wearing nothing but a pair of shorts. Leaning against the wall, he had the casual confidence of someone accustomed to turning heads. His physique seemed more sculpted than muscular—lean rather than bulky, like a living statue. With a jawline that looked as if carved from marble, his smile could make headlines.

19

Dulcie's eyes flicked upward, and she reacted instinctively to the newcomer. She made an effort not to stare, but it was hard to act casual when someone so breathtaking appeared out of nowhere.

"What's going on in here then?" Asked the vision. "I step into the shower, and when I come out, a charming stranger appears in the lounge." Pulling a sports top over his head, he added, "Excuse my state of undress, I didn't realise we had a visitor."

"Hi Tristan," Owen said. "This is Dulcie, the girl I was telling you about. The one who has moved in downstairs."

Dulcie smiled politely and held out her hand.

"Nice to meet you!" Tristan's grip was firm and friendly. "The girl who was supposed to be a Chicken Tikka Bhuna and a Peshwari naan?"

"That's me." Dulcie confirmed, her voice warm and light, "It's been nice to meet you both. Owen has been very kind and made me tea"

Glancing at Owen and then at Dulcie, Tristan threw his towel onto a chair. "He's really kind, though a bit clueless, but that's part of his charm. You're the first attractive young woman he's brought to the flat in a while."

"Thank you for that, mate." Owen protested.

"I guess that's a compliment of sorts." Dulcie's eyes sparkled. "I'll take it."

Owen winced. Sharing a flat with Tristan was generally a good thing, as he was easy-going, financially stable, and had an almost mystical talent for keeping the fridge stocked. But as a wingman, he was the worst, given that Tristan always looked like he had his own invisible spotlight. Owen stood and wandered over to the open window, fiddling with the blind as if it desperately needed realignment. It didn't.

Flopping onto the sofa beside Dulcie, Tristan stretched out and positioned his arm casually behind her head. He launched into a story about riding the night bus home, missing his stop, and the strange chain of events that ensued. Dulcie laughed, leaning in, clearly engaged. Owen gave the blinds one last, unnecessary tug before returning to the armchair across from them, dropping into it with a bit more force than needed. "So, Dulcie," he said, interrupting Tristan's story about hitching a lift on a scooter, "you mentioned something about a new venture. What kind of work do you do?"

Dulcie sat up a little, the question catching her off guard. She hadn't intended to explain her plans tonight, but since he had asked, the urge to explain and perhaps show off a little was irresistible. "I'm going to upcycle furniture," she said. "Find old, unwanted pieces and fix them up. Paint them, repair them, give them a new life."

Genuinely puzzled, Tristan tilted his head. "Up… what now?"

"Upcycle. You know, like recycling but… fancier? Instead of just throwing things away, you put them back together, better than before."

"Oh, right," Tristan nodded slowly, trying to recall if he'd heard that word during one of his gym sessions podcasts. "Like, making old kitchen dressers look cool again?"

"Exactly," Dulcie said. "I love giving things a second chance. Plus, it's creative, and I get to work as my own boss. Doesn't hurt that it's environmentally friendly, too."

"Sounds pretty awesome." Tristan moved his arm lower, so that it was brushing the back of her neck. "Do you paint furniture all day, or is there some kind of magic involved?"

"The magic is mostly in not smashing your thumbs with a hammer. But in general, things only need a little tender loving care."

"I get that," Tristan nodded thoughtfully. "Like when I fixed my phone screen… well, actually, I took it to a repair shop, but still…" He nodded slowly as she launched into her story. Something about turning old junk into… not junk? Interior design for those who apparently couldn't afford new stuff. "Yeah, yeah, makes sense," he said. He furrowed his brow and pursed his lips like a man lost in thought. Long ago, he'd discovered that if your expression is serious enough, people stop explaining things to you in detail.

"So, you'll be working outside, or rather in the outbuilding?" Owen re-joined the conversation. Something clever or charming to say would be good at this point, but nothing came. His mind fumbled, blank where wit should be.

"Yes, that's the plan," Dulcie said. "I want to make it a proper workspace, away from distractions. The only challenge is that I'll need to refurbish the shed a bit before I can start working on anything inside it. Les has been keeping all manner of treasures there. He can't bear to part with so much as a bent nail, in case it comes in handy."

"My dad was the same," Tristan said. "I wonder what else we have in common?"

Owen ferociously tugged at the blind, causing the slats to clatter against each other.

Hey, mate, you should try upcycling too," Tristan said, giving him a pointed look. "That old chair in your room could probably become something cool, with a bit of attention."

"I think that chair is probably too far gone to save." Owen returned his look with a piercing one of his own.

Oblivious to any building tension, Tristan leaned back, flashing his perfect smile once more. "See? I'm already throwing out ideas. If you ever want help with the shed, just let me know," he added with a wink. "I'm always willing to lend a hand for a worthy cause."

"Thanks, it's always handy to have input," Dulcie said, although it generally wasn't.

Looking up, she noticed the time on the kitchen clock. "Wow, is it that time already?" She placed her cup down with a gentle clink, brushed her hands over her jumper, and stood up. "I'm supposed to be calling on Big Maccie in the basement flat. I was on my way there when I ran into Owen and helped rescue his bike." She turned and headed for the door. "Sorry to dash, but I really should get going now, if you'll both excuse me?"

Owen jolted upright, driven by a sudden need to do something, anything, to leave an impression on this lovely girl. He attempted to open the door for her, but she was faster, already halfway there with her graceful stride.

"Dulcie," Owen called, louder than he meant to.

She paused, hand still on the doorknob, and turned back toward him.

"You're new to the area, right?" he asked. "London can feel a bit tough at first, on the social side – the whole 'surrounded by people but still alone,' kind of thing." He hurried on, "The point is, there's a pub just down the road. It's called The Witch & Stable, and we're both meeting a group of mates there next Friday night. You're welcome to come along too, if you'd like. No pressure. Moderate pressure. Just... medium pressure."

"Is that one of your awkward attempts at small talk?" Dulcie asked.

"I haven't even warmed up."

"Alright then. Sounds fun. Thanks." With a quick look over her shoulder, she stepped out into the hall and disappeared from view.

Tristan followed her exit with his eyes, then glanced at Owen and whistled softly. "Living here just got a lot more interesting; don't you think?"

CHAPTER 3

The entrance to the basement flat nestled discreetly below street level, concealed behind a low wrought-iron gate and a steep brick staircase. Gripping the rust-speckled handrail tightly, Dulcie descended to the small landing, which was scattered with fallen leaves, many forming a pile against the dark red front door. Above the doorframe, a tiny canopy protruded, decorative rather than functional against the weather. She rang the doorbell, and the sound echoed through the basement flat.

Inside, Maccie stiffened. He rose from his chair with the careful precision of someone who knows their muscles are no longer taking requests. "That'll be her," he informed the indifferent feline who shared his home. Moving carefully, he opened the door, bracing for any strain it might cause. Dulcie stood there like a springtime crime scene: a long yellow jumper, green leggings, and a bright smile.

"Hiya! You must be Mr. Maccie!" she said brightly.

"I'm Maccie. Drop the Mister. Makes me sound like a headmaster." He gave her a long look. "And you must be the niece."

Big Maccie had an impressive build and looked like someone who had once been nimble on his feet. Younger than Dulcie expected, he was probably in his early fifties, yet still muscular and square-jawed. His impressive height and broad shoulders were clearly the cause of his nickname. With a clean-shaven head and smooth, clear skin, the strong shape of his skull emphasised the bold lines of his face. A neatly groomed beard framed his jaw, trimmed close along the cheeks but fuller around the chin and mouth, with streaks of silver running through the dark shadow of stubble.

"Pleased to meet you." Dulcie held out her hand.

"Are you, indeed?" He sounded doubtful, but shook her outstretched hand. "Normally, I'd ask you to prove who you are before you gain entry, especially given you are about to have access to all ma worldly goods. But I've seen your photo. Les has been flashing it since he heard you were coming to stay. You'd better come in, hen."

Maccie held the door open, stepping aside to let Dulcie pass. "Watch your step, the carpet's a wee bit uneven there. I've been meaning to fix it."

The flat was unmistakably a bachelor's residence. Not like the one Owen and Tristan shared, but in the no-nonsense, comfortably cluttered way of a man who knew exactly where his TV remote was because it hadn't moved in six years. Framed police memorabilia lined the walls: old commendation certificates, grainy black-and-white photos of moustached men in uniform, and a proudly displayed Metropolitan Police cap, preserved under glass.

"Make yourself at home," Maccie closed the door with a practised flick. "You want a coffee?" he asked. "Or something stronger? I've got whisky older than most of my neighbours."

Dulcie politely declined, glancing around the shelves filled with books on crime, sport, and a pristine cookery book. A set of fine porcelain dancers and a pair of painted plates rested on the top shelf of a wall unit. All the furniture was sturdy, mismatched, and old-fashioned. In the corner, a brown leather armchair loomed like a retired general, facing the telly with unwavering loyalty.

"This is Missy-Mae Meowski," he gestured towards a tortoiseshell cat, lying supine across the top of the chair. "Missy to her friends. Don't touch her without asking. She hates dogs, other cats and the woman next door. In that order."

The cat stared at them both, lazing on the armchair like a sunbathing lion.

"You behave yerself," Maccie muttered, addressing his pet. "This young woman will be popping in to look after you whilst I'm away. No scratchin'. No climbing the curtains. No murderin' the porcelain ballerinas, OK?" He said, glancing at the cabinet where the delicate figurines balanced on their toes in pastel agony. He had inherited them from his gran. Or perhaps her gran. The memory was hazy.

Missy-Mae opened one eye, then closed it again, deep in thought.

"You met the boys upstairs yet?" Maccie asked, grasping for conversation. "Good lads, the pair of them. And at the top of the house, there's Jamila Odhiambo. She lives in the attic flat. Works at The Witch & Stable. Strong as an ox, sings like a dove. She's a really good sort. Your uncle has a lot of time for her, as it happens.

"I haven't met Jamila yet." Dulcie wondered whether he was hinting at something.

"Oh, you will. This house is like a crewed ship. You hear everything and get involved with everyone." Maccie assured her. "And Kay Kenneths lives next door. She's appeared in lots of telly programmes. Dunno if you remember her from the "On Location" series on TV?" His voice was low, the gentle burr of his Scottish accent softening the edges. "Probably before your time, and probably before Noah sailed by, two-by-two, come to that. She thinks she's still famous. Bit stuck-up."

"I'll be sure to curtsey." Dulcie bobbed slightly on her toes.

Maccie cracked a smile. "Good. You're not completely soft, then. Anyway," he seemed keen to end their meeting, "I appreciate you looking after the cat whilst I'm away. I've left her food on the kitchen counter; everything you need is in there. Here's the spare key to the front door." He handed it over. "I'll be taking myself off to the hospital later today, but she is all set for now. If you could pop down tomorrow, that would be grand. I shouldn't be more than a day or two away, unless the cure is worse than the cause."

Dulcie gave the key a little rattle with her fingers, the way people do to show they have a firm grip on a precious item. They shook hands with surprising formality, and she spun on her heel. "Right! You go and get yourself fixed up. I'll hold down the fort."

As the door clicked shut behind her, Maccie frowned. "I don't trust anyone who smiles that much."

The cat purred in agreement.

CHAPTER 4

Armed with determination and cleaning supplies, Dulcie followed her Uncle Les into the back garden, like a new apprentice entering a head office. In this case, the foyer was filled with dandelions the size of hamsters and dominated by a rotary line creaking mournfully in the breeze. Dulcie thought that naming her new home 'the garden flat' had given the shabby backyard delusions of grandeur.

"Right," Les waved an arm towards a large, timber-framed outbuilding which dominated the space. "There she is. The Old Girl. Bit rough round the edges, but she's stood longer than most of our prime ministers."

"This is so exciting. I love her." Dulcie took in the dimensions of her new premises.

Les snorted. "You would, you're easily pleased. Come on then."

Inside the workshop, the air smelled of dust, old varnish,

and a faint hint of pigeon. A few long-abandoned crates lined the back wall, with faded stencilling that read "Champion Flyer. Speckled Sally, owned by Les Staples, 1984. Flight time 5.5 hours."

"Those crates saw glory," Les puffed his chest with pride. "One of my girls flew from Carlisle to Croydon in five and a half hours—Olympic standard for wings.

Beyond its contents, the space itself had great potential. It was well-built and durable, with a concrete floor and two shuttered windows. There was a sturdy workbench, a functioning tap, a worn but operational sink, two modern plug sockets, and a light switch.

"It's perfect."

"I don't know about perfect, but it's practical," Les corrected. "The electrics were installed so Margaret could use a twin-tub machine on wash days. It would bounce across the floor like a demon on the spin cycle. Now and then, she'd do arts and crafts out here too, 'I'm just pottering,' she'd say." He sighed at the memory. "It got too cold for her in the winter, mind. But I suppose you'll be alright, what with all the lifting and shifting you'll be doing."

The following hour was spent airing out the place, dragging the pigeon crates outside and sweeping away years of sawdust, spider webs, and assorted clutter. In the corner, a small crate held a pair of children's wooden stilts, a tiny metal tea set, some skittles, and a selection of beanbags marked with the word 'Evelyn' in black felt-tip pen.

"Did these once belong to my mum?" Dulcie asked.

"Yes! I'd forgotten about those. Your Great-Gran used to

31

keep them here for her to play with when she was little. Gran had a real soft spot for your mum, who was named after her, as it happens. Everyone called them 'Big Evelyn' and 'Little Evelyn'. I put those toys aside for your mother to collect on her last visit, but she told me her cottage was too small to take them."

Rather than assist Dulcie with the clearing and cleaning, Les sank into the worn, candy-striped garden chair, which was set like a throne on the last patch of grass. His self-appointed task was to offer helpful criticisms from a safe distance, and he took pride in being rather good at it.

"Too gentle with that broom," he called. "You're not petting a hedgehog."

"Thank you, oh wise one," she nodded at him, fruitlessly. "Don't mind me, I was born to sweep like Cinderella, on my own, with no help."

"And bend your knees when you pick up those heavy sacks; you don't want the curse of a bad back."

"I've got a few curses already, and you'll be hearing a loud one in a minute," she muttered. "What about all these tools? They look like they've stood here so long they're taking root."

"Mind the spade, Dulcie! That one's older than you and twice as rusty," Uncle Les called out from his gently swaying seat. He fished a well-thumbed Racing Post from his jacket and slid a pencil behind his ear, torn between pretending to be the site manager and marking his bets.

Dulcie paused while pulling out a tangled mass of old garden netting. "Why do you have a scythe?" she asked, holding one up between two fingers, as if it were infectious.

"Ah! That was for the cabbage front." His eyes twinkled beneath his flat cap. "Back in the day, this garden was a fortress. Rows of spuds like trenches, carrots like bayonets. And rabbits—oh, the rabbits were the true heroes."

"Please don't start giving me the full history, Uncle Les," Dulcie pleaded.

Too late. He had already taken up his storytelling stance: arms crossed over his stomach, face turned towards the sky, and one foot wagging rhythmically.

"We had twelve hutches down the back. You could hear the whole lot twitching at dawn like they were preparing for roll call. But they were a docile lot, for the most part. Except for Sandra, she kept us on our toes."

"Named after Sandra Dee?" Dulcie knew Les was a fan of the American icon.

"No, after my mum's friend at the Women's Institute. Clever little madam, that rabbit. Escaped three times. First time, she ended up in the coal scuttle. Smelled like soot for a week."

Dulcie leaned against the shed doorframe, intrigued despite herself. "And you kept them for fur?"

"Fur and stew." Les was lost in reverie "Your great-aunt Mabel had a recipe that could turn rabbit into something that tasted like the nectar of the gods. Onions and a bit of wild garlic; delicious. My dad sold the pelts to a man in Bermondsey who claimed he made gloves for the troops.

"Grim." Dulcie frowned; she could do without the finer details.

"It was the war. Everything was grim. Rationing went on for years after D-Day. Hobbies had to be productive. I was born later, of course, but I took on the rabbits when I was old enough. We kept them going for years, but in the end, no one was buying."

"Did you make much money out of them, back in the day, I mean?"

Uncle Les let out a wheezy bark that sent a robin flapping indignantly from the guttering. "We made *plans* for the rabbit money. Dreamed of it. New shoes, a radio, even a bicycle. We used to spend it in our minds several times over, but like any other kind of money, it wasn't elastic and never stretched that far." He gazed wistfully at the patch of lawn, which nowadays was occupied mainly by weeds, three empty plant pots, some trailing ivy, and a lone splash of colour from a vermilion rose. "It was hard work, mind. You had to be careful with breeding. Get the pairings wrong and you'll end up with so many little critters that you had to start tagging them alphabetically." Until now, he had forgotten that he'd given them all names, despite his parents' strict advice.

"What letter did you get to?"

"Q. for Queenie"

"I'm not sure I believe half of what you say." Dulcie sniffed.

"That's because I only remember half of it," said Uncle Les cheerfully. "The rest I embellish. You can't let too many facts get in the way of a great story."

Dulcie held up an old enamel mug that read *"Dig for Victory!"* "What happened when the war ended?"

"The rabbits won!" He laughed at his own joke. "Not really. We carried on with them for a long time, but I got too busy to help out. I'd discovered the delights of the fairer sex by then, and I got my HGV licence and began driving lorries for a living. My dad used the last of the hutches for firewood." Uncle Les carried on with his anecdotes until Dulcie opened a box labelled 'Shed – Misc (Important??)' and pulled out a single, shrivelled carrot.

"Ah, 1943 vintage," he nodded at it sagely. "You can still taste the Blitz."

After another hour of hard work, sweat beading on her brow and a minor incident with a rogue nail and her elbow, Dulcie stepped back to admire her progress. "She's going to be a wonderful workshop. I can feel it," she declared. With the floor now cleared, the area both inside and outside felt wonderfully spacious. In her mind, she envisioned each phase of the restoration process unfolding, with distinct sections for sanding, painting, and finishing. All that remained was to add the new contents.

"She's breathing again," Les admitted.

"Now for the next steps."

"We'll start by asking the neighbours if they've got any old furniture they want gone," Les read her mind.

"Exactly," Dulcie perked up. "But I don't want just to go knocking on doors."

Les eased himself against the pillows. "So, what then?"

"Once I'm up and running, I'll use all the online socials to promote the business. But to start, I'm going to have to go old school: a leaflet drop." She had given it a lot of thought. "Nothing fancy. Simply asking if people have old furniture they don't want. I'll collect it."

"You're the expert," he conceded. "There's a shop on Percy Road that does a decent job. They offer instant printing, as long as your project isn't urgent, important, or printed in colour. But the manager is a mate of mine, so I'll ask him to pull out the stops."

"Perfect. We'll be a proper operation by tomorrow."

Taking one last look at the cleaned and organised workshop, Les gave a short, satisfied sigh. "Alright then. Let's get the next chapter underway."

They returned to the flat, and Dulcie went directly to her room, eager for a shower. Covered in dirt from hours of hauling, sweeping, and trying to organise the chaos in the backyard, she was longing to feel the splash of hot water on her skin. Les, meanwhile, made a beeline for the kitchen like a man on a mission. They met at the table, where mugs of tea were poured with military precision, and a pack of Bakewell Tarts was deployed to boost morale. Dulcie opened her laptop, and Les plonked down a battered notebook labelled "Ideas & Lists."

"We'll need a headline," Les searched for inspiration. "Something bold. Impactful. Rousing. How about adding in a family name?" he suggested. "What about 'Staples for Salvage'? In my day, most businesses had family names like 'Timothy Lewis and Sons.' No? 'ReDulcieated?' I suppose that's a bit forced. A bit naff."

Dulcie scribbled, crossed out, and pondered. "Second Chances," she declared. "Simple. Like the furniture. Like me." She thought for a moment, trying to picture exactly what would grab attention. Something punchy. Something persuasive. Something that didn't make her sound like a woman who once tried to reupholster a wingback chair with nothing but a glue gun. She needed to inspire them to take action and contact her. Then she typed:

'Got Old Restorable Furniture? We Can *Refurbish, Recycle or Get Rid.'*

"Not bad," Les granted. "Now include something about being Brixton-based, or you'll get calls from all the posh folk in Camden who can't be bothered to go to the dump."

Dulcie added to the wording: 'Local, reliable & just starting out – let us give your old treasures a new life!'

"Very you. Bit sentimental. But worth a whirl." He dunked a biscuit with the satisfaction of a man offering invaluable advice.

They planned the drop: starting with Minet Road, then the three long streets on either side, one leaflet per letterbox — unless it was guarded by anything larger than a West Highland White Terrier. Neither fancied getting their ankles bitten in the line of duty. They could afford to wait before expanding their patch, if they got a good response. The last thing they wanted was to overpromise and end up with a house full of broken furniture. Les offered to assist with the mailshot, saying he'd join in for moral support, which Dulcie assumed meant he would walk alongside her, enjoying a chinwag, while she handled most of the posting. Meanwhile, her workspace was prepared, and her message was ready for launch. She was eager to see if the world was prepared for someone with a shed, a sander, a toolkit, and the drive to transform the world one broken chair leg at a time.

CHAPTER 5

The main doorbell rang as Dulcie was placing a bolt of calico and a box of upholstery foam on top of her wardrobe. She gave the bulky items one last push and went to answer the call. Padding out in her stockinged feet, she made her way into the cool, echoing hall and walked to the front entrance.

At the same time, a tall shadow materialised at the top of the stairs. Tristan came down as if in a coffee commercial —wearing an artfully wrinkled shirt, tight jeans, and that effortless charm which seemed to cling to him like static.

"Hiya," he said, catching sight of her and flashing a smile that had no right being so bright at that time of day. "I was just heading out."

"Is that so?" Dulcie brushed a curl off her cheek. "And here was I, thinking you'd heard the bell and were expecting a line of starlets, clamouring for your attention."

He grinned. "You say that like it hasn't happened before."

Dulcie rolled her eyes and opened the door.

A deliveryman stood holding a large cardboard box that looked as though it wanted to collapse in on itself. "Delivery for... Dool-sy?"

"Dulcie," she corrected, signing with a flourish.

He handed over the box with an apologetic grunt. "Bit of a lump, this one."

Dulcie grasped it, bracing herself for the weight, but she still staggered backwards under its heft.

"Whoa, there." Tristan's arms were under the box before she had a chance to protest. He didn't even seem to notice how heavy it was. The container, which had momentarily threatened to end her, now appeared as light as feathers. "Were you planning on deadlifting this into the kitchen, or has Les ordered a small car?"

Dulcie straightened herself with as much grace as she could muster. She noticed how his bulging forearms tensed at the edges of the box, and how his shoulders shifted beneath his shirt. Her stomach did an inappropriate swoop, like a rollercoaster with a poor safety rating.

"It's mine," she explained. "Tools. Paint stripper. A small lathe."

"Planning to update the décor in your flat, from its current 1950s vibe?"

"It's for the furniture, to use in the workshop." She reached forward to take the package back. "It's no problem, I've got it —"

"I've got it." He was already turning with the parcel in his arms as if it were weightless. "I was heading out anyway, just not through the back garden," he smiled reassuringly to show it was no trouble.

Watching him walk out into the morning light, she chose not to protest further. If a handsome hunk wanted to carry heavy loads for her, it wasn't the moment for indignant feminism. After all, she was only human. Grabbing her trainers, she followed him outside. They went through the snicket between the tall, brick-walled houses, where the scent of grass carried a hint of mint, thanks to a stubborn patch of wild herbs growing along the fence.

"So," Tristan glanced over his shoulder, "you're settling in alright? Still speaking to your uncle?"

"I am," she jogged a couple of steps to keep up with him. "So far, so good. Though his idea of 'settling in' included watching me clear out the shed, single-handed."

They arrived at the back gate. Dulcie dug the key out of her pocket, her elbow brushing his arm as she leaned in closer than necessary. Entering the yard, Tristan surveyed her small setup, taking note of the solitary garden chair, the stacked firewood, and the discarded clutter. He placed the box down with a loud thud. "There you go. All yours, Miss Projects."

"Thanks. That was good of you. You didn't have to."

"I know." He rubbed the sides of his arms. "But I couldn't miss the chance to be chivalrous to someone who appreciates a bit of muscle. A little box like this is one is a mere bagatelle to a man who can deadlift his own body weight."

"You think I'm easily impressed?"

"Maybe not, but I think you're the kind of person who judges a man by whether he can pick out a Phillips head screwdriver."

"...I mean, can you?" Dulcie asked.

"No," he admitted, grinning. "But I make a decent cocktail, and I can lift heavy things."

"I'll keep that in mind."

"Good. Because given the chance, I intend to make the best kind of screwdriver for you, the kind you can drink. Shaken, not stirred."

"I'll hold you to that, Tristan."

"I'm relying on it." Cocking his head, he offered her a smart salute and turned back along the way they had come. Dulcie watched him go, her heart doing things it really shouldn't over a man who, by his own admission, regularly missed the last bus home. Turning back to the box, she tore open the flaps and pulled out her prized lathe. It was solid. It was perfect. It was upside down.

CHAPTER 6

Armed with Dulcie's advertisement, copied onto a USB stick, Uncle Les set off to the print shop first thing the next morning. Meanwhile, Dulcie was assigned to check on her promise to feed the downstairs cat.

Big Maccie appeared to be a nice chap, and Dulcie was eager to build a good relationship with the people she would be living with. with. However, she regretted agreeing to be on pet duty the moment she reached the basement flat. The air inside was thick with the smell of feline activity and the scent of forgotten tinned fish.

"Missy-Mae?" she called, voice cracking like a nervous Victorian governess. "I come in peace."

A shadow streaked across the floor. A low meow followed.

"There you are," Dulcie murmured, spotting the cat crouched behind an upturned laundry basket. Amber eyes locked onto hers, wide and unblinking. Ears half-back, with a disdainful expression, Missy-Mae remained perfectly still, curled up like a discarded cottage loaf. "What's up, Pussycat?" she whispered, cautious that speaking loudly might break the safe mood. "I'm the temporary food human. And I have snacks." She extended a single treat, which she set down gently, like an offering at an altar. A paw moved forward hesitantly, then withdrew. Backing off, Dulcie turned and headed to the sink, pretending to browse her phone as she looked sideways at the basket. "You need fresh food. And I need to clear my lungs." Leaning over the sink, she pulled the window handle and pushed it open. Clean, sweet air poured in. Missy-Mae saw this as an unexpected stroke of luck and shot out through the gap like a guided missile.

"Oh, for the love of…Missy! Missy! Missy-Mae! Come back!" Dulcie reached out despairingly from the window just in time to see the tabby cat's rear end vanish over the garden wall. Snatching up the door key and running as hard as she could, Dulcie dashed out of the flat, onto the pavement and through the alley between the houses and began the chase. Missy was a blur of fur, weaving along the tops of walls and darting across the paving stones, with the speed of a spy on the run and the cunning of a hunted weasel.

Racing around to the back of the buildings, past communal bins, a scooter with a lovingly duct-taped seat and a forlorn supermarket trolley, the two of them engaged in a chase that led them into the next street in double-quick time. Scanning the area with frantic haste, Dulcie stopped and looked for any sign of Missy, calling her name and parting bushes like a naturalist on a new planet. Finally, in the ginnel between the terraces, behind the last bin, two glinting eyes stared out.

"There you are," Dulcie breathed, crouching slowly like someone trying to defuse a bomb made of whiskers. "No sudden movements. Let's just be cool." She inched forward with her hand outstretched.

Missy twitched her nose and looked hopefully at the extended fingers. Given that there were no treats on offer this time, a brief standoff ensued. Then, miraculously, she jumped right into her arms.

"I *am* the Cat Whisperer," Dulcie announced, weak with relief.

Cradling Missy like a disgruntled bag of sugar, she returned to the flat, deposited her inside, and locked the window. She poured kibble into a fish-shaped bowl and watched the unabashed cat gobble it up eagerly. Even though their escapade had lasted only minutes, the food disappeared at a rate that suggested Missy was a long-term convict who had starved whilst on the run.

With her main objective completed, Dulcie took a breath, steeled herself, and approached the final, most dreaded task: the litter tray. It was... full. Spectacularly full. A grand achievement of feline digestion. She used a small scoop to transfer the clumps into a little sack, tied it shut, and held it away as if it might detonate. Outside, she marched towards the bins, swinging the bag as far from her body as physics would allow. Unfortunately, the corner had a hole in it. A steady trail of greyish litter dotted the concrete behind her like the breadcrumbs in one of Owen's fairytales.

"Brilliant," she muttered. "Could today get any better?"

Aiming to sweep the trail into the gutter, she kicked at the mess, sending clouds of dust swirling around her boots. By the time she reached the bins and threw away the offending item, she looked as if she had lost a fight with a gravel pit. Back at the flat, Missy-Mae was perched on the windowsill, grooming herself smugly. Dulcie pointed at her. "You're lucky you're not mine. And to be alive. And not posted to Belgium." She locked up, trudged back to her flat, and collapsed onto the sofa with a groan.

This initial attempt to please her Uncle Les had gone poorly. Her intentions were good, but she hadn't covered herself in glory. Releasing the pet that she was responsible for and running around the streets like a madwoman wasn't going to earn her any brownie points. She'd learned a few lessons: cats are faster than they appear, bystanders often gawk or record instead of helping, and emptying litter trays demands caution and an unbroken carrier bag. The next time Missy needed feeding, the doors and windows would stay firmly shut.

CHAPTER 7

Armed with a canvas tote overflowing with supplies, including a bottle of water, a leaflet distribution map, and a stack of freshly printed flyers, Dulcie and Uncle Les took to the streets as though born to the job. Dulcie took out the first copy and gave it her undivided attention. The paper was a little too white, and the font lacked character, but the cartoon of a wobbly three-legged bench added a touch of whimsy. She marched up to the house next door to theirs, on the east side of the terrace. This was the home of Gerald Waring, the road's self-appointed guardian of lawns, lamp posts, and proper bin placement. Small in stature but mighty in indignation, he ran the Neighbourhood Watch with the zeal of a man who believed society was only a stray dog poo away from collapse.

Slipping the leaflet into the letterbox, Dulcie paused for a moment, then pushed it halfway through. The door swung open suddenly, as if Gerald had been waiting behind it with his forehead pressed against the wood.

"You there!" He was gesturing toward the slot. "What do you call this?"

She blinked. "It's a leaflet."

"I can see that." He pulled it out and held it up with two fingers. "It's litter. You're putting litter into my home." Gerald looked at her as if she had delivered one of Missy's specials through his door.

"It's information," Dulcie tried to explain. "About furniture upcycling."

Gerald gave her a hard stare. "Do I look like a man with broken furniture?"

She regarded him. Smart trousers, buttoned shirt, and slippers with a natty tartan design. "Honestly? You *do* have the look of a man who has a cracked side table somewhere."

His eyes narrowed. "Well, I don't." He crossed his arms.

"Alright," Dulcie conceded. "You can recycle the flyer."

"Not the point," he snapped. "It's unsolicited."

Behind them, Uncle Les appeared on the front path, surveying the scene with a seasoned eye. He was the sort of man who could size up two opponents in a wrestling ring in a heartbeat, but, looking between Gerald and Dulcie, he wasn't sure where he'd place his bet. Perhaps, he concluded, this was less of a match and more of a standoff, and it might be time for him to step in as referee.

"Morning, Gerald," he greeted his neighbour cheerfully. "Why so chipper?"

Gerald unfolded his arms and waved the piece of paper at them. "I suppose this is the niece you were talking about in the pub last week. You didn't mention she is launching a pamphlet campaign."

"Brilliant, isn't it?" Les enthused. "Got you socialising before eight-thirty in the morning. That's a new record."

"If I wanted a leaflet, I would have asked for one."

"But still," Les added, "if you *do* have any wobbly chairs, she'll take them off your hands. Do you have anything in the wobbling department?"

Gerald gave them both a long, pained look, folded the leaflet in half as though it might be contaminated, stepped back inside, and firmly shut the door.

"Don't worry about him, love. It's being so cheerful that keeps him going." Les adjusted the strap of his bag. "Only sixty-three houses to go. I'll take the left side," he declared, striding off with the confidence of a man who had once canvassed for an independent council seat and knew no fear.

Moving briskly along Minet Road, Dulcie tucked the bundle of leaflets under one arm and slipped them through letterboxes one by one, many of which seemed to bite back, snapping at her fingers. Sticky gates and squealing, rusty hinges couldn't deter her; she ducked and dodged past overgrown hedges and cluttered doorsteps. In an hour, the job was done, and they headed home, with Les grumbling that his feet were on their last legs. By lunchtime, a text arrived:

Hi. I've a small cupboard & bookcase for u 2 collect if u like. Marjorie Donaldson @ No. 52 Gordon Grove.

Dulcie beamed, holding out her phone to show her uncle

the result of their labours. "Success! I can't believe someone has responded already."

Les nodded sagely. "If there's one thing I've learned in life, Dulcie, it's that exciting things happen when you make them happen. I knew it wouldn't take you long to get going. And so—it begins."

The next day, it truly did. Dulcie borrowed a parcel trolley from Les to aid her first collection. It was a large wheeled contraption, used to move compost or cases of bulk-buy lager. She headed out to gather the promised donations.

The bookcase on offer was crafted from solid pine and carried the scent of old potpourri. The bedside cupboard that matched it was covered in stickers and lacked a door, but Dulcie saw promise in its rounded edges and squat shape. She wheeled both of them home like trophies from a game show. By Wednesday, she had fully committed to being a woman of enterprise. She had purchased a new outfit, consisting of dungarees and a work shirt with big buttons. To complete the look, she added a tool belt which hung from her waist and a lead pencil to tuck behind her ear. She also trimmed her fingernails short into a neat, practical shape, which she regarded as a sacrifice both mature and slightly heroic.

But with great ambition came the spectre of admin.

"You'll want to get a licence," Les said at breakfast, whilst he buttered his toast. "Or a permit. Something official-looking. Otherwise, someone'll report you for running a 'furniture racket' out of a domestic back garden."

"Who would do that?"

"Janice up the road," he pointed with his crusts.

"She reported me once for 'unconventional topiary,' the miserable old hatchet face. She had it in for me, just because the lads upstairs have the occasional party. Can't stand to see other folk enjoying themselves."

"Was it unconventional?" Dulcie couldn't imagine what form that would take.

"I shaped her autumn hedge to look like a witch's hat. It wasn't personal, it was seasonal," sulked Uncle Les.

Dulcie wasn't entirely sure if a permit was needed, but if her uncle wanted her to find out, she was happy to oblige. An online application would save her from a trip to the civic offices, with its fluorescent lights and plastic chairs, but it also meant waiting weeks for a response. Dulcie was eager to begin, which meant an in-person appointment with numbered tickets, passive-aggressive posters, and the hum of shared boredom.

With a sense of foreboding, she headed for the bus stop at the end of Minet Road, which was more of a sheet of graffiti-covered plexiglass than a proper shelter. She spotted Owen before he noticed her. He was standing at the stop, hands in pockets, shoulders hunched, a paper carrier bag dangling from one wrist.

As she approached, Owen looked up. "No bike today? Where's your noble steed?" she asked.

His expression shifted from brooding to one of defeat. "Gone," he said flatly. "Someone nicked it."

"What? *Your* bike?" Dulcie tried not to sound amazed that

anyone would want to pinch such an ancient old crate.

"Lifted it right off the front step. I left it briefly when I popped back up to the flat. I was only gone sixty seconds, just enough to grab a copy of 'Mabbs Cautionary Tales', which is somewhat ironic, since I should have been more cautious myself." Owen sounded exasperated. "When I came out, it was gone."

"That's rough. I guess it's just not your day."

He caught her eyeing the paper shopping bag he was holding, which was slightly wet at the bottom. One corner of a pre-packed sandwich poked through.

"I'm picking up groceries for a friend," he explained. "I had already bought a few items and packed them into the saddlebags on the bike. Perhaps the bulging panniers made it an irresistible target."

"Something must have done. Who would want it otherwise?"

"Helpful. Thanks. That makes me feel *so* much better." Owen looked slightly annoyed, then he conceded the point. "If it was the food they wanted, then I suppose someone really needed it. Desperate times." He gave a slight, resigned shrug. "I ran up to Bunces' shop to replace what I could, and now I'm massively behind schedule."

"So let me get this straight. Your bike got nicked, you're late for work, and you still stopped to pick up someone else's shopping?"

"I said I would," Owen replied, as if it were obvious. "She can't manage on her own. I'd feel worse if I didn't."

"What happens now? Have you reported the theft of your bike to anyone?"

"No point. It's not worth much. The groceries probably cost more to replace. In fact, the more I think about it, the more I believe it might have been the food they were after in the first place. Either way, it gives a whole new meaning to 'meals on wheels."

Dulcie studied him. His shirt was creased, his left sock halfway down his ankle, and his hair was doing something indecisive. Unkempt and miserable, he looked like a noble, gracious knight in crumpled clothes.

She gave him a gentle nudge with her shoulder.

"You're kind of a sap, you know? A worthy, caring one, of course, but perhaps you should try being a little more cynical."

"I've been told," he said, his lips twitching. "I'm working on it. Don't tell anyone. It'll ruin my image."

"What image? You've been robbed of a bike almost as old as a penny-farthing, you're wearing sleepy socks, and you own a bookmark that says 'Librarians Do It Quietly." Her tone was light and teasing, attempting to lift him out of the slump that had settled on his shoulders. "I think your reputation can survive." She watched him for a moment longer before turning away, puzzled by the fact that her heart had just given a little flip. What would an entire day with him be like, she wondered? Not just a quick chat at a cold, smelly bus stop, but an actual date. Coffee, conversations, perhaps a casual lunch at a cosy spot with mismatched chairs and a view of the park.

"I'm sorry about what's happened," she said. "Really. That sucks. You know what they say about 'no good deed goes unpunished,' and it sounds to me like you've experienced the truth of it."

"I suppose it's one of those things, but I could have done without it today." Owen gave a small, strained smile that didn't fully reach his eyes, but it was a noble attempt nonetheless.

A city bus approached from the main road, emitting a low, mechanical groan as it slowed to a stop. Rounding the corner from behind the bakery, its wheels ground against the pavement. Owen stepped forward and stuck out his hand, fingers splayed in that half-confident, half-hopeful way regular bus riders seem to perfect. The vehicle came to a stop at the curb, releasing a pungent cloud of exhaust fumes that drifted across the tarmac and into the morning air.

He looked at her. "You waiting for this one?"

She shook her head. "No. I'm off to the council offices. Hoping to get an official permit to trade from the workshop."

"Of course you are," he said, stepping toward the bus as it let out a sharp hiss of compressed air. A mechanical whir followed, then a soft thud as the doors folded open, revealing the dim interior with its scuffed flooring, faded seat fabric, and the scent of warm upholstery. He paused at the foot of the steps.

"Dulcie?"

"Yes?"

"Do you want to—" He caught himself. "Never mind. I mean, I wanted to say... I'm looking forward to going to the pub with you. And the others." He lifted his hand in a small wave. "I'll see you around?"

"I only live one flight down. You'll definitely see me around."

He gave an awkward nod before vanishing inside. The doors stuttered to a close, and the bus pulled away, leaving Dulcie standing on the pavement, watching as he was swallowed up and carried away in the wheezing belly of the bus.

CHAPTER 8

The council building was a dull, grey block, unwelcoming and squat. Inside, a sign read "Take a number," and below, someone had scribbled, "and a deep breath." Tearing a ticket from the grey dispenser, she took her seat on one of the moulded chairs, which were bolted to the floor. Time slowed. A staff member walked past wearing so many lanyards that he looked like a human keyring stand. He headed to do battle with the office photocopier, which took up the challenge with relish. After ten minutes, the machine had cheerfully eaten several documents, wrapping them around the internal brushes, and celebrated by lighting up every button on its menu. Now covered in sprays of ink from the toner, the employee slammed the lower door shut on the machine and conceded that the Xerox had won. Giving up the unequal fight, he stalked off, thereby ending the only entertainment that the room offered. After that, Dulcie counted the ceiling lights and examined each leaflet in the nearby rack so thoroughly that she felt qualified to stand for election.

Next to her sat a man of average height and slim build, wearing a beige overcoat and a football scarf. Leaning over, he said, in a confidential whisper, "I'm here because they rejected my girlfriend's conservatory. Told us it was too imposing." No subject was too dull or insignificant for him to discuss at length. When his name was finally called, Dulcie had to stop herself from cheering.

In time, she was summoned to a desk by a woman who enjoyed rules, not just knowing them, but enforcing them, preferably without any exceptions.

"Name?" she demanded, peering over her spectacles.

"Dulcie Staples."

"Nature of business?" asked the clerical officer, her face as stony as the marble busts in the corridor behind her.

"Er... upcycling. Furniture restoration." Dulcie stuttered, her face beginning to flush.

"Do you intend to trade from your premises?" Thus far, the woman seemed unimpressed.

"Yes. Well, sort of. It's more... passionate salvaging."

The administrator sighed and settled back in her chair. Having a sense of humour would have disqualified her from her job. Besides, she dealt with would-be jokers daily and was an expert at dismissing them quickly. She pressed on with the questions, unmoved.

"Do you intend to make a profit?"

"Eventually. In a small, joyful way." Dulcie was still trying to lighten the mood.

Her interrogator believed she had the measure of this

opponent. "You'll need Form 76-B. Possibly 91-C if your hammering exceeds permitted decibels."

Dulcie began to sweat. "How loud is passion, legally speaking?"

Handing her a stack of papers so thick it could deflect a crossbow bolt, the clerk allowed herself a smirk of satisfaction. "Return these with copies of your risk assessment, waste disposal plan, and a drawing of the premises."

"A drawing?" This was a surprise.

"Doesn't have to be good," the clerk said, indifferent. "Just accurate. No stick men."

Staggering outside, clutching a stack of forms, Dulcie caught the bus home in a daze. That evening, Uncle Les found her sitting at the table, surrounded by papers, and asked how she had fared. "I'm not sure if I've started a business or joined a secret society." She lifted the papers, slightly dropping them in her arms to exaggerate their weight.

Les peered at the rules and regulations. "Oof. That's a lot of ticking," he sympathised. "I'd say a challenge that calls for refreshment." He fetched the ever-reliable biscuit tin. It was fair to assume that form-filling would usually be done online nowadays. However, if it had to be done the old-fashioned way, he knew they would need to keep up their strength with Hobnobs and Custard Creams.

"I don't even know what a 'Class 3 Repair Zone' is," Dulcie moaned. "Why is there a section on poultry?"

"Standard form." Les dunked his snack. "They use the same one for egg farmers, scrap dealers, and falconers. Just tick

'No' unless you plan to reupholster a chicken."

By suppertime, the documentation was filled in. Dulcie had sketched the workshop, with some artistic licence, had devised a waste plan involving a skip, and ticked "No" to poultry thirteen times.

She gazed at the final line: 'Business name (if applicable):"

Taking a deep breath to mark the solemnity of making her company official, she wrote: "Second Chances."

"This must be how Lord Sugar felt, once upon a time," Les speculated. "Start small and grow fast. Then before you know it, you'll be on the telly firing people with a pointy finger."

Later that night, Dulcie posted the forms in the letterbox, sealed in an envelope brimming with hope and biscuit crumbs. She wasn't sure how long the approval process might last. It could be weeks or months, or perhaps until someone found the paperwork during a distant audit. In the meantime, she saw no reason not to respond to anyone willing to trust her with their family heirlooms.

Lying in bed that night, she hoped the morning would bring more messages from potential customers; otherwise, her time at the council had been wasted. She set her phone alarm, in case success decided to turn up early. Success did turn up, but not until midday, when a note was pushed through the letterbox of the main door.

From: No. 61 Minet Rd
Subject: Some stuff!
  Dear Dulcie,
Mum's got a single-door French armoire in the back room. She

says you are welcome to it for free, and if you take it away, you can have some of her second-class redcurrant jelly too. (It's very tasty, just a bit runny.)
Best, Amaya Lainy

It was precisely the kind of note she had been hoping for. Although the council may require a complete audit and the approval process could be lengthy, today felt like a victory. So far, two people had reached out to her about upcycling, and Missy had been fed without escaping, scratching, or biting. In about a week, she would head to the pub with two attractive housemates to meet others her age, marking the beginning of her new social life. Everything, it seemed, was going remarkably well. From experience, she knew that this usually meant something was about to go terribly wrong. But for now, she intended to enjoy it.

CHAPTER 9

The only apartment Dulcie hadn't visited in the whole house was No.3, the top flat. With a crumpled leaflet in her hand, having squeezed it at least three times between the first and second flights, she walked up the stairs to the attic. The smell of toast and shea butter drifted across the landing, and someone inside was humming—not a melody Dulcie recognised, but a soft, bouncy tune that suggested: this is a happy place.

She took a deep breath and rapped hard on the door.

A brief moment went by before the door swung open with a faint creak. Standing there was a tall, graceful East African woman in her late fifties, with a confident, upright posture. She greeted her visitor warmly, with an enthusiasm usually reserved for long-lost relatives or deliveries of champagne.

"Hello, my darling!" Mrs Odhiambo beamed at her. "You must be Dulcie."

"Er—yes. Hi." She offered the leaflet. "I live downstairs with Uncle Les. I thought I'd... introduce myself. And give you this."

Mrs Odhiambo accepted it with a flourish. "Oh, wonderful. Come in, come in. Call me Jamila, everyone does."

Dulcie entered a home brimming with personality, where vibrantly patterned throws and cushions were artfully arranged across low, inviting furniture. Woven baskets decorated a shelf by the window, and the walls displayed vivid, abstract artwork and line drawings which illustrated stories from distant places. A small radio on the windowsill played a lively highlife song, with notes that hung in the air, scented by the breeze.

"This place looks fabulous! I love your style."

"Thank you, sweetheart." Jamila gave her a wink. "I like to be surrounded by things that remind me of home. Kenya, originally, but I've been here long enough to develop a taste for marmalade and rainy Sundays." She ushered Dulcie to the centre of the room. "Please, take a seat. Will you take some refreshment?"

Dulcie nodded and settled onto a pouffe decorated with what appeared to be kente cloth. Tucking her feet beneath her, she took a moment to observe the intricate details around her, delighting in the hand-carved rhinos on the side table, the colourful beaded curtain at the kitchen entrance, and a stunning Kitengela glass vase filled with fragrant yellow freesias.

"You want ginger or lemon?" Jamila asked from the kitchenette, her head half in a cupboard. Her voice had a light, gravelly edge, like pebbles shifting gently on a shoreline.

"Ginger, please," Dulcie replied, hoping for herbal tea but prepared to be surprised.

A low hum emanated from the free-standing freezer, and a whispering gust of air flowed across the roof and through the open window of the attic flat.

"I've run out of the good stuff," Jamila said, emerging with two mugs and a glass jar of crystallised ginger slices. "But these are fiery enough to take the edge off." She passed a mug to Dulcie and settled on the other end of the low, squashy sofa, legs tucked up like a cat. The tea had a murky tint and a spicy kick, which suited the ambience of the room.

A dog collar hung on the wall by the bookshelf. It was a simple, cracked leather loop with a small brass tag. "That belonged to Toots. He was a funny-looking little thing," Jamila said, following Dulcie's gaze. "Fox-red coat. Stumpy legs. Silky ears like flaps in a wind tunnel."

"Did you have him for a long time?" asked Dulcie, who loved dogs and had grown up with an Old English Sheepdog and, more recently, a lively little cockerpoo.

"Twelve years. Which was long enough for him to believe he was in charge of absolutely everything." She sipped her tea. "He had strong ideas about my bed. It needed sharing."

"Was he bossy?"

"Opinionated. Also, rather gastric. I fed him charcoal biscuits for the last three years. Flatulence like a small engine. No warning. No shame. I'd be reading, he'd let one go, and I'd pretend it was the plumbing."

Dulcie laughed softly. "Did it help?"

"The charcoal? A bit. I'm telling you, I used to think, 'Oh my days, two sniffs of that and you're greedy! But he couldn't help it" Jamila threw her head back and laughed.

"He must've been very loved."

"Indeed, he was. Still is. I talk to him sometimes."

A pause followed as Dulcie watched her hostess add another slice of ginger to her cup. Jamila moved gracefully; her generous curves highlighted by a bias-cut dress. Her sleek, inverted bob of jet-black hair framed her face, with sharp angles emphasising her high cheekbones. Scarlet nail polish on her manicured nails tapped rhythmically against her teacup.

Jamila pointed to the far corner, where a small woven basket sat next to a half-deflated football.

"That was Toots' happy place. In the daytime anyway. He slept with his nose in that basket and his hind legs hanging out. Always half-finished, that dog. He loved it here, even if he didn't have a garden." She raised one finger for emphasis, "You know, the one thing I miss about living on the top floor is not having a patch of my own, full of flowers."

"I know what you mean. The yard here is practical rather than pretty. I used to do gardening when I lived at home." Dulcie said. "One summer, I worked in the greenhouses at a stately home. It was lovely—I spent my days packing pots with soil, planting seedlings, and helping to set up displays of fruit and flowers for the visitors." She had enjoyed that job, even though it was short-lived.

"A stately home," Jamila chuckled "Girl, that might be taking things a bit far for me. People dream about life in a big country house, but I've always thought it would be like living in an empty hotel." She shook her head. "I'd settle for a small patch of earth and a few pots."

They sat in silence for a while, listening to the occasional thud of pigeons landing on the roof. The flat was high enough to feel separate from the world, yet it wasn't isolating—a peaceful oasis at the top of a noisy, chaotic house.

"Will you be living with Les now for the foreseeable future?" asked Jamila.

"Hopefully, yes," Dulcie replied. "He needs someone to keep an eye on him."

"Really? That's funny. I always got the impression he thought he was the one doing the looking after."

"He pretends he doesn't need help, but last night I saw him fall asleep in his chair halfway through eating a sandwich."

"Oh, that man. Grumpy as an old goat when he wants to be, but soft underneath it all. He likes to moan about my cooking, you know, but last week I caught him sneaking a third helping of my Mutura. I told him it's quite a smoky sausage, and he said, 'It's not one of my favourites, but it's not too bad...probably better with chips.' Jamila shook her head at the memory. "Now, let me see this flyer of yours properly."

She unfolded the paper as if it were something of great importance. "Second Chance: Upcycling for Homes with a Heart.' Oh, I like that. Got a lovely ring to it."

"I'm hoping so," Dulcie tried to sound casual. "It's early days, but I've already got a bit of interest."

Jamila nodded as she read. "I like your idea. Make do and mend, but with flair."

"That's exactly it," Dulcie agreed emphatically. "People toss out lots of furniture. Scratched, stained, wonky legs. They think it's rubbish, but most of it simply needs a bit of love."

"Like people," Jamila tapped the edge of the leaflet. "You give them a fresh coat and a little attention, and suddenly they are bright-eyed and bushy-tailed."

"I hadn't thought of it like that, but yes. Exactly."

Settling into her chair, Jamila rested her hands gently on her lap, her eyes drifting with quiet concentration. She remained silent for a moment, as if weighing her words carefully. "Well, I don't have anything in need of a second life just now." Setting the flyer on the coffee table, she looked up. "But I can spread the word. I work part-time at the pub down the road. Ten years behind the bar and I know them all. Plenty of chatty folk down there. I'll tell them what you are up to."

"That would be fantastic, thank you," Dulcie gushed. "I've heard all about the pub. Actually, I'm going to visit The Witch & Stable on Saturday with Owen and Tristan, from the flat below you. They gave me the impression that it's the unofficial neighbourhood hub."

"Oh, it's very official if you ask me. The gossip alone is worth the price of a drink. Those two boys are often in the thick of it. Charmers, both of them."

"Thank you, Jamila. Honestly. Even one person showing interest in my project would mean the world."

"I'm sure you will be allowed to put a leaflet up on the pinboard at the pub. And the charity shop I work at too, if you'd like. We get a steady stream of people there rummaging for furniture to 'do up,' or more realistically, to leave in the corner for six months while they think about it."

"That would be amazing. Do you work in the shop on your own?"

"Oh no, we have a couple of volunteers. Retired teacher, a lovely chap who used to do drama before life got him down, and Jill, who's an old hand and has been there longer than I have. Faith, Hope and Charity. That's us."

"This building feels like my lucky charm. Ever since I moved in, everyone here has been so kind about my plans."

"Well, you're part of it now. Welcome to the madness." Jamila reached over and patted Dulcie's hand. "And next time, bring Les up here with you. I've got some leftover stew in the freezer that could do with a backhanded compliment."

"It's a deal." Dulcie smiled. "I don't think he'll need much convincing."

"Oh, he'll come. He's always keen to taste my cooking. Just tell him there'll be horse racing on TV and double helpings on offer."

"Noted. Thanks again for the ginger tea—and the advice. If you find any more places to put up my flyers, I'd be so grateful." Putting down her teacup, Dulcie smoothed the front of her sweatshirt. She pulled out a few more leaflets from her back pocket and set them on the dark brown occasional table, which had legs resembling elephant trunks curled inward like question marks.

"My door's always open," Jamila said, walking her to it. "Well, not literally, but if it's closed, just knock."

Stepping back into the stairwell, feeling lighter than when she had climbed up, Dulcie paused for a moment on the top step. Behind her, the door clicked gently shut, sealing in the small, sunlit room. Jamila had resumed her humming. The melody was low and winding, with no clear beginning or end, and it floated down the stairwell, accompanying Dulcie to the lower floors. She stood listening for a moment, and then turned and went back into the garden flat.

Walking into the kitchen, Dulcie found Uncle Les reading a trade magazine and making what he claimed was Bovril, though it looked suspiciously like instant gravy.

"Well?" he asked, without turning around.

"She's amazing," said Dulcie. "Your neighbour upstairs."

"Told you," Les had the unwavering certainty of a man who viewed all his opinions as universal truths.

"And she told me that you like her casseroles."

He made a noise halfway between a grunt and a chuckle. "She puts peanut butter in it. It's not right. But yes, I might've asked for seconds once or twice."

"She's going to take my flyer to the pub and the charity shop."

"Course she is." Les turned to her, holding a mug of something murky. "If there's one thing I've learned in life, the secret to success is not what you know, but *who* you know. Jamila could sell a pencil to a penguin. Everyone likes her."

"Her and her cuisine. She said you moan about her cooking just to get invited back for more."

"She says lots of things." He raised the mug. "Want some of

this?"

Dulcie peered inside. "What even is that?"

"It's brown. It's warm. It does the job." Les took a sip, puffing out his cheeks and blowing on the hot drink.

"I'm good, thanks. I'm happy to make my own."

Les shrugged. "Suit yourself."

Dulcie sat at the table, running her finger over its faint scratches. She imagined delicately polishing it with fine wool wire, working carefully until the grain was visible again. It could become beautiful, restored, and full of character.

"So," Dulcie said slowly, drawing the word out like a fine thread. "You and Jamila. Anything I should know?"

Les stiffened. He blinked twice, then turned a page in his magazine to closely examine an image that seemed to show nothing but a close-up of tile adhesive.

"Do you fancy her?" Dulcie leaned in to stare with unabashed interest at her uncle's face.

"I appreciate her lentil bake," Les answered, hastily. Then he folded Modern Grouting Quarterly with the resignation of a man caught doing something saucy. "I'm sixty-six years old," he said. "At my age, romance is mainly rubbing in ointment and holding hands to help each other out of a chair." But I will say, she's a good woman. With an impressive grasp of spices."

"So, you admit it?"

"Admit what? Do I have a fondness for someone who feeds me occasionally and listens when I complain about streetlighting? Heaven forbid!"

A pause lingered between them. It expressed the finality

of a subject swiftly closed, strong enough to suggest that further discussion was forbidden.

"Well," Dulcie quickly finished her coffee, "I'm going to bed. I have to get up early to collect that armoire. Redcurrant jelly included."

Les nodded, reaching for the crossword. "Sleep well, love. Big day tomorrow. Try not to bring back anything that's too far gone."

"I won't." She stood up. "That's the last thing I need." A few steps down the hallway, she paused and turned back, gripping the doorframe and peering back into the room.

"Oh—and Les?"

"Yes?"

"If you ever decide to take Jamila out on a date, maybe skip the grout talk. Lead with turmeric."

"Cheeky madam." He growled.

"Goodnight, Uncle Romeo."

Les grunted, but Dulcie caught the small smile tugging at his mouth as she walked to her room. Somewhere in the hall, the radiator clanked as if it were applauding.

CHAPTER 10

Big Maccie had returned.

Dulcie knew this because the sound of his front door closing echoed through the whole building like a backfire. Moments later, she carefully descended the steps to his home once more, this time holding a shopping bag filled with 'provisions' Les had cobbled together from the kitchen: a loaf of bread, two tins of soup, a brown banana, a tin of corned beef, a pint of milk and a packet of apple pies.

She knocked. The door flew open. "Dulcie!" barked Big Maccie, looming like a giant in the doorway. His face was red and puffy with anger. "Explain yourself!"

This was not the warm welcome Dulcie had expected. They weren't close friends, but she'd hoped for some indication of gratitude, perhaps even effusive praise, for her selfless feeding of his cat. Instead, he appeared furious with her.

"I, well I brought you some supplies," Dulcie hoisted the thin carrier bag like an offering of appeasement.

Maccie squinted at it. "Good Lord, is that corned beef?"

"Yes."

"Are we at *war?*"

Dulcie looked confused.

"Never mind." Maccie sighed and shifted to one side "You'd better come in."

Dulcie entered and was instantly enveloped by the familiar, eye-watering scent she recognised as unmistakably 'Eau de Feline.' At that moment, the sleek tabby cat strutted out of the bedroom with its tail held high. It wore the smug expression of one who had committed several misdemeanours and would do so again without a moment's hesitation.

The pungent aroma was much stronger than anything Dulcie had experienced in her visits to the flat in the last couple of days. She wrinkled her nose. "Wow, what's that terrible smell?"

"I'm glad you mentioned it," said Maccie sarcastically. "I thought it must be you."

Deciding Maccie must be in an awful mood due to pain from his procedure, Dulcie ignored the comment. "How are you feeling?" she asked politely.

"Full of morphine and betrayal," Maccie declared. "I came home and thought I'd been burgled!"

"What do you mean?"

"I found all my top-shelf china smashed on the floor. And, bugger me if there wasn't a *shite* right in the middle of my coffee table! *And* you were meant to feed my cat."

"I did feed your cat," Dulcie protested, looking at the feline.

"That," Maccie pointed, enraged, "is not *ma fekkin'cat!*"

Dulcie stared at the cat, and the cat stared back.

"You mean… I've been feeding a random cat?"

"Look at its collar!" Maccie snapped.

Dulcie knelt and peered at the tag. It read: "Princess Peppa" The cat purred.

Maccie was fuming. "You opened my window, didn't you? You let a stray in, fed her Missy's food, and then left her to break all my porcelain figurines!" The tall, lean Scotsman remained stiff in the doorway; his weathered face flushed with fury.

"Okay, okay, I shouldn't have cracked the window open." Dulcie held up her hands. "Missy escaped through the gap, and I chased all around the houses to find her. How was I supposed to know a doppelganger was living in the street?"

"It's basic feline protocol, Dulcie! Is anything going on in your head, or does it whistle when the wind blows?" The man's voice thundered through the room, reverberating off the walls with the force of astonished disbelief.

"I can't understand how it happened! I mean, I can, of course I can." Dulcie gabbled in her eagerness to put things right. "I'll tidy everything up right now and go straight out to look for Missy. I'm so sorry, Maccie, I really am." She looked completely stricken.

"Is that so? All I hear is weeb, weeb, weeb." He gestured with his hand, mimicking the shape of a mouth opening and closing. The cat, Princess Peppa, trotted to the open door and casually let herself out, as if her con was complete and she was off to find her next mark. They both watched as the furry vandal leapt up the steps and disappeared into the street.

Silence lingered heavily as the two humans gazed at each other glumly. Finally, Maccie let out a grunt. "You'd best get started with the clean-up. I'm meant to be resting. This shock will have knocked me back weeks." He stepped aside stiffly, allowing Dulcie to squeeze past him into the sitting room, where the worst of the destruction lay.

When she saw the shards of china, the dust, and the disarray, her face crumpled in dismay. Maccie, watching her, softened slightly. "Aye, well," he muttered, "it probably looks worse than it is. Though it looks bad enough."

"It's awful. I can't believe it." Her voice trembled as tears started to glisten in her eyes. "And Missy's lost out there somewhere... It's all my fault."

Maccie flinched. His coarse words and rough attitude were reflexes; beneath his bluster, there beat a compassionate heart. "Aye, well, she's done this before." His temper faded quickly, as it usually does in a man with more bark than bite. "Gone walkabout for a week or two. She's tough enough —bit of a scrapper, that one. She'll be out there going ten rounds with the local toms, and I don't need another vet bill landing on my doorstep" He lowered himself gently into his armchair. "I'm not even supposed to be up and about yet, so you'll need to keep a lookout. And this time," he jabbed a finger for emphasis, "if you do find her, make sure it's the right ruddy cat before you go locking her in here again."

"Fair enough." Dulcie squared her shoulders at the wreckage Princess Peppa had left behind. "I'll go and find something to clean up all this mess." Emptying the shopping onto the sideboard, she used the carrier bag to scoop a pile of cat poop from the coffee table, which she then scrubbed with such ferocity that the surface gleamed like a commercial for polish. Next, she looked for a dustpan and brush, which were in the coat cupboard beside the vacuum cleaner.

By some miracle, one of the dancing figurines had survived. The porcelain ballerina had landed upright, completely unharmed. The rest were beyond saving, broken into pieces too small to repair. Two decorative plates had exploded, shards scattered across the floor like oversized confetti. Dulcie swept everything into the pan and dropped the pieces into the kitchen bin.

After cleaning everything up, she mustered her courage and, lingering near the sitting room doorway, asked if Maccie could manage something for lunch. He sat with his arms folded, staring at a spot just to the left of her, his face unreadable. Then, slowly, he gave a slight shrug. "A snack would hit the mark," he said. "And I'll take an apple pie."

It wasn't much, but it was a small crack in the ice. When she handed him his sandwich of white bread, corned beef and a thin layer of pickle, Maccie regarded it warily. Then he took a bite, chewed thoughtfully, and gave a slight nod of approval.

"To be honest, I never really liked those little dancers," he admitted. "But what can you do when you've been left someone's precious possessions? In a way, I suppose you've done me a favour, hen," he said, as if declaring the incident closed.

They chatted for a while, discussing light, neutral topics such as the unexpectedly good hospital food and the logistics of transferring a wardrobe using a parcel trolley.

Maccie sat with one hand lightly on his plate and the other holding a mug of coffee. A flush of colour returned to his cheeks, and the tough set of his jaw softened. He looked, if not completely happy, then at least at ease. Taking stock, it seemed he had everything he needed for now, and for the first time since she'd walked through the door, Dulcie allowed herself to hope that everything would turn out right. "Well," she brushed her hands together, "I'll leave you to it. I'm going to have a thorough search for Missy, and as soon as I find her, I'll bring her back home where she belongs."

Giving him a wave and a quick smile, not too bright or expectant, just enough to show she meant it, Dulcie took her leave of him and made her exit: swift, quiet, and as dignified as one could be when holding a cat poo in a Sainsbury's bag.

CHAPTER 11

After an extended, unproductive search through the streets, calling out for Missy and looking everywhere she could think of, Dulcie reluctantly went back to work. She hoped to clear her mind and ease some guilt by concentrating on one of the most challenging projects on her list. Kneeling close to the cabinet, she carefully removed layers of cracked varnish using a flat-edged scraper. The workshop door was propped open, allowing a breeze to enter, carrying the scent of grass clippings and the sounds of the city. But a recurring thought kept invading her mind: Missy—gone in an instant.

Reflecting on the entire fiasco, Dulcie had to admit that Maccie had been surprisingly stoical. "Missy's survived worse than this," he'd told her. "She once stowed away in a Tesco delivery van and ended up in Basingstoke. They brought her back, but I think that's how she developed a taste for international travel."

Still, Dulcie hadn't stopped glancing out of the window since, which played havoc with her schedule. Wood shavings curled up in the corners, and a jar of cloudy turpentine sat nearby, abandoned next to a half-used tin of beeswax polish and a stiff-bristled brush. The air was filled with the scent of resin and aged varnish, and every inch of the space spoke of a work in progress, waiting to be given attention. Switching to fine-grit sandpaper, Dulcie sighed and began to smooth the edges of a drawer, and before long, she heard the unmistakable sound of leather boots on the gravel pathway.

"Don't pretend you didn't hear me coming," Uncle Les called from outside.

Dulcie didn't look up. "You stomp about like a hippo in Doc Martens. Not easy to miss."

Stepping into the workshop, Les dropped a clinking tote bag onto the workbench, knocking over a handsaw. "I've brought you ginger beer and a meat pasty, as solace for your conscience," he said, giving her a knowing look. "I bumped into Big Maccie. He told me you haven't made a great impression, since you've managed to drive away his only companion."

"Don't remind me," she groaned.

"It looks like you've been sanding that same bit of wood all morning," Les observed, briefly changing the subject. "Keep it up and you'll be left with nothing but matchsticks." A thick layer of sawdust covered everything, softening the outlines of clamps, chisels, and screwdrivers spread across the workbench.

"I'm staying occupied to distract myself," Dulcie said,

shrugging her shoulders. "I still feel terrible about everything that happened."

"So you should! How do you think I felt? Like a proper Charlie, that's what. I mean, I made a promise to Maccie that he could entrust his pet to safe hands, then you let her make a bid for freedom. Not to mention locking a random moggy in his home and letting it run amok."

"You don't need to go on about it. I feel bad enough as it is. I know I should've looked harder at the other cat."

"You looked. You didn't see. If there's one thing I've learned, those are two very different things."

"I thought the one thing you'd learned was that jam needs scrunch?"

"I've learned many things, thank you," Les retorted. "What counts is that Maccie took the pet-sitting fiasco better than I would've."

"I know. He was surprisingly decent about it. He told me that Missy often wanders off. We had quite a good chat, and he appeared to forgive me. By the end, he was calling me 'hen' and offering whiskey."

"That's practically a full amnesty. All we need now is for the wanderer to return."

"I've left some sardines by the fence, along with a clean towel, in case Missy comes back looking like she's been living rough and needs a quick clean-up before we head home." Rifling through the shopping bag, Dulcie pulled out the can of ginger beer, lifted then threw away the ring pull, and took a sip.

"That'll attract every cat in the neighbourhood," Les warned. "Offer a buffet, and a crowd of strays will gather.

You'll have to pick Missy out of a line-up." He glanced at her, noticing she wasn't in the mood to be teased. Quickly altering his tone, he said, "Never mind. She'll turn up. She's probably out there now, sitting on some rooftop, laughing at us."

The sound of an overground train drifted past, its clattering noise building up and fading away as it trundled into the distance. A familiar voice broke the silence.

"Hey, Dulcie! Are you in?" Tristan ducked through the side entrance, a crooked grin on his face and a small, battered table balanced on one shoulder. "I found treasure," he announced, lifting it like a trophy. "And by treasure, I mean this complete wreck."

Les muttered something that sounded suspiciously like "rubbish disguised as an excuse to wrangle a date," but Dulcie ignored him.

Tristan set the small card table on the bench. Its surface was chipped and scratched, with the once-luxurious veneer peeling at the edges to reveal the raw wood beneath. A crack ran down one side, splitting the frame near the corner like a fault line. Despite its battered state, there were still hints that it had been something special, a piece of delicate craftsmanship. "I thought you might work your magic on it." He placed it at her feet, like a cat presenting a mouse.

She bent down to examine it, her fingers already searching for the damage. "Where on earth did you find this?" she asked.

It was in my mate's attic. He was going to throw it out, but I said, 'No way. I know someone who can make this look really good, and I've brought it to you.

So, you told your friend that I restore vintage furniture, and he gave you this broken card table?

"Well, I told him I knew someone who's very good with her hands," Tristan said, with a subtle wink.

"Unbelievable," Les muttered. "Well, we'd like to help you out." He stepped in front of his niece. "Which way did you come in?" he continued, deliberately changing the meaning of his first statement.

"Uncle, please don't." Dulcie urged him to stop interrupting.

Squinting into the faint light, Tristan faked a surprised look on his face. "Hello, Les. I didn't notice you there." He smiled broadly at the older man, giving him his brightest toothpaste-commercial grin, and leaned against the bench. Then he turned away. "Dulcie, if I bring you more broken furniture, does that guarantee I get to see you in your overalls, or is that just a happy bonus?"

"It depends." She held the card table by the leg, swinging it onto the workbench. "If you bring me an actual antique, I might let you watch me sand something down."

"Really? Dangerous talk." Tristan enjoyed their flirtation, treating it as the first step in a familiar game. Giving her the table was a planned gesture, designed to foster an initial connection. So far, the wheeze seemed to be working. Her tender touch on the table and the focused look in her eyes convinced him that this was the promising start he had hoped for.

"Dulcie, can I talk to you outside for a moment?" Uncle Les was a man not to be underestimated. Despite her earlier rebuke, he believed protecting his niece's honour was his duty. They needed a private talk, and he walked through the door confidently, expecting her to follow.

She hesitated. "Can it wait? I'm working out how to reinforce the joint without replacing the whole leg."

"It'll only take a minute."

Tristan threw up his hands. "What's this? A father-daughter talk?"

"I may not be her father," Les said, straightening up to his modest height. "But I've got an honorary shotgun for times like this."

Dulcie rolled her eyes but still followed him into the yard, while Tristan stayed behind and waited, idly picking up and putting down the tools of her trade. He flexed his muscles under a rolled-up flannel shirt as he leaned in, fingers brushing the cold steel, prodding at the vice with mild curiosity, straining his ears to hear their conversation.

Outside, Les crossed his arms and faced Dulcie like a grown-up about to impart the wisdom of Solomon. In his mind, he was responsible for her, acting in loco parentis while she lived under his roof.

She pre-empted him. "I know what you're going to say."

"Do you?" He looked unconvinced. It probably wasn't his place to interfere, but it wasn't in his nature to ignore metaphorical red flags, fluttering in the wind.

She faced him confidently and, in a voice just above a whisper, stated, "You think Tristan is superficial, unreliable, easily distracted, and flirts as a way of breathing."

"I was also going to mention that his last three romantic entanglements lasted roughly the same time it takes to boil an egg."

"He's not proposing, Uncle Les. He brought me a table to fix."

"Along with his dimples and a wink."

"I'm not twelve years old." She was exasperated. It was one thing to have conversations like this with her mother, but surely clashes like this should be a thing of the past?

"I know you're not, which is why I'm saying this. You have taste, skills, and patience. You deserve someone who recognises all of that." He gestured toward the shed. "What Tristan sees is a cute girl in overalls who can glue his problems back together."

"I appreciate the concern. Really. But it's fine."

"Is it?" Les was unconvinced.

"I can enjoy a flirt, a harmless one," she stressed. "I may fancy the bones of someone, but it doesn't mean I'm picturing our future children."

Les realised he was fighting a losing battle. It was one he hadn't signed up for and certainly wasn't equipped to win. He grumbled something that sounded like 'hopeless' and stormed back to the house. Along the way, he was heard muttering darkly about errant libidos, diminishing brain cells, and the overall decline of civilisation.

Dulcie lingered outside for a while, letting the breeze cool her flushed cheeks. Missy was probably watching from some secret perch, silently judging her complicated path to romance. Fair enough.

Returning to the workshop, she stood in the doorway, wiping her hands on a rag as she observed her visitor. Now seated on a wooden stool, Tristan leaned forward with elbows on his knees, thoughtfully flipping through her collection of old repair manuals. Sunlight sparkled in his tousled hair as he studied diagrams and traced the brittle pages with his long fingers. He looked up at her, his eyes resting on the curve of her mouth.

"How did it go? Are you alright, or have you been threatened with banishment to a nunnery?"

"That's *exactly* where I'm being sent," Dulcie confirmed. "But the good news is that black and white suits me, so wearing a wimple is a win-win."

"That image of you will live rent-free in my mind for some time." He studied her slowly, from head to toe. "Unfortunately, Les likes me as a tenant but not as a suitor."

"Suitor? Very fancy. You're getting a bit ahead of yourself." Dulcie picked up a piece of sandpaper and waved it coyly in front of her face like a fan. "Don't mind him, he's just protective."

"But I'm harmless, honestly. A genuine, run-of-the-mill guy with a dodgy card table and nowhere else to take it. My intentions are respectable, Scout's honour." He lifted two fingers to his forehead in a salute.

"I know what scouts use wood for, and if anyone needs to rub things together to start a fire, it will be me."

"Well played," acknowledged Tristan as he watched her lift the broken table and carefully position the leg back into place. "If I brought you something else to fix, would you let me bring snacks along, so I could spend a tea break with you?"

"That depends."

"On what?"

"On whether you can find Missy-Mae and bring her back,

too."

"Challenge accepted." He stood up and backed out of the door. "I'll leave you to your endeavours whilst I go on my quest," he said, tipping an imaginary hat. "But if I manage to slay the dragon, or at least catch a cat, I promise to return and claim my reward."

Watching from the house window, Les could see Tristan swaggering away through the garden gate. He was on red alert to a situation developing with this well-known Lothario. If so, the problem would require careful handling and advice from a panel of experts. An immediate consultation was needed, and there was only one thing for it. Grabbing his jacket, he set off to the pub.

CHAPTER 12

How to collect her donations from far and wide was a challenge Dulcie hadn't quite figured out, which is why, on Tuesday morning, she found herself wheeling an ancient, unwieldy armchair along the pavement, using the parcel trolley that Uncle Les had offered for the more ambitious tasks.

The chair, a yellow-gold monstrosity with stuffing like hard popcorn, was strapped to the trolley with a belt and half a bungee cord. Dulcie was about to push it into the narrow alley to the back gate of No. 67 when she heard a sharp snip, then the unmistakable sound of someone inhaling in polite disapproval.

"Excuse me," came a voice as crisp as a starched tablecloth.

Dulcie turned, squinting against the sunlight.

The owner of No. 65 stood in the tiny front garden, carefully pruning a rose bush. Dulcie saw a beautifully tended flower bed, in the centre of which was a woman of a certain age, dressed in linen trousers, pearls, and a wide-brimmed hat. Petals lay scattered along the path, one or two more fluttering down as she adjusted a wayward stem.

"Are you planning to throw that chair in the alley, or is this some kind of performance art?" the woman asked.

"Neither," Dulcie halted the load just before it reached the curb. "Mrs. Odhiambo, who works at the charity shop down the road, told me this was left outside the door. But they can't accept furniture like this, without fire safety labels. So, it's being rescued."

"Rescued," the woman repeated, carefully trimming a flower with precise, surgical movements. "How quaint." She looked painfully thin, with her collarbones visible under her ivory blouse and her wrists as delicate as a bird's. Her face, suspiciously smooth, had features that once drew attention: high, sculpted cheekbones, a straight nose, and delicately shaped pink lips. Long, artificial lashes highlighted her eyes, while her stylishly arranged, blonde hair was styled in an intricate updo beneath a large hat.

"Well, as it seems we may be neighbours, we had better introduce ourselves. My name is Kay Kenneths." She waited, a flicker of anticipation in her eyes. "And before you ask, yes, I am *the* Kay Kenneths. The one who played Jemma Francis in "Downley Lodge". Of course, I have many other television credits, but that's the show most people your age would recognise me from.

Dulcie nodded. She'd never watched the series, or even heard of it.

"Before you ask, I'm afraid I won't agree to being in a selfie with you; my policy is always to say no. If you say yes to one, you must agree to all, or it's not fair." Kay relayed her rule with some reluctance.

"I'm delighted to meet you anyway, even without a picture," Dulcie said, trying to look suitably disappointed. "It's quite a thrill to live next door to a bona fide star"

"So I'm told," Kay said without false modesty. "I must say, it's refreshing to witness enterprising initiative, albeit one that involves dragging upholstery along the street."

"Thank you. I'm Dulcie Staples, and I've moved into 67 to start a little business refurbishing old furniture. This chair's got good bones. Bad smell, but good bones."

Kay sniffed, as if the phrase "bad smell" had conjured a palpable reek. She paused; an idea had come to her unbidden. "As it happens, I have a chaise longue that needs some attention," she said cautiously. "Velvet. Chartreuse. Contemporary. It belonged to my second husband's first wife," she continued, as though that explained everything. "That harridan was a dreadful woman, but she did have taste. The chaise longue is gorgeous. Or at least it was, before time and tragedy took their toll."

"That's a pity. What sort of tragedy?"

"Just wear and tear. The normal hurly-burly that a chaise longue guarantees," Kay said flatly. "None of which was caused by me. Alas."

They stood in a brief silence, broken only by the snip of the rose clippers. It was a touch surreal, Dulcie thought, to be talking to a public figure while she was calmly tending her plants, just like any gardener on a quiet afternoon. Her eyes wandered to Kay's arms, noticing that above her gloves, deep scratches showed through the skin, thin red lines shimmering in the light as she moved. "Those look sore," she said, nodding towards the red welts.

"Oh, it's nothing. These roses are such a pretty shade of pink, but they have the most terrific thorns." Kay pulled down her sleeves. "Would you like to come in and see the couch? I'll permit entry. It's well worth seeing. It's a rather valuable piece, but it needs some restoration. Not to its original glory, of course, but to a point where one wouldn't feel the need to cover it with a shawl when guests arrive."

"I'd love to take a look." It wasn't every day you got a chance to visit someone who used to be on television. Even if Kay hadn't been on screen for years, she was still nominally famous. It would be a privilege to see behind the scenes, and, honestly, anything was better than struggling with a mustard-coloured armchair in full view of the street.

"Excellent. You can leave that chair monstrosity there, just inside the gate." Kay turned and headed up the stone steps. "Follow me. Try not to touch anything. Shoes off at the door, of course." She led the way inside the ornate, gilded house, beyond the embroidered doormat and along a short hallway, leading to an opulent front room. "What do you think of my little sanctuary?" she asked.

Velvet curtains pooled on the floor, gold-framed mirrors reflected the light from ornate, tasselled lamps, and cushions were scattered in every corner like decorative sentinels. Shelves bowed under the weight of glass, framed photos, and awards, while the glossy furniture shone as if polished twice that morning. The faint smell of roses and old perfume, one of those rich, powdery scents that clings to heavy fabrics, hung in the air. Altogether, the room had a peculiar charm, presenting as half stage set, half museum to a life once full of entrances and exits.

Dulcie considered her words carefully. "It's... very, very detailed." Her face stayed neutral, hiding her actual feelings.

With a flourish, Kay swept back a large, silky pashmina, revealing a chaise longue underneath. The fabric was unmistakably chartreuse—a vivid, almost defiant shade that straddled the line between green and yellow. The fabric shimmered faintly in the light, catching on the nap of the upholstery as if it were still performing, even in retirement. It was in reasonably good repair, requiring work on the upholstery but not the frame. "Well?" Kay asked. "Isn't it marvellous? It's a designer piece, of course, an original Lucy Weldon."

Dulcie whistled softly and mentally increased its worth tenfold. She crouched and gave the seat a tentative poke. "It definitely has potential."

"Don't we all, darling. Some of us just need the right lighting." Kay moved across the room. "I do so love to be surrounded by beautiful things." She lifted a small bronze ornament from the mantel. "This came from the set of 'Beyond Birdbrook,' where I played Aaliyah DePaul. The harshest critic at the time said that I made the role my own." She lifted the object to shoulder height, as if to catch the footlights. "I wasn't exactly presented with this little souvenir, but after five sold-out weeks and standing ovations every night, it was only fair that I should have it. The company owed me that much." A guileful smile crept across her face. "And... well, the director and I were rather close at the time. He was such a dear man. He told me I could have anything I wanted. Within reason." Kay placed it back on the shelf, an old secret hiding in plain sight. "Luckily," she added, "I've always had an excellent sense of reason."

Each corner of the room whispered stories of a life fully lived: ornate frames, silk cushions, and souvenirs from distant travels. To an outsider, it might appear cluttered or overly extravagant, but for her, it was a personal gallery filled with echoes of stages, hotel balconies, and midnight trains. In this space, she was more than just an older woman fluffing pillows and dusting. Here, she was the woman she had always been. A star.

Unable to resist showing off, Kay continued to detail the most desirable items in her collection. "As someone who appreciates objects d'art, I dare say you've already noticed that I have an original Jo Jackson on my wall," she remarked, gesturing towards a vibrant contemporary painting of a polar bear, depicted in turquoise and mauve swirls. "Naturally, I prefer not to name-drop," she added, immediately dropping another name, "but you may be surprised to know that Annabel Theodore created that charming statuette on the chiffonier." She gave Dulcie a knowing look. "Both were gifts to me from well-known admirers, very high-profile fans, household names, you might say. Not that I could ever, *never,* even under the most persuasive interrogation, disclose who they were."

Dulcie didn't take the bait.

Disappointed, Kay indicated that they should sit down. "Do mind the cushion," she said. "It's decorative, not practical."

Perched on the edge of the antique settee, her hands neatly folded in her lap, Dulcie dutifully scanned the room in appreciation of its many treasures.

"So," Kay said, drawing out the word as if it were the opening note of a performance. "You must be the young relative who has come to stay with Les?"

"That's right."

"Mm. I've always liked Les, though I've never known him well." Kay reached over to a small silver tray and plucked a sugared almond, then seemed to forget about it halfway to her mouth. "I've spoken with the two young men in the other flat," she continued, waving the sweet vaguely upward. "They go in and out at all hours, like moths. You never can tell what they are up to. They wear such casual clothes for every occasion. And then there's the sleuth in the basement. Duncan McCallie. A very curious fellow."

"Yes, I've met him." "He's actually quite—"

"Alone," Kay interrupted. Lives entirely alone. Just him and that cat. A great, hairy creature. The cat, not Maccie, although..." She trailed off, eyes thoughtful. "Given he's a bachelor devoted to his pet, I must admit I'd rather assumed that he was gay. A certain flair about him, you know. Well-dressed and observant. I have several dear friends with those qualities. The theatre has given me so much more than simply a career."

Dulcie wasn't expecting to share confidences. Nor did she know if she was required to comment. She settled for a two-beat hum.

"But no, I was wrong on that count," Kay sighed. "Several lady friends have come and gone from his flat over the years. Let's say my radar may have short-circuited in his case. I find it odd," she added, "A mature, single man with no steady romance. Good-looking, too, in a rough diamond way. Either he's terribly particular or simply... undisciplined. I've always thought there's a difference between choosing solitude and being alone."

"Maccie lives life on his own terms. I suppose it's not that unusual these days."

"My darling, that's the very problem. Unusual has become usual. No wonder we're all so terribly *bored.*"

Dulcie wasn't sure whether to agree or not. Kay had the kind of presence that made pauses feel like a cue to deliver a line.

"You're a sweet little thing, aren't you? Like chamomile tea, which is so comforting that it goes unnoticed, until one realises they've been somewhat stressed."

"Thank you?"

"I mean it kindly. I don't invite just anyone into this lounge, you know. Most people wouldn't appreciate it. It doesn't suit every taste."

Suddenly, a faint noise came from somewhere in the background that sounded like rhythmic, fluttering thumps, followed by a sharp, high-pitched clatter. Both women hesitated, tilting their heads to listen more closely. The muffled yet distinct sound echoed again from the back of the house.

"Did you hear that?"

"Of course," said Kay casually, "it's one of the ghosts. Various spectres haunt these houses. Didn't you know?" She spoke with indifference, then paused, looking thoughtful. "It's either that, or the pipes are acting up again." She turned sharply and strode out of the room with an unreadable expression. "Come along," she demanded. "If you've seen enough, let's go back outside." Startled by the sudden shift in tempo, Dulcie stood up to follow her into the hall and outside into the cool air, leaving the noises behind.

"Well," Kay said briskly, picking up her clippers and waving them like a wand. "Back to the roses for me. They grow as fast as an enchanted forest. I half expect them to start singing or trap me in a briar."

"Would you like me to give you a quote for repairing the chaise longue?" Dulcie asked, trying to keep her tone between professional and 'I'm capable of miracles.' The potential commission was irresistible, and the opportunity to work on the chaise would be a thrill. Plus, a glowing testimonial from someone whose name turned heads could do wonders for her reputation.

"Yes, yes. Just post the details through my door, would you?" Kay had grown rather tired of granting an audience. She turned her full attention to the flowers, her focus on the blooms intensifying; each snip served as a gentle but unmistakable dismissal. The message was clear: the show was over, the curtains were drawn, and their conversation, as far as she was concerned, was finished.

With a sigh and a lurch, Dulcie retrieved the donated chair and pushed it forward. She wondered if her new career would often involve dealing with people who, for lack of a better term, were a bit weird. Perhaps odd encounters would be part of the job. An occupational hazard of working with people and their eccentric belongings. Nevertheless, she hoped that the next challenge she faced would only involve basic upholstery and not whatever the hell was going on with Kay Kenneths.

CHAPTER 13

The golden slant of the early morning sun poured across the back garden like a spilt bottle of honey. Tiny motes of sawdust floated in the air, shimmering stars dancing in the sunbeams. With her sleeves rolled up and hair in a neat knot, Dulcie was focused on a vintage cabinet door. She gently slid a sanding block along its curved edge, uncovering pale, swirling wood beneath the chipped varnish. On a tall shelf, an old radio played a slow, nostalgic tune, its melodies mellow and relaxing.

Lost in her work, she barely noticed the knocking at the garden fence until it repeated, louder and more insistent. Wiping her brow with the back of her wrist, Dulcie crossed the flagstones and opened the back gate. Owen stood there, looking flushed, tousled, and frazzled. "Disaster," he said, holding up his hands. "I've locked myself out. Again. Phone, keys, dignity. All gone." He stood with one hand resting on the fence post; his face showed a mix of hope and shame.

"I saw you were busy working, so I thought I'd ask if you would take me in for a little while." He made a display of crossing his fingers. "I really hope that's okay with you. Or do you think it's a bit of a cheek?"

"Where's Tristan? Can't he let you back in? Doesn't he have his keys?"

"He stayed out last night, and now he's nowhere to be found." Owen appeared exasperated, but in truth, he was rather glad to have a reason to mention Tristan's overnight tryst. "Jamila has called a locksmith for me, but he won't arrive until 10 a.m. It's the same chap I used when I made a fool of myself last time. Forgetting my keys is becoming an expensive habit."

Dulcie moved aside, giving him a knowing look as she let him in. She lowered her protective facemask that covered her nose and mouth. "You'd better make yourself at home. Feel free to sit on the stool inside the doorway," she suggested. "Just avoid touching anything sharp."

He entered the workshop as if stepping into a chapel, careful not to disturb anything sacred. The wooden stool creaked under him as he settled, folding his long limbs neatly and resting his hands on his knees like a schoolboy during a time-out. "It's amazing to see such a whole workplace out here."

"It's where things come to life, if I get it right." She was already immersed in her work. She replaced her mask and continued sanding in slow, deliberate circles, forming small dust piles around her. Owen noted the curve of her spine as she leaned forward, the tip of her tongue caught between her lips in concentration. It was like watching someone craft poetry in grain and texture.

"Did you always want to make old things feel new again?" he asked.

She glanced at him, then at the wood, and lowered her facemask, resolving to stop and have a proper conversation rather than this scattered back-and-forth. "I've always enjoyed repairing items and reselling them in the second-hand market. Sometimes they get snapped up, sometimes they don't. But I mainly enjoy the process itself."

"There's something really...honourable about that."

"Honourable?" It wasn't a term she would have used.

"Yeah. Like... hopeful. You know?" he tried to convey how worthy he believed her career choice was. "I think it's commendable."

That surprised her. Most people nodded and moved on when she discussed her work, but he seemed genuinely interested. He leaned in as they spoke, listening as if every word she said mattered. Owen inquired about the different types of wood, why she chose beeswax polish over synthetic sealant, and whether she had a preferred antique period. It made a refreshing change from those who found it difficult to articulate an interest, genuine or not.

The conversation floated like dandelion fluff onto new topics. They discovered they both loved 1970s album art and agreed that "Rumours" by Fleetwood Mac was perfect in sound and style. Dulcie shared her childhood obsession with illustrated books, while Owen revealed he still remembered every word of "The Wind in the Willows," even the strange bits. "My dad built a Toad Hall treehouse one summer," he recalled. He swore it would last ten years. We had five minutes. My sister Emma and I climbed in, and it completely collapsed. Boom!" He mimed an explosion with his hands. "It turns out that enthusiasm is no substitute for expertise when building palaces."

For the umpteenth time, Dulcie wondered anything fascinated him more than pixies, old stories, and vintage bikes. It was hard to tell if she felt anything beyond friendly energy, but the conversation had flowed, and time had never slipped by so quickly.

After a little while longer, it became clear that Tristan wasn't coming to the rescue. She wondered where he had spent the night and tried to decide whether it would matter to her if he had a girlfriend. It would be disappointing if he did, she concluded. It's not every day that the heavens deliver a drop-dead gorgeous charmer into your lap. Only time would tell.

"Do you fancy a coffee?" she asked Owen. "I've got a kettle out here, all mod cons. Though I can only offer the instant variety, and there's no milk."

"That'd be great."

She boiled the water and poured it into two mismatched cups from the collection by the sink. His mug was the one that read "*Dig for Victory!*" and he accepted it without comment. They sat in the sunlit corner of the workshop, surrounded by sandpaper, tins of finish, and the comforting scent of old pine. A half-painted cabinet was propped against the back wall of the shed—her first donation, which was now beginning to take shape. A coat of matte sage green and new brass knobs would give it the elegant look she aimed for.

"This is brilliant," Owen said, running his hand over the top of the bench. "I know you told us you would be working with furniture, but I didn't realise you did all this back here."

"I try to keep the power tools quiet during 'respectable' hours. The neighbourhood prefers to pretend I don't exist when I'm sawing." Dulcie grimaced.

"I don't mind a bit of noise. Way more interesting than marking."

"Exam papers?"

"Essays on 'Folklore to Fiction: The Enduring Legacy of Fairies in Modern Literature." He responded to the face she pulled. "I know, I know, riveting stuff."

The lecturers that Dulcie had come across at college hadn't captured her attention, but to be fair, her subject didn't leave much room for imagination. Still, she might have appreciated them more if the teachers had been more like Owen, whose passion for his subject and engaging way of sharing knowledge made the dullest details feel like interesting discoveries.

"I've got a chair that needs attention. If you want to have a go at something," she said suddenly.

"You're offering me a project to try?"

"It's pretty broken," she warned. "One leg's completely shot. But the frame's good. I've been meaning to figure out what to do with it."

"I'm in," he said, already rolling his sleeves. "Teach me your ways, master artisan."

She pulled out a chair from under a pile of tarp, which had a mid-century design, a spindle back, and one leg that was cleanly snapped at the joint. Owen crouched beside it, feeling along the break as if reading braille. "Okay, this is fixable," he said.

"You say that now, but you'll have to earn your stripes."

They worked together for a while, with Dulcie guiding him as he measured, glued, and clamped the pieces. Their fingers touched several times, and when he leaned in to steady the frame, she caught his strong scent of citrus and musk and the clean freshness of his gentle breaths.

"You're a natural," she said when the leg was clamped back into place.

"I only followed your lead."

"Well, you did a great job. But don't let it go to your head." She was surprised at how well they worked together. Usually, she disliked collaborating, often frustrated that others couldn't grasp or fulfil her vision.

Owen cleared his throat, seizing a lull in the conversation. "So," he began, acting casual and missing by a mile, "are you still planning to come to the pub with me and Tristan on Friday?"

"Yes, I'm looking forward to it. Uncle Les told me he's a big fan of the Witch & Stable. I hadn't realised it was his local too, but I suppose, being the nearest pub, it would be."

"Yeah, almost everyone nearby heads there," Owen said, shifting his weight to lean on the bench. "Not only your Uncle Les and Big Maccie, but also some less welcome folks. Gerald, for instance, the one who believes his neighbourhood watch badge grants him diplomatic immunity."

"Sounds... welcoming."

"It is, surprisingly so, Owen laughed, the sound light and easy. His finger flicked towards the roof. "Jamila from upstairs in the attic flat works there behind the bar. She has a way of making everyone feel like they belong, even the oddballs. Every night there feels like a family reunion, which is sometimes brilliant, sometimes a bit of a worry."

"Reunions can be like that."

"True," Owen agreed. "But don't worry—there's a younger crowd too. A couple of university grads who have moved back home to save money, some artists from the co-op down the hill, and Evie, who's in a band, and always trying to convince people to come to open mic nights."

"Is she any good?" Dulcie was more of a supporter than someone who would get up and sing.

"Pretty good," Owen said with a grin. "She's got lots of enthusiasm and bags of stage presence. You won't be stuck talking to Gerald all evening, I promise."

"Good to know. What else goes on in this den of iniquity?"

"Don't mock, it's lively stuff. Every other Monday, tickets are sold behind the bar for the notorious meat raffle. Sausages from the butcher, a leg of lamb, or chops. Gerald claims he never wins, but often walks away with the biggest prize. Curry night on Thursdays, pie night on Tuesdays."

"I'd be the size of a *house* if I went to all those events."

"It's a temptation," Owen agreed. "Just brace yourself for Les's attempt at karaoke on a Saturday. That's when the party really gets started."

Outside, the garden was peaceful, no noise except the occasional rustle of wind through the trees. They stood close together in the workspace, the overhead bulb casting warm shadows across the walls. They looked at each other, and whatever they saw sat comfortably with them both. The space between them closed slightly. They weren't touching, but the air felt charged. Owen glanced at her forehead, then back to her deep, brown eyes. "This is... really nice," he said. "As rescues go, this has to be up in my top ten."

Suddenly, there was a knock on the fence. Jamila Odhiambo, dressed in a silky blouse and a floral apron, appeared through the slats. "Owen, dear," she said softly, "I believe someone is trying to reach you. I can hear your phone ringing over and over again, inside your flat. If you think you know who it is, you can use my phone to call them back." She handed him her mobile with the reverence typically reserved for new kittens or grandchildren.

"Oh. Sorry about that. Thank you." He stood, nodded towards the garden, and ducked out of the door. Jamila followed, calling that she would see them both later, then swiftly returned to the house.

Dulcie returned to her sanding, but now her hand lacked rhythm. The strokes were uneven and distracted. Through the fence slats, she could hear his voice, muffled yet distinct enough.

"It should be fine... yes, I didn't mean to miss your call... No, I just got held up... I know, me too." Owen's words were cheerful and heartfelt. "Thank you ever so much, Jen. Where would I be without you?"

She tried not to listen, but his heartfelt tone made it impossible to resist. Earnest, familiar. Too intimate for a stranger. Her chest tightened. What with one thing and another, things were not going well on the romantic front today.

When Owen returned through the gate, she had already packed up her tools and was polishing the cabinet with a wax finish. He hesitated in the doorway. "Hey. Thanks for the drink, the seat, the shelter, and... the story hour."

She didn't look up. "No problem."

He waited, half hoping she might offer more. A smile. A joke. Anything.

"The locksmith should be here soon," she said, with the polite finality of a closed sign.

From the depths of the garden flat, a voice bellowed like a foghorn powered by breakfast porridge. "No need for a locksmith. It's expensive to call one of those out. I can open the door for you, no problem." Uncle Les emerged carrying a bent wire coat hanger and a butter knife, waving them in the air like the keys to the kingdom.

Dulcie groaned. "Are you absolutely sure you know how to open a lock, Uncle Les?"

"I am a man of many hats," Les replied, winking at Owen. "And if there's one thing I've learned in life, it's how to open locked doors. Besides, we can't have you two youngsters flummoxed by something as petty as a flat door. A landlord's work is never done," he concluded. "It's just a shame you borrowed the spare key last time you got locked out, Owen. We wouldn't be in this mess If you'd given it back." He scratched his chin. "What's more, if I hadn't seen Jamila in the hall earlier, I'd be none the wiser about the crisis." Les sounded a little hurt that he hadn't been consulted, straight away. "Never mind, all I needed was a quick wash and brush-up. Then I dug these out." He waved the coat hanger in the air again. "Now it's all systems go. Come with me and we'll soon get this sorted out."

Les beckoned to them with the authority of a sergeant major who would brook no argument, his hand slicing through the air in a gesture that said 'Hurry Up.' With the resigned obedience of schoolchildren, they dutifully fell into line, trailing behind him. In single file, their shoes crunching on the gravel path, they headed back to the house and climbed up to the second-floor landing, where Owens' new bike rested against the banister. Coming to a halt outside the door of Flat No. 2, Les knelt gingerly on the carpet, his face shifting into one of solid concentration as if the door was a complex puzzle, which only he could solve.

"Now, I once saw a YouTube video where a fella opened a door using a credit card and sheer bravado. Have you got something like a loyalty card? Coffee stamp one will do," he asked.

Owen shook his head. Everything he owned was inside the flat. Les sighed, pulled his wallet from his back pocket, took out a plastic payment card and attempted to push it into the tiny crevice near the lock. After a minute of hard labour, he had managed to wedge the card, bend the butter knife, and drop the coat hanger. "Just wait," Les said confidently, sweat gleaming with determination. "It's all about finesse. You insert something thin into the slit at the side of the door and slide it up, like so." He shifted his position, mindful of his knees, then wiggled the card and pushed really hard.

Click.

The door swung open, and Les fell through the gap like a diving turtle. He landed face down with his nose on the floor and rump in the air.

Dulcie and Owen stared in astonishment at the open flat.

A locksmith stared back.

"What the bloody hell is going on?" demanded Les, sitting back on his heels with as much bruised dignity as he could muster.

"Hi, Owen," the tradesman said, holding the door handle and jiggling it up and down. "I've fixed the lock. I was making sure it worked both ways. You are fast becoming my best customer," he went on. "Jamila answered the front door and let me in downstairs. As you weren't about, I thought I might as well get on with the job."

"Well," Les spluttered, getting to his feet with injured grace. "I don't have time to stand about here all day, debating who fixed what, where, when and how," he hurried on, deflecting like a man who had been upstaged once or twice before. "If you ask me, the more interesting question is why this happened at all?"

Owen looked confused. Dulcie choked on air. "Uncle Les!" she hissed.

"I'm just saying," Les continued, already walking away, "maybe fate locks you out so someone else can let you in." He then spun around and headed back down the stairs, humming a tune that sounded like the theme from' Love Actually'. Dulcie trailed after him, complaining loudly about his choice of melody, her voice bouncing off the walls. Owen stayed behind to pay the locksmith and then re-entered his home, the door clicking satisfactorily shut behind him. He paused briefly, keys in hand, contemplating how to steer this extraordinary day back on course and wondering whether Les had a clearer grasp of the situation, a deeper understanding of their feelings, and better instincts than he did when it came to romance.

CHAPTER 14

That Saturday evening, Owen and Tristan set off together, intending to collect Dulcie along the way. Tristan walked down the stairs with the self-assurance of someone who never questioned the effect he had on people. There was a bounce in his step as he adjusted his shirt cuffs, rolling them up just enough to reveal his well-defined forearms and his glossy new smartwatch.

Owen fell into step a few paces behind, quieter than usual, a flicker of anticipation curling in his chest. He liked Dulcie. Liked her more than he was comfortable admitting to. So much so, that he was doing his best not to notice how Tristan had gone the extra mile to impress her: his hair blow-dried, subtly waxed, and tousled just so, styled to look as though he hadn't tried at all.

They reached the garden flat together, and Owen rang the doorbell. A gentle, melodious chime rang out from inside, and Dulcie answered the door, looking utterly captivating.

Her copper-coloured hair was casually tied back, her eyelids were smudged with soot-coloured powder, and a touch of gloss highlighted her lips.

"Hello, you two!" Her smile was bright and full of excitement for the evening ahead.

"Wow, you look catwalk ready." Tristan flashed a smile that had derailed many a good intention.

Owen gave a short nod, less polished but no less genuine. "Hi, Dulcie. Ready for the pub?"

"As ready as I'll ever be." She stepped outside, locking the door behind her. She had spent a fair amount of time in her room getting ready and had checked her phone more than once to make sure the plans hadn't been called off. The group of friends she was about to meet felt like a big unknown, and she made sure to dress in a way she hoped balanced being friendly and fashionable. "Who exactly am I going to be meeting, then?" She asked. "You've both been vague about these mates of yours."

"You'll see," Tristan offered his arm, which she took, while Owen fell into step beside them, trying not to feel like the odd one out.

"Okay," Dulcie announced, "I'm in your hands. Let's go and charm some strangers."

The street was deserted, calm and shaded, with the peaceful hush of early evening. A handful of leaves skittered across the pavement. As twilight fell, the windows began to light up one by one, shining yellow beacons of comfort.

"So," Owen said, "your first visit to The Witch & Stable. It's not fancy, but, as I said, the food's good, and the company is weird and wonderful, so you'll fit right in."

"She'll fit in because she's weird?" Tristan teased, glancing down at her. Dulcie grinned and tilted her head towards Owen.

"I take it that was a kind of compliment?"

"The highest kind," Owen said. "Honestly, there are too many normal people in the world. You'd hate it if we took you somewhere full of them. Besides, we're going to the pub your uncle frequents, and he rather sets the bar on eccentric."

"I'll tell him you said that," Dulcie said, giving him a playful nudge.

Tristan took the lead in the conversation. He shared a story about a magpie that dive-bombed him during his morning run, holding his arms wide like wings and mimicking the attack for effect. Dulcie was in fits of laughter. Owen laughed too, but mainly kept watch, trying to see what made her laugh the hardest and where her attention lingered. Tristan's eyes were the front-runners.

As they approached the pub, the buzz of early evening chatter spilled out through the partially open doors. Warm light bathed the entrance, and the background of laughter and clinking glasses invited them in.

"You'll like them," Owen said as they stepped through the entrance, the cheerful clang of the bell overhead announcing their arrival. He looked at Dulcie and offered her a sincere smile. "They'll like you too."

The pub was lively, filled with the murmur of conversation and the low drone of football commentary playing on a screen above the bar. The decor featured a cosy blend of mismatched chairs, vintage horse brasses, and gentle yellow lighting. Glasses rattled as someone hurriedly approached the dartboard, making a chair leg screech. The subtle aroma of malt and roasted peanuts lingered in the air. Dulcie paused just inside the door, taking it in. "This is very... traditional," she murmured, adjusting the sleeves of her jacket.

"You say that like it's a bad thing," Tristan replied with a grin, leading her towards the cluster of tables at the back where his friends were already mid-pint and the conversation was flowing freely. "Alright, everyone," he called. "This is Dulcie, our new neighbour, come to add a bit of glamour to our gathering."

The three of them slid into a seat spanning the bottom of a window, covered in cracked red leather that was slightly sticky and cold to the touch. Introductions fizzed around like beer foam—frothy, fleeting, and hard to catch. Dulcie gave them all a slight wave of her hand and tried to pay attention, striving to match names to faces. First on the list was a young couple: Megan and Rob looked welcoming but rather tired, their faces showing the exhaustion of broken nights and managing childcare. Rob was tall and lanky, with a beard more overgrown than stylish. Megan had golden, tanned skin and wavy black hair, worn in a loose ponytail. As Megan turned to greet her, Dulcie noticed a small oval stain of baby sick on the back of her cardigan, recognising it as the universal badge of new motherhood. A youth who stood to their right, was introduced as Tom, an emerging artist with long bare arms and paint-smeared fingers. Tousled brown hair gently curled at his temples and fell over the shoulders of his vintage-inspired tank top. His greeting was warm and genuine; the sort of person who never met a stranger.

Next, Owen introduced the two recent graduates he had mentioned before. Ellie was all sharp features and vibrant colours, with a close-cropped buzzcut dyed a fiery orange-red that seemed to glow under the pub's soft lighting. A constellation of silver studs traced the curve of one ear, and a tiny nose hoop sparkled as she moved her head. In contrast, Jessie had long, chestnut-coloured hair that nearly reached her waist, parted neatly in the middle. She wore an oversized, light grey wool sweater, with the sleeves pushed up to show delicate wrists and bitten nails.

To one side, a young man, introduced as Iden, was seated alone at a table, his slim frame hunched forward with his elbows resting on his knees. He wore a regulation football jersey and scuffed trainers, and sat with his jaw clenched as he watched the match on the screen. His short, dark hair looked damp, as if he had just come in from a quick shower. Lost in the game, he was oblivious to the busy room and everyone in it, totally focused on the unfolding drama on the pitch.

Taking their drink requests, Owen went to place their order with Jamila, who was on duty behind the bar. He returned, balancing a tray as if he were auditioning for a low-budget Western. "Here we go: two white wines, a prosecco, three lagers, one cider, an orange juice and a glass of Malbec." He handed them round. "Cheers," he said.

They all clinked glasses as their conversation shifted from work gossip to TV shows and, inevitably, to local scandal. "Did you hear about Mrs. Donaldson's window box?" Ellie leaned in. "Someone stole all the plants from it, leaving it looking as bare as an empty nest. It's not a crime that will make headlines, but I feel for her. That display is her pride and joy, and it's a real shame that it keeps getting ruined."

"Strange stuff indeed," Rob shuffled up, voice dropping conspiratorially. "But that wasn't even the craziest thing to happen last week."

"I had no idea I'd moved into the middle of the wild, wild west. Do tell," said Dulcie.

"Well," Rob began, "it seems we're in the middle of a small but growing crime wave."

"Don't listen to him," Megan interrupted. "The two of us haven't been in public for some time, so he's a bit overexcited." She smiled at him indulgently. "Having a baby means falling in love with your dressing gown; neither of us has been fit to wear anything else or go out for weeks. Too busy getting parenthood wrong."

"Sounds tough," Dulcie sympathised. "I'm told the key thing about babies is they won't *remember* if you were bad at changing nappies, or soothing them at 3 a.m. in the morning."

Rob interrupted. Much as he loved his newborn, he was determined to steer the conversation away from the nursery, even if it meant exaggerating the local scandal. "The chip shop got hit earlier this week. Twice, I heard."

"They didn't get *hit*," Jessie clarified. "Someone stole a box of fish just after opening. No break-in, no smashed lock. Just reached over the counter apparently and... gone."

"Very Ocean's Eleven," Tom interjected. "If Ocean's Eleven had fewer casinos and more vinegar. What about you,

Owen? Didn't I hear someone stole your bike the other day?

"They did. I've had to raid the savings and get a replacement."

"Don't be sorry for him," Tristan chipped in. "That bike was in terrible shape, so much so that the thief left behind a fiver and a note of sympathy." Jeers rippled through the group. "Now he's bought a fancy one, and keeps it on the landing, where it lurks as a trip hazard."

"That wasn't my fault," Owen said, giving his friend a shove. "If you come back at two in the morning, three sheets to the wind, with legs as wobbly as a crane fly, you're going to end up on the floor." Everyone cheered.

As the conversation continued, Dulcie was impressed by how involved everyone was and how genuinely they cared about the place they called home. It had been a while since she felt connected to a community, where people looked out for each other. She didn't feel like an outsider; she already felt involved.

"The corner shop lost half its stock of premium Swiss chocolates." Iden had lost interest in the football after his team drew their match, and now he joined the chat. "No sign of forced entry. Just… boom. Chocolate gone," he added.

"It's baffling," Owen said, taking a sip of his beer. "The residents' WhatsApp group is in full meltdown. You'd think someone had taken the Crown Jewels." In truth, he rather enjoyed reading the lengthy exchanges, which were filled with outrage and bristled at every minor misdemeanour.

Rob mimed typing furiously on an invisible phone. "Whoever stole my Twix is a menace, and I will not be silenced."

"So," Dulcie said, resting her chin in her hand, "if the fish outlaw strikes again, are you two planning to intervene?"

Tristan raised his pint. "Naturally. Heroes of the haddock."

"Protectors of the peas."

"Avengers of the vinegar. All for one and one for all," Dulcie added, and they all clinked their glasses again. Ideas bounced between them, partly serious, partly amused. Someone suggested setting a trap. They weren't just aimlessly talking; they were plotting in a light-hearted, harmless way, including her in all the chats, as if she had always been part of the group.

"I'm telling you," Rob said, with the confidence of a man holding a pint and a theory, "it's a gang. Possibly teenagers. Possibly geriatric vagabonds."

"But who steals flowers?" Jessie asked. "Pulling blooms out of window boxes is vandalism, but taking them away with you is a bit psycho."

"We need help to resolve this." Ellie speculated, "Someone with a genuine investigative background. What about Big Maccie?" A moment of silence descended over the table, only interrupted by the hissing of the espresso machine behind the bar.

"That could be a solid suggestion. After all, he's a retired cop. Something of a legend by all accounts. I heard he once chased a shoplifter through a car wash and came out cleaner than he went in," Tom replied. "Have you heard of him, Dulcie?"

"Heard of him. Met him. Lost his cat"

They looked at her in surprise. "It's a bit of a long story."

Owen stepped in. "Missy will be fine; she's the queen of the street cats. However, if you do see her around, could you please message one of us? It would give us some brownie points with Maccie."

"You think he'd agree to lend a hand with this other stuff?" Iden asked. "I thought he'd sworn off crime-solving in favour of enjoying a peaceful retirement."

"I could ask him," Owen offered. "He likes me. I think. When he first fell ill, I'd carry his shopping, including that enormous scratching post he'd brought for Missy. It was the biggest one in the shop; carrying it home was like tossing the caber."

Dulcie pondered for a moment. "Let's do it. Let's ask. From my experience, his bark is worse than his bite. It's not like he can arrest us for just asking."

As evening fell and drinks kept coming, the idea of using Big Maccie as the local detective grew more convincing. Fuelled by the kind of boozy enthusiasm that turns half-baked schemes into heroic quests, the group united around their clever plan to protect Minet Road from further treachery. They jotted notes on napkins and debated timelines with the confidence of amateur sleuths who had watched enough crime shows to believe they knew what they were doing.

Dulcie saw the momentum build with a combination of amusement and curiosity. It appeared that Big Maccie now had no say in the matter. His reputation as a professional who was somewhat nosy and blessed with free time had predestined his fate. Whether Maccie would accept this, or if it would spiral into the most absurd mystery of the year, was anyone's guess.

"To Operation Battered Justice!" Owen said, lifting his beer. They raised their glasses and sealed the deal, clinking them together once more.

CHAPTER 15

Even though it was Saturday, Gerald Waring at No. 61 adjusted his tie with military precision. Navy blue with tiny clocks on it, his "casual" tie. He wore it to convey that while this was technically his day off, he remained a man to be reckoned with.

A single mattress leaned awkwardly in his hallway, propped like a drunken relative against the wallpapered wall. It had belonged to Gerald's late mother, and he had been meaning to get rid of it for a while. He gave it a salute. "You served her well," he said. Then, gripping it by the corners, he began the long, sweaty shuffle out of the building.

He could have taken it to the tip. Indeed, he should have taken it to the tip. But that was before he knew the young woman in the garden flat at No. 67, one Ms. Dulcie Staples, was touting for old junk. It appeared that she was working from that old workshop in their backyard. If there was a shed, Gerald reasoned, then by rights there must be storage. And if there was storage, who was he to deny that mattress a final, peaceful resting place within it?

Lugging the old mattress down the garden path, its sagging bulk awkward in his arms, Gerald made his way into the empty road. The cool night air was illuminated only by the porch behind him and the occasional flicker of a streetlamp. Scraping against the pavement, the mattress left a faint trail as it gathered up leaves and grit from the ground. He wrestled it through the narrow gap beside the houses, shadows closing in around him. Finally, he reached the back gate, his breath visible in the cold, sweat sticking to his collar despite the chill. He carefully moved the mattress into the backyard to the shed at the far end of the garden. Gerald glanced around; the coast was clear. He pulled the mattress towards the shed with the cautious reverence of someone attempting to infiltrate a foreign embassy.

Locked.

Of course, it was locked.

He stared at the workshop, as though it might open out of respect for his efforts. It didn't.

No matter. Gerald wasn't a quitter. He was a solutions-oriented professional. Beside the shed was a narrow strip of concrete, perfect for propping a mattress against. With a satisfying flop, the mattress came to rest, looking somewhat deranged, as if it had tried to escape and been caught mid-flight. Nevertheless, leaving it here was a gesture of resourceful generosity to a budding 'upcycler'. Not that he was entirely clear what that title meant. He inspected his work before dusting off his hands and marching back up through the ginnel, feeling very pleased with himself. However, that sense of satisfaction vanished the moment he stepped out of the side passage, just as Tristan, Owen, and Dulcie appeared around the corner after returning from the pub.

"Good evening, Gerald," Tristan weaved slightly as he walked towards him.

"Evening," Gerald replied, stiffly. He hadn't anticipated bumping into anyone during his mission.

"Lovely clear night," Owen offered, peering up at the stars with mild wonder.

"Yes, indeed. I was just out for a short constitutional," Gerald straightened his collar. "Very good for the health," he added. "Still, one can have too much of a good thing, so I'd best be off." He turned on his heel. "I bid you all a goodnight."

With that, he strode smartly up his front steps and disappeared inside.

"I wonder what on earth he was up to, skulking in the shadows like that." Dulcie watched the door click shut. Perhaps he is our phantom thief," she mused.

"I wouldn't put it past him, funny little man. And they say he's tight with his money—could be a criminal mastermind hiding in plain sight," said Owen.

The three stood in contemplative silence, gazing at Gerald's door for a moment longer before tipsily meandering home.

Just beyond the hedges, under the rose bushes, Missy the cat watched them carefully. Her newfound freedom turned the town into her kingdom, and she intended to rule it. She padded through the deserted streets of Brixton. An empress in her element, stealthy sovereign of the night.

CHAPTER 16

Les stepped into the dimly lit Witch & Stable pub, the scent of ale and aged wood curling around him. As his eyes adjusted to the low light, he scanned the booths but saw no sign of Gerald, only the usual regulars nursing their pints. Les was confident that his neighbour would be there somewhere; he was a creature of habit. When at last he spotted him standing at the bar in the corner, Les greeted him with the enthusiasm of a long-lost friend.

"Gerald!" he bellowed. "How are you?"

"Oh, you know," replied Gerald without lifting his head from his customary slump. "Another day, another dollar down the drain."

"Great to see you enjoying yourself," said Les heartily. "Can I offer you a Jack Daniel?"

"Jack Daniel*sss*, surely?" Queried the pedantic Gerald.

"Oh, you want more than one?" asked Les, enjoying his little joke. "Make it a double then, Jamila," said Les.

Les knew the only way to interact with Gerald was to disregard most of what he said and plunge into conversation. Listening politely only encouraged the man, who possessed a rare ability to drain the joy from any cheerful gathering. Luckily, this method suited Les, who had never been one for delicate conversational footwork. He noticed that Jamila was doing her best to stay at the far end of the bar, busy polishing glasses that didn't need a polish. She also tended to avoid their neighbour, agreeing that he was as much fun as Eeyore on a down day, minus the charm.

"Give us a smile, Gerald. You know what they say about smiles being infectious. One small smile can travel around the World," said Les

"I don't tend to go about grinning like an idiot. And I don't touch hard liquor, so if you are buying, I would rather have a bitter shandy. Half a pint, please. Below room temperature, if possible."

"You don't want a full pint? We're off duty. Let your hair down."

"I prefer moderation in all things, thank you very much."

Les gave Jamila a nod, prompting her to stop wiping the already spotless counter and expertly pour their beers. As the glasses filled, she exchanged a look with Les that spoke volumes – somewhere between 'good luck' and 'rather you than me.' Without a word, she set the drinks down and stepped away, leaving the men to talk. Les lifted his glass.

"Bottoms up."

"Quite." Gerald paused, attempting to sip his drink without letting his mouth touch too much of the rim.

"So," Les swirled his pint, "I wondered if it was you who

moved your mum's old mattress into my yard yesterday?"

"Yes, indeed," Gerald said, opting for honesty—Les clearly already knew what had happened. "The item in question *was* moved to the back of your premises," he admitted. "Your niece appears to be collecting a variety of discarded bits and bobs. I understand she can craft something clever from them, and I thought I would add to her collection. It was time for me to, you know, clear the decks."

"Mm-hmm. Right. I was going to do some gardening early this morning when I noticed the mattress. Dulcie mentioned she saw you out last night, so I thought it must have been your donation." Les pursed his lips. "Not that she's requested any mattresses. She can't use them, especially not ones that block her shed."

"Interim placement, in that case," Gerald understood that he had been caught out and wriggled like an eel on a stick. "Pending proper disposal."

"Funny you should say that, because I did you a little favour. Took it off your hands permanently. You won't have to worry about it anymore."

"Oh. That was… considerate. Where did you take it?"

"A friend of mine's got an allotment on Mitchum Way," Les waved vaguely. "Already had a big bonfire on the go. Got rid of it in no time."

"You burned it?"

"Well, yes. It was a health hazard, Gerald. Mouldy. Probably full of spores."

"That mattress belonged to my *mother*." Gerald was profoundly offended. How could anyone think he would possess a household item that was inferior in any way?

His shirts were perfectly pressed, his lawn carefully maintained, and his front porch inspected for litter. He credited his discipline to his military background, even though he never saw combat, having served in the catering corps. Yet, he proudly displayed his service as a badge of honour, and viewed any breach of his self-image as a personal insult.

"Your mum didn't need that old mattress any longer, did she? You wanted rid of it and, as a good neighbour, I've sorted that out for you."

Gerald opened his mouth, closed it, then opened it again. He felt wrong-footed and wasn't quite sure why.

Having achieved the reaction he wanted, Les reached into his pocket and took out a small, singed object. He laid it on the table like a tarot reader revealing a cursed playing card. It was, in fact, the corner of a ten-pound note. Burnt, blackened, but unmistakably legal tender. "I wasn't sure if I should tell you about it, but this was found in the ashes." Les held the piece up for inspection. "Makes you think, doesn't it? I wonder if your old mum had money tucked under her bed, or in a slit in the cushioning? She was a canny woman by all accounts."

Gerald blinked. He felt like someone had poured cold soup down his spine. "You don't suppose, I mean, she never trusted banks... but she'd never hide her savings there. *She wouldn't,* would she?" he spluttered.

"Hard to say," Les looked downcast. "I would have thought that it's *unlikely* she was squirrelling money into her mattress. But old folk always used to put their spare funds under the bed, and it's a hard habit to break." He shook his head sadly. "Of course, if there *was* a lot more notes in there, they'd probably be ashes, too. There isn't much that can be done about it now."

"I have to go," Gerald announced, jumping to his feet.

"What, now? You've barely touched your warm beer."

But his neighbour was already halfway to the door, shouldering past a man in a dart-themed waistcoat and knocking a couple of chairs aside like bumper cars.

Eyes twinkling like a fox in moonlight, Les turned and made his way back to the bar. "Care for a drink, Jamila?" he asked. "I'm feeling generous."

"Well, I never," she replied. "Yes, I'll have a bitter lemon with you." Les had bought her plenty before, but she noticed something different about him tonight. He glowed with a barely contained energy, like a kettle just shy of the boil. His eyes had a glint of mischief, and unless she was much mistaken, he looked ready to burst into song. She was happy to raise a glass with him, but wondered what exactly they were drinking to.

Les waited until Jamila had a drink in hand. Then, in the tone of a man who'd just pulled a coin from behind a child's ear, he said, "Did you see our new piece of garden art earlier today? The mattress?"

"I saw it from my window this morning. I thought it was odd."

Les chuckled, a low, wheezy sound that made it unclear whether he was laughing or suppressing a burp. "Gerald took it upon himself to dump it there, the cheeky blighter," he said, raising his glass in mock solemnity. "But you'll be pleased to hear justice has been done."

Jamila took a sip. The pub was quiet, and she had a moment to listen to his story.

Les leaned in. "I may have... suggested that a friend of mine took on the mattress at his allotment, needed kindling, and gave it a Viking send-off."

"You set the mattress on fire?"

"No! You can't get away with burning anything like that around here," said Les, eyes dancing. "But I told Gerald I did."

"What have you been up to, Les?"

"I told him it was burned to ashes. And I may have shown him this," he reached into his pocket and pulled out the charred corner of what had once been a ten-pound note, blackened at the edges only.

"Wait, was that actually there? In the mattress, I mean."

"Oh, give your head a wobble!" Les remonstrated, "Of course not! That mattress didn't go anywhere near an allotment. It's down the back of Nev's garage, waiting for the next trip to the recycling centre. But I told Gerald it'd gone up in flames, and implied that this," he wiggled the bit of ash, "was all that remained of the small fortune his dear old mum had stashed inside it."

"You are a wicked man." Jamila's face slowly split into a grin, understanding why Les was so pleased with himself. He had pulled off a fantastic prank, with just the right mix of cheek and ingenuity to earn him bragging rights for months to come. The story would spread among the regulars like a dropped pint skittering across the floor, gaining more embellishments with each retelling. It had all the ingredients of a timeless pub legend, sure to be shared repeatedly and always with Les at the centre, grinning like the cat that got the cream, the pint, and the punchline.

"I thought it would be good for him," said Les. "Teach him not to preach about anti-social behaviour, then use my backyard as a rubbish heap." He paused. "I don't suppose I can pay for my next beer using the rest of this tenner, can I?" He pulled out the remainder of the torn note, which had donated its corner for the joke.

"No, you can't." Jamila laughed, shaking her head. "How did he take it?"

"Ran out of the pub like a man possessed. I gave him the location of the allotment, of course. He'll be rooting through someone's double-dug patch right now. Looking for the remains of his family fortune."

"Remind me never to cross you, Les."

"Too late." He gazed at Jamila fondly. "You offered me an afternoon watching the racing and promised double helpings. But I've not heard anything since."

"You'd better come up tomorrow night," she offered. "But there will be no mattress burning of *any* kind in my attic."

"In your dreams," scoffed Les. But his cheeks flushed pink, and he struggled to swallow the last mouthful of beer. He was sure he'd had more enjoyable days in his life, but at that moment, he couldn't remember any.

CHAPTER 17

The scent of linseed oil and scorched pine lingered in the summer air as Dulcie ran a hand plane over the edge of an old drawer front. The scrape...scrape...scrape of the plane was hypnotic until it was interrupted by an unexpected thunk, followed by a grunt and the sound of something heavy grating along the gravel. She didn't look up. The workshop behind the house was warm with late-afternoon light, and her hands were stained with walnut oil and the fine, dark dust of sanded oak. A half-finished back panel rested in her vice. She was smoothing its edges, quietly focused, chin tucked, the soft scrape of sandpaper and the breeze in the fig tree her only companions.

Then came another muffled clang, the sound of something heavy against concrete. She glanced toward the open door. A few ripe curses drifted across the yard, followed by the low shuffle of metal being dragged. Tristan and Owen appeared, wrestling an enormous metal filing cabinet through the narrow side gate. It was tall, gunmetal grey, and weighed more than the two of them were comfortable admitting.

"Watch your side!"

"I am watching my side. Maybe you try lifting instead of critiquing?"

"Good grief!" Dulcie set her tools aside. "What on earth are you doing?"

At the front, Tristan was half-smiling, sweat darkening the collar of his shirt. "Special delivery."

"Someone left it on the pavement next to our steps," Owen said, adjusting his grip on the back end. His voice was calm as always, but his brow was furrowed with the weight. "Didn't knock, didn't ask. Just… left it. We thought bringing it around the back here could be our good deed for the day."

"Speak for yourself, mate. I just thought it looked heavy and wanted an excuse to flex." Tristan placed the end of the cabinet on the ground, stretched both arms together and swung them in an arch, showing off impressive biceps, with muscles that danced in line as he moved.

"Mission accomplished," murmured Dulcie, appreciating the view.

"Apparently word's out," Tristan added. "You're the girl who turns trash into gold."

"I wish that were true." She walked around the cabinet. It was tall, four drawers deep, with chipped paint and rust blossoming along the sides. She ran her fingers along the edge of the metal, earning herself a fine line of rust and a high chance of needing a tetanus shot. The drawers were stuck fast. This was the kind of thing someone abandoned because it had become obselete in it's current form. It stood bravely, if unsteadily, on the ground, forlorn and bemused at being discarded after a lifetime of service.

Owen folded his arms. "Some people are given flowers, but you get office furniture." She caught his eyes for a moment, and a fleeting look passed between them.

Tristan stepped closer and nudged the cabinet with his boot. "You think it's salvageable?"

"Oh, definitely. Once I get these drawers unstuck and sand off the remaining paint."

The wind shifted, flapping the edge of the tarp covering her pile of salvaged wood like it was trying to fan the flames of their conversation. Tristan leaned against the frame, glanced at Owen, then looked back at her. "I can stay here for a bit to help you out," he said. "I'm always willing to give you a hand, and I don't like to think of you trying to shift this thing on your own."

"I've got a spare twenty minutes," Owen interjected, his expression so obvious you could project a movie onto it without missing any plot points. "I can help you too, if you need it. As it happens, I know Tristan has an event he needs to get to soon, and there's no need to delay him, as I don't have to set off for a while."

"I could come back later, if that works better for you, Dulcie?" asked Tristan.

"I'm fine. It's good of you both," she said. "But thanks."

She looked back and forth between the two men. They stood close to her, careful not to overshadow each other, yet still discreetly competing. There was a delicate tension among the three of them, a tentative shape beginning to emerge. Not quite a triangle, but a fragile, shifting situation. No one voiced these feelings; none wanted to be the first to declare their position.

"Well," she said at last, brushing her hands together, "thank you for the cabinet. It's going to look amazing once I work my magic."

Tristan sighed, stepping back. "Guess we'll leave you to it, then"

"Back to work," Owen agreed, though his eyes lingered on her as he turned to leave.

The two men walked away together, resuming their joking as they disappeared into the alley. Dulcie watched them go, then turned to the cabinet and leaned against it with a sigh. She wasn't sure what to do with it yet—this large, rusty object dumped unceremoniously at her door. But she'd figure it out. She was still inspecting the metal drawers when the workshop door creaked open. She lifted her gaze quickly, curious which of her admirers had come back for her.

Instead, Big Maccie stepped inside, his silhouette instantly recognisable. Moving with the cautious pace of someone accustomed to assessing a situation before entering it, he got straight to the point of his visit. "I hope it's all right to come in. I wanted to let you know. Missy came home this morning."

"She *did?*" Dulcie let out a long breath. "I'm so glad to hear it. I've been worrying about her."

He nodded. "At about seven. I was making tea. Heard the catflap, looked over, and there she was. Calm as anything. Walked in, jumped up on the radiator, like she'd never been gone," he continued. "She's fine. No injuries, no signs of a fight, and as sleek as a seal. She's either been taken care of by a personal trainer or been living in a bin behind Greggs. Never seen her in better shape."

"That's wonderful news. Thanks for coming to tell me." Dulcie was delighted. What a relief." Assuming Maccie must be in high spirits, given the happy return of his feline friend, she seized the moment to bring up the delicate topic of asking for his help. "I thought your ears might be burning last night," she began. "The pub was buzzing with tales of your crime-fighting days. It seems you've become quite the folk hero." She felt that a generous dose of flattery couldn't hurt.

"Oh? I regard that as highly unlikely."

Stepping away from the bench, Dulcie busied herself by swapping the coarse-grit sandpaper for a finer grade. "Yes," she continued. "Your reputation precedes you. Everyone agreed on how much good you've done over the years."

"Usually right before adding, 'He once nicked my nephew on Christmas Eve.'" Maccie muttered.

"The thing is," Dulcie pressed on, "a few odd things have been happening along Minet Road. Not serious, not enough to bother the police. But people are unsettled."

"Unsettled how?" Maccie sounded bored rather than curious.

Unclamping the sanded backing, Dulcie placed it on the workbench. "Someone snatched a box of fish right off the chip shop counter. They turned their backs for one minute, and it was gone. Plus, there's been an increase in parcel pirates and plant thefts from window boxes and gardens, and the sweet shop regularly reports missing boxes of expensive chocolates." She feared she was losing her audience, so threw in some intrigue. "I know it's not a catalogue of serious offences, but it's clear that a mysterious pattern is beginning to form."

"You think all these things are connected?"

Picking up a small handheld drill, Dulcie turned its handle and enjoyed the satisfying chirping sound it made. "I don't know," she admitted. "But it's always the same stretch of road—nearly every night around nine or ten. There are no signs of break-ins. Nothing unusual. Whoever it is, they don't leave much behind."

"The police won't pay much attention to that; they're hardly the crimes of the century."

"No one's even bothered to report it." Dulcie began handdrilling holes in the back of the chair seat. She felt increasingly awkward but was determined to make her request. "Everyone seemed to agree that it might be worth asking you about it. What with you being the best in the business at feeling a collar."

"That was a long time ago. I don't think your average crook can be found wearing an actual collar these days."

"Doesn't mean it's not true."

Maccie gazed out the window for a long, reflective moment. Retirement didn't suit him as well as he had expected. He missed the routine of his work, craving the sense of purpose and the thrill of the chase. These days, television bored him, and newspapers were portents of doom. Searching for a needle in a haystack might be futile, but at least it would give him something engaging to think about.

All right, he agreed. "I'll keep watch and ask some questions, but don't expect miracles. If someone is cautious, they'll be hard to catch. It could be random teenage kids fooling around or passing strangers." He gave a wry half-smile. "Maybe your haddock bandit has a sweet tooth and a flair for the dramatic. But let me know if you find out anything more, okay? I won't be able to go very far myself in the next few days. If something specific happens or if there's anything new, stop by and knock on my door."

"Brilliant," said Dulcie, beaming. She was thrilled, both because he agreed to the plan and because she would have the pleasure of telling her new friends that she had pulled a proverbial rabbit out of the hat.

"I should get going. The cat won't forgive me for spoiling our big reunion by lingering too long." He raised a hand in a casual salute and stepped back into the glow of the late afternoon light. As he reached back to close the door, he leaned in slightly and added, "Of course, if Missy is involved in this mystery in any way," his eyes twinkled, "you never saw me."

"It's a deal," smiled Dulcie, misquoting a famous poem; "you may meet her in a by-street, you may see her in the square. But when a crime's discovered, Missy-Mae is *never* there!"

CHAPTER 18

Tuesday marked a long-awaited milestone: the first time Dulcie sold an upcycled chair to a bona fide customer. Not only did she sell it, but she also made a clear profit since it was the one she had picked up for free and wheeled home from the charity shop. The upholstery had been a battle to replace, but the actual structure hadn't required much beyond a bit of spit and polish. A couple of well-presented photographs online, and hey presto!

Uncle Les had cheered at the news and done a little 'finding gold' dance. He insisted they mark the occasion with a slap-up supper. In his vocabulary, this meant fish and chips from the local fryer, which went by the legendary name of '*Absolutely Battered*'.

"You're gonna love it, Dulcie," Uncle Les promised. "My friend Angie runs the place with her cousins, Sheila and Barbara, who have been frying chips since before your mum was born. What Barbara doesn't know about a King Edward potato isn't worth knowing. I'll tell you something else: when that woman laughs, it's a delight. Her nose turns red and her eyes run with tears. If you can once make her howl with laughter, you'll dedicate your life to making it happen again. Come and watch how it's done. Food and entertainment!" he winked.

"If you like," agreed Dulcie, who would have preferred something less stodgy but could see the opportunity this presented for her investigation. "Whilst we are there, we can find out if anything else has gone missing from their stock recently. I'm supposed to give Big Maccie a report."

"Well, get your coat on then, Miss Moneybags. Those chips won't eat themselves, will they?" He reached for his jacket and opened the door for her.

After a short walk, they reached the shop, its neon sign flickering and winking at them. Inside, two women worked quickly, cooking, coating, and serving. One woman was so short that a sturdy beam was fixed to the floor as a step, helping her see into the fryers and reach over the counters. Dulcie thought it was no surprise she was so trim—each shift probably doubled as an aerobics class. The air in the fish and chip shop was filled with the strong, familiar smell of hot oil and vinegar. The deep fryers hissed and bubbled constantly, creating a steady chorus of boiling fat. Steam stuck to the windows, blurring the view and leaving streaks of condensation on the glass. The white-tiled walls had acquired a faint golden sheen that no amount of scrubbing could remove. Fluorescent lights flickered overhead, casting a harsh glow over the counter and trays of battered fish, sausages, and golden chips.

"Les! You old rogue," Barbara cried, her eyes lighting up. "And who have we got here?"

"This is my great niece, Dulcie," Les pushed her gently forward. "She's just sold her first upcycled bit of furniture. A chair she restored with her very own hands. A big day, eh?"

"Bravo. I'm all for women making their own luck." Barbara leaned over, handing Dulcie a laminated menu. "I expect you'll want the Tuesday Night Tea? Fish, chips, mushy peas or pie? The pies are homemade. Angie rolled the pastry, and Sheila made the gravy, so it can't be beaten."

"I can't decide." Les looked mischievous. "What's written up there on the wipeboard? Haddock or Plaice?"

"Plaice"

"Yours or mine?"

"You cheeky beggar." Barbara grinned and poked Les's ribs with a long metal spoon. "You'd go pale if I took you up on it, wouldn't you?"

"Never!" exclaimed Les, tongue in cheek. "But, as it is, we'll content ourselves with two Tuesday night fish suppers as they're on special offer. I'm not made of money." He proceeded to launch into a couple of jokes: "What is the world's fastest fish? A motor-pike!" Then, "What do you call a fish with no eyes? A Fsh." Barbara's eyes twinkled but stayed this side of amused. "You should try writing comedy, Les," she said, "and stop putting us to the trouble of listening to it."

"Don't give up the day job," warned Angie, her colleague, who was eavesdropping while skilfully wrapping large portions of chips. "Your gags are only good for a Christmas cracker, Les."

"I'm thinking bigger than that," he replied grandly. "A one-man show. 'The Hilarious Halibut.' Tickets at the door. Here all week!" But none of his puns were landing, so he chose to reconsider his strategy and smoothly retired, leaving the line of customers and walking with Dulcie to the back of the shop to wait for their food.

A few other customers waited in line, shifting their weight from foot to foot, eagerly examining the warming cabinet. An older man wearing a flat cap glanced at his watch impatiently, and a woman in a high-visibility jacket leaned against the wall, holding a can of fizzy drink. The scene had a soothing rhythm: the rustling of paper, the clattering of tongs, and the occasional squeak of trainers on the aged linoleum floor.

"I have to admit," Dulcie told her uncle, "This was a good idea. Especially as I was considering a quiet night in."

"Quiet? You've got to celebrate the wins, Dulcie! Especially the ones where you've managed to transform something from what was rubbish into a prize worth treasuring. You're helping to save the planet – a superhero armed only with a saw and sandpaper."

Barbara nodded. "And if you want to make it official, there's always the 'Chip Shop Champions' board," she pointed over their shoulder with a chip fork. "We can put up a before-and-after photo of your restoration project. Think you're ready for that kind of fame?"

"I am. All publicity is good publicity, so they say. Can I really?"

"Certainly. We'll put it on the noticeboard, above the business cards and adverts. It gives customers something to browse, and a success story is a popular read."

Les was warmed to this theme. "After that, you can design a fish dish with a secret blend of paint chips. Do you see what I did there?" he demanded happily, "Paint *chips*?"

"Oh, please. Stop while you're ahead," Angie pleaded.

"Tough crowd." Les shook his head. "But I'm not defeated; a thankless audience is no barrier to success."

"It's not all success on this side of the stage either." Barbara shook her head. "I've had two bottles of vinegar stolen from the counter this week. Who pinches vinegar? It's not as if it's costly or there's a national shortage. But it's very annoying." She continued, adding batter to a batch of sausages. "Isn't that right, Angie?"

Angie nodded and sighed heavily. "It's a wonder we have any left." She turned and went into the stockroom at the rear, where she tilted a heavy barrel of chipped potatoes and rolled it back into the shop in a zig-zag motion.

Dulcie watched the colleagues as they undertook their everyday tasks. "I know you are very busy this evening, but we've been told about the box of haddock that went missing last Thursday; can you tell us anything more about it?" She tried to sound professional. "Our friend Maccie's trying to track down the thief who's been targeting this area."

"Angie's been referring to it as The Great Fish Robbery." Barbara didn't look up from the fryer as she prepared the following order. "But it was more a vanishing trick than a theft. Here one moment, gone the next."

"Right. Yes, that's exactly what we heard. Do you have any thoughts about what happened?"

Barbara carefully placed the coated fish into the fryer,

which hissed and sputtered. She didn't think anyone would be held responsible. However, she believed that 'it isn't what you know, but who you know' that matters; in this case, she knew Big Maccie. Given his past as a respected policeman and his current retirement, involving him seemed sensible. "Well," she said thoughtfully, "there was one man in the shop around the time the fish disappeared. Bit of an odd sort. Shoulder-length brown hair, a bit straggly, average-looking. One of those beards that's neither one thing nor another. He wore a long beige raincoat, a wool hat, and a football scarf. If I had to pick someone likely to ask for chips and then sneak off with my haddock, it would be him."

This description rang a distant bell with Dulcie, and her eyes lit up. "Oh! I think I know him. I've met someone who is exactly like that!"

"You have?"

"Yes! At the council office! He was droning on like a broken podcast about his girlfriend's conservatory. He fits the description perfectly. I thought there was something off about him at the time."

Their food was ready. Golden, crisp, and steaming. Barbara swiftly bundled the fish into paper boxes lined with paper, wrapped them tightly, and tucked them into a bag. Uncle Les, who'd been sitting at the window bench eyeing a newspaper, picked up the carrier and put a hand on Dulcie's shoulder.

"Well, love," he said, "sounds like you've cracked the case. I'm sure Scotland Yard will be round any minute with a medal and a letter of commendation."

"I suppose it is a long shot," Dulcie noted the sarcasm. "But we know he must be fairly local, and his description fits. It could be him, if you put those things together."

"Or me, come to that. I own a beige raincoat."

"Wait a minute—where were you last Thursday night?" She turned to him, eyes narrowing.

Les was wrong-footed. "You made me watch 'Bake Off' with you." He was convinced she was joking. At least, he certainly hoped so. He had better things to do than sneaking around stealing condiments from neighbours or pocketing chocolate bars from the local shop. While he wasn't perfect, some lines he would never cross. Mischief, maybe. The occasional white lie, perhaps. But theft? Absolutely not!

Barbara dropped a new batch of chips into the fryer, apparently unexcited by the revelation that Les could be a suspect in the crime of the century.

"Have you got any security cameras, Barbara?" Dulcie asked hopefully, moving her investigation forward.

"Just a dummy one. Blinks when it rains, scares no one except me. Makes me jump when it flashes."

"Anyone else who seemed suspicious hanging about lately? Or perhaps just a new face that stood out?"

"Not that comes to mind." Barbara maintained a sense of continued indifference. It wasn't that she didn't care; instead, she had accepted the series of light-fingered incidents as an inconvenience and expense that any small trader had to face these days. But she searched her mind. "Last week, a woman I hadn't seen before walked in, dressed in an orange Afghan coat and purple leggings," Barbara recalled, squinting as she tried to remember more details. "I think she requested vegan fishcakes."

Les scratched his chin. "That's not a suspect, that's a tragedy."

"They're very popular." Barbara handed over an extra cone of chips. "On the house, for the lady detective." She wanted to express her gratitude for the interest they were showing in the pilfering. However, the chippy was getting busy now; Angie needed to change the card machine receipt roll, and customers were waiting.

"Thank you," said Dulcie. "I may not be right about conservatory man, but we are gathering lots of facts, and I think the case might be heating up."

"Lightly simmering, more like," said Les, lifting the carrier bag to waist height. "Come on, let's get home before this masterstroke of culinary delight starts to get cold."

They said their goodbyes and squeezed out of the now-packed chip shop, nudging their way past a queue that had started to spill onto the pavement. Behind them, the fryer hissed and spat, like a fuming, furious oracle.

CHAPTER 19

It was early, perhaps too early for most of the household to be awake, when Dulcie stepped out into the garden carrying a cardboard box in her arms. She noticed something fluttering on her workshop door—a note, taped just above the latch, slightly crinkled by the morning dew. She placed the box on the bench and carefully peeled the note off. It read:

Dulcie,

I know this is short notice (and retro, leaving a note, but I don't yet have your number, and I have to go to work.) I'm in a bit of a social bind, and I'm throwing myself on your mercy.

Jamila roped me into attending one of her charity events this evening. It's something to do with birds or wildlife, I think. I bought two tickets in a rare moment of optimism since I've never mastered the art of mingling alone.

Would you consider coming with me? It's at the town hall tonight. The dress code is smart-ish, but I would never judge your work boots. I'll even walk you there.

Say yes?

Tristan

Dulcie read it twice more, a small smile forming at the corners of her mouth. The note was typical of Tristan: cheerful and cheeky enough to distract from the fact that he'd probably forgotten about the occasion until now. Still, he had thought of her as his plus-one, and apparently, he was expecting to get her mobile number soon. You had to admire his nerve.

"I'll think about it," she murmured to the quiet garden before heading back to work, trying not to feel too pleased.

Upstairs, Owen was supposed to be grading essays. Instead, he stood by the bedroom window, the coffee in his mug cooling as he watched Dulcie work in the garden below. She moved with purpose, her sleeves rolled up, auburn tresses neatly tied back, industrious as a figure in a Lowry painting. He didn't realise he was smiling until Tristan came into view. Owen stiffened, leaning closer to the window for a better view.

Tristan strolled through the garden with a polished, effortless air. He carried a bottle of water and had a jersey casually draped over his shoulders, as if a professional had styled it for him. Dulcie looked up when he approached, tilting her head. Tristan probably said something clever or agreeable, because she folded her arms and nodded slowly. From his body language, Tristan appeared delighted about something. Dulcie pulled a scrap of white paper from her jeans to examine it. They were chatting animatedly and enjoying their conversation. He saw Dulcie give Tristan a gentle push. First contact.

Owen stayed put, his forehead lightly pressed against the glass. His reaction to the scene didn't surprise him; flickers of envy shot through his core. He knew he had no claim to Dulcie's company; they were neighbours, acquaintances, maybe even friends. She couldn't possibly know how often he thought of her, or the clever things he wished he'd said when they first met. His longing for her had become a persistent ache.

He took a sip of his coffee. It was stone cold.

With a quiet exhalation of breath, Owen placed the mug aside and opened a folder of essays. The title on the front read 'Folklore and Symbolism in Modern Storytelling'. The words on the page blurred as his thoughts wandered back to the girl with copper-coloured hair, the main character in his personal, anguished storyline.

As the light dimmed and evening approached, Dulcie tidied away her tools, took a shower, changed her clothes, and headed out into the street. A breeze stirred her curls, pulling loose strands from the style she had spent too long perfecting, given that it wasn't an actual date.

Tristan was already waiting near the ginnel, holding his phone in one hand and casually tucking the other into the pocket of his tailored, tan-coloured coat. He looked like a perfect embodiment of autumn, dressed in layers of burnt orange and rust brown, and sporting just the right amount of stubble on his dimpled chin. "Hey, Dulcie," he said, his eyes taking her in at a glance. "You look... utterly ravishing, if I may be so bold."

"You may." The word 'ravishing' sounded like something from a cologne advert, but she graciously accepted his flattery. "You are looking very... Tristan tonight."

He grinned, taking it as a compliment, which it almost was.

The charity event, hosted for "The Birds, Bees and Bugs Trust," initially gave the impression of being thinly disguised chaos. On arrival at the door, they were greeted by Jamila, who was resplendent in a floral blouse that could stop traffic and carried a clipboard as if it were military issue. "There you are." She studied them, eyes narrowing. "Tristan, you owe me an apology for pretending this event hadn't slipped your mind."

Tristan opened his mouth, likely to charm his way back into her good graces, but Jamila cut him off with a single glance. "Don't bother," she said dismissively. "I know you well enough to recognise your greatest talent is for disappearing when you could be helpful, especially when it comes to doing the washing-up. Luckily for you, my friend's niece, Hallie, has taken on that task; otherwise, you'd be up to your elbows in teacups and soap suds right now. You have the timing of a magician's rabbit."

Muttering something about strategic delegation, Tristan managed to look both contrite and slightly wronged.

"I can't stand here listening to you make excuses," Jamila

declared. "Make yourself useful and start spending money. We've got a target to hit." She pointed to the enormous picture on the wall, depicting a kingfisher perched on a large thermometer. The mercury indicator was painted red about a quarter of the way up, with large arrows pointing to the top. Jamila marched off, clipboard held aloft, leaving the two of them to navigate the maze of tables.

The town hall was alive with chatter and the clatter of teacups. Fold-out tables drooped under the weight of cakes, jams, and homemade chutneys. Children with painted faces ran through the crowd, while a small folk band played near the back, mostly in tune. Tristan paused every few steps to greet people, many of whom said they recognised him from school or a cousin's party. Magnetic amidst the crowd, he smiled, waved, joked, and leaned in to chat with passersby. Despite herself, Dulcie felt a flicker of pride standing beside him. "Is there anyone in Brixton you don't know?" she asked, sipping the tea they bought from a counter where several ladies served refreshments and jostled each other. The tea was so weak that it barely had the strength to be sipped.

Handing her a slice of lemon drizzle cake with a flourish, he said, "I grew up here. Working in the events industry means I collect names the way some people gather fridge magnets. I'm a freelance hospitality professional," he explained. "Basically, I'm the guy who keeps champagne flowing, makes any crisis vanish, and keeps drunk uncles away from the microphone. Weddings, galas, corporate disasters—I show up, smile, and somehow make everything look intentional. Besides, you haven't been here long, and you've already made many friends. Look," he pointed out, "over there is someone you already know."

In the corner of the hall, Kay Kenneths held court. Dressed in silk and topped with an exotic turban, she waved them over with theatrical delight. Making their way towards her, they weaved through the crowd, sidestepping toddlers and avoiding eye contact with a man dressed as an owl. Kay rose and welcomed them graciously. "Oh, darlings," she cried. "Come, come, do sit. You've arrived in the nick of time to rescue me from a very dull man who collects pheasant feathers," she added in a stage whisper.

"You look lovely, Kay. Dulcie smiled as she sat. "Radiant."

"Thank you. You are *very* sweet. A generous hand with the blush covers a multitude of sins," she trilled.

"Is that the secret to showbiz, or is it simply that you have the cheekbones of an angel?" Tristan asked her flirtatiously, putting a hand across her back and drawing her close.

"That, and saying yes to everything." Kay tilted her head and winked at the handsome young man holding her in a loose embrace. "In this case, I agreed to support a worthy cause. They know I bring that extra sparkle, and of course, I draw the crowds."

Tristan glanced around at the bustling but indifferent attendees. "Right. Quite the fan club tonight."

Kay either did not hear or chose not to listen. She lowered her voice confidentially. "They've asked me to introduce the guest speaker. Naturally, I've agreed."

"They're lucky to have you," Dulcie said, ignoring Tristan's sideways glance. "By the way, did you get my quote for the chaise longue?" She had taken her time calculating the price, grappling with the numbers, adjusting them up and down until she was confident the total would be irresistible. "Was it in the right ballpark?" she asked. "I can use a different fabric or finish if you had something else in mind."

Kay was momentarily embarrassed. The quote had been received, but she was currently short on funds. Her home and investments made her wealthy on paper, but hefty fees and royalties no longer flowed into her bank account. She straightened her chin. "I did receive it, yes. However, I will be hosting several of my *Sunset Soirees* in the coming months, and I won't have enough seating for all of my friends if you're working on the piece." The impression was given that the issue was purely logistical rather than financial. "We will review the situation when my social calendar is a little less full. Now it's been lovely talking to you, but I must dash," she said, changing the subject. "The speaker will be on stage soon, and I've barely glanced at the script. I find preparation so very dull; besides, improvisation keeps things fresh." Slipping free from Tristan's arm, she swept away in a flurry of purpose and perfume.

Tristan turned to Dulcie. "She is aware that this isn't the BAFTAs?" he asked. She nudged him firmly. It was unkind to mock when Kay was relishing the limelight, such as it was. They found seats at a table close to the stage. Soon, Kay stepped in front of the curtains and, with her customary poise and professionalism, she introduced the speaker. The audience responded with polite applause as a robust woman from the ornithological society moved forward to deliver an 'unmissable talk on bird and wildlife rehabilitation.' Kay had her doubts about calling it *unmissable.* It had the ring of something you'd say before locking the exit doors. Nevertheless, she knew how to engage an audience, even in the role of master of ceremonies.

Shifting the position of his chair, Tristan brushed his leg against Dulcie's. "You have a habit of frowning when you concentrate," he whispered. "It's adorable."

"And you have a bad habit of whispering during speeches," she said, irritated. But she still allowed herself to enjoy his nearness, the intimacy of their hands resting on the table, close but not touching. She reminded herself that life wasn't a Jane Austen novel. Even if it were, she'd probably be the sister running family errands and feeding the horses, while everyone else got proposed to.

Unable to fake interest in the speaker any longer, Tristan stood, brushing lint from his sleeve. "I'm going to help with the raffle. I'll be back victorious," he whispered into her ear, stepping away from the stage.

"Try not to sprain anything. " Dulcie watched him go with a flicker of regret. She would have liked to go with him, but stayed seated, which seemed the polite thing to do. He moved away with unhurried ease, his long, languorous strides carrying him out of sight, past the tables and towards the tombola.

Ten minutes passed. Then, fifteen.

The presentation ended, and Dulcie wandered towards the back of the hall, pretending to inspect some of the more unusual items on the donated bric-a-brac stall. A cheerful, young lad working behind the stand said, "Can I interest you in the purchase of this truly dreadful, gaudy knick-knack? It's only a quid." He leaned across the trestle table conspiratorially. "I compete with my brother to see who can sell the most shockingly repulsive donation."

"I would buy it from you, I really would. But I've already got two of those at home," Dulcie said, sounding hurt. "Which is why I gave *that* one to the charity to sell today."

The young man looked stricken. "I'm so sorry! I didn't mean to be rude." He was spluttering with embarrassment. "You didn't *really*, did you?"

She took pity on him. "No, I didn't." She grinned and shook her head. "But I still don't want to buy it."

"Thank gawd for that." The boy breathed out. "Good one, by the way. You had me there," he gave her a look of undisguised admiration. "What about a pack of notelets? Then we'll call it quits?" As compensation for teasing him, Dulcie bought a bee-covered bookmark.

It took another five minutes of aimless browsing before she spotted Tristan. He was near the windows, deep in conversation with a tall, elegant brunette, whose tailored jacket hugged her figure like a second skin. She stood with one hand on a chair, her feline focus fully on him, content to see how the conversation would unfold. A cascade of silver earrings winked against her neck whenever she tilted her head, which she did several times. Tristan leaned in and said something that made her pick up a napkin and push it toward him. He jotted something on it and handed it back. She took it, folded it once, and slipped it into her pocket without even glancing at it.

Dulcie paused by a shelf of second-hand books, captivated

for a moment by the woman's calm confidence. Gazing at a row of greeting cards and stuffing her hands in her pockets, she tried to contain her emotions. It wasn't her concern if Tristan was using a local event to make connections, romantic or otherwise, yet she couldn't shake a feeling of humiliation. Perhaps the truth was that he really had only taken her to this event as a last resort, to avoid facing Jamila's wrath alone.

It wasn't much longer before Tristan returned to her side. He held out two gingerbread men and handed her one of them. "I've been looking for you," he stated, sounding mildly put out.. "I saw the speeches had finished and went back to the seats, but you'd vanished."

"So did you. I've been walking around the stands, but you were nowhere to be found."

"They had me shifting crates," he jerked his head in the direction of the refreshments. "Kept me busy all this time." He grinned at her. "I think they only wanted me for my animal strength."

Dulcie looked him in the eyes and bit the gingerbread man's head clean off his shoulders.

They walked home later that evening beneath a starless sky. The city streets remained lively with bright lights and activity, the shops still open, and the pubs bustling. Tristan talked nonstop about music, travel, and his favourite TikTok workouts. Dulcie murmured back now and then, but her mind was elsewhere. It was interesting to learn more about her companion, of course, but the real takeaway from the evening was this: he was easy on the eyes and just as easy on everyone else's, too.

If she were considering a fling with this man, which she knew in her heart that she was, resilience would have to be the name of the game. No strings, no swooning, no writing his surname after hers in her notebook margins. That was the idea. However, in her experience, plans involving the heart had the strength of wet tissue paper, and all it took was one well-timed smile, and she would be dreaming of a romantic weekend for two.

At the front door of No. 67, he turned towards her, and she lifted her face in response. "This was fun. We should do it again," he said, gently cupping her chin and tilting it upward. Instead of the full smooch she was expecting, he brushed past her lips and gave her a light kiss on the cheek. "Sweet dreams, Dulcie," he whispered. Then he stepped away, catching her off guard. She hadn't been expecting to fight him off exactly, but this peck was more of a "thanks for coming" than "I can't live without you." *Maybe he doesn't fancy me after all,* she thought. That would certainly spare her a lot of late-night overthinking, but she couldn't help feeling just the tiniest bit dismayed. It was one thing to choose not to fall for someone; quite another to realise they'd never tripped over you in the first place.

She waited patiently as he inserted the key into the ground-floor lock. A sudden shiver, an instinct that she was being watched, caused Dulcie to look up toward the centre of the house. The bright light from the kitchen window in the flat above caught her eye, and she thought she saw a shadowy figure retreating into the room. Immediately, the light went out, subtly dimming the evening glow that bathed the quiet street. It marked a troubling end to what had been a disconcerting day.

CHAPTER 20

Just before eleven on the following morning, Dulcie spotted Owen getting ready to head to the university, wheeling his new bike into the street. His hair looked tidy, and his clothes were styled for work, although his padded jacket had a small, torn hole at the elbow, with some stuffing peeking out and fluttering in the breeze.

"Morning," she called, noting that the faded panniers slung over the rear rack were once again overstuffed with books. One strap looked like it could give way at any moment, and the saddlebags themselves tilted slightly, as if barely clinging on.

He looked up, but only briefly. "Hey, "he nodded.

"It looks like this bike is better at carrying a heavy load than the last one."

"For now. I'm hoping it will get past the first junction, but you never know."

"Oh." She paused. He sounded tense. "Is everything

alright?"

"Fine. Just busy. Better be off, I've got a lecture to give in an hour." He cast her a fleeting glance, pressed down on the pedals, and rode off, his gaze fixed ahead.

Dulcie stood and watched him ride away. Something in their budding friendship had changed. It was a shift in dynamic that needed further investigation at some point, but in the meantime, she was due at the pub. Big Maccie was back on his feet, and they had planned to meet for an update, a debrief and a visit to one of the petty crime scenes.

The Witch & Stable looked dimmer than usual. The windows were fogged from inside, and the ever-present fire burned low. Familiar conversations buzzed through the air alongside the soft murmur from the muted television screen. Maccie had not yet arrived, so she settled onto a barstool and watched Jamila working behind the bar. She was skilfully pouring a pint with one hand while ringing up the total with the other. They nodded to acknowledge each other.

"I think I'm going to need a glass of Chardonnay. Can you make it a large one, please?" Dulcie asked. "I'm here to meet with Big Maccie, and things might get intense." She pulled out her phone. "He wants to compare notes. Crime-related."

"Is that so?" Jamila enquired. "Well, before he arrives and turns everything into a detective show, tell me, how was your evening with Tristan after the town hall? Not well? Is that the reason for the look on your face?"

"What look?"

Jamila settled herself, her arms resting on the bar, her expression all ears. "The one that says you are pretending to be fine when you are not. Come on. Tell Auntie."

"If you must know, he gave his number to another woman at the charity event." Jamila didn't react, retreating to pour Dulcie's wine and handing her the payment device with calm efficiency. Like all bar staff, she was used to customers revealing secrets, especially those about complicated love lives, dramatic breakups, and questionable late-night texts. She had gained a good deal of insight from many years of witnessing people break down over their drinks.

The transaction was swift. After making sure Dulcie had a sufficiently large glass to mark the occasion, Jamila resumed her role as a trusted advisor.

"How did he do it? Grand gesture? Sneaky pass?"

"Napkin," Dulcie muttered.

"Classy. At least it shows he didn't go prepared, if he had to use something close to hand."

"I know. And it's not like we're officially paired up, or anything like it. But I had hoped we were on our way to it. He is so undeniably my type." She ran her finger around the rim of her glass. "He probably has half of Brixton listed in his phone. It shouldn't have been a surprise that he's a bit of a player."

Jamila tilted her head. "Why do you think that?"

"It is the way he speaks, as if he studied charm in night school. He knows precisely how to make you melt. I have fallen for that sort before, and it never ends well." Dulcie sipped her wine, dejectedly.

"So, what's stopping you this time?"

"Because I know myself. I get attached too quickly. Even when I say 'it's just a fling', it never stays that way, and it always ends in tears. Usually mine. That's how I ended up living here in the first place."

"Maybe the real question is not whether Tristan is a player. Maybe it is whether you are ready to deal with it if he is?"

"That's exactly what I'm trying to figure out. I'm in a somewhat unique situation. A first, at least for me. Two men live in the flat above, and I like them both in different ways. Owen is lovely, kind, and thoughtful, while Tristan makes me feel both on fire and a little crazy. But last night, Tristan seemed to cool off somehow. And Owen... he must have known I was out with Tristan yesterday. Today, he barely spoke to me."

"Owen? Now that one is a slow burn." Jamila wiped the counter. "But I know he likes you too."

"You think so? How do you know? Has he said something?"

"No, but I know so. He watches you like you are a secret he's afraid to say out loud." She began polishing the taps. "Tristan, on the other hand, looks at most women like dessert."

"This is ridiculous. I'm here to sort myself out; I've got a business to build and a new home to adjust to, but instead, I find myself tangled in a love triangle."

"You can handle all of those things," consoled Jamila. "Listen to me. Tristan is fun, yes. But people who are like him? They chase attention because they need it to breathe. Don't get me wrong, you will have the time of your life in his company, but the chances are you will always be competing with someone new."

"And Owen?"

"Owen, doesn't compete. He waits. And that shows more

character, if you ask me."

They stood silently on either side of the bar, with only the clinking of teaspoons near the coffee machine and the crunching of crisps breaking the silence. Jamila decided it was important for her friend to have all the facts. After all, there's little sense in tying yourself in emotional knots, only to discover a few key details you weren't aware of. She wiped the bar and added, almost casually:

"Have you met Jennifer?"

Dulcie looked up. "Jennifer? Who's that?"

"The girl who sometimes leaves books at Owen's door. Lovely hair. Big eyes. I assumed she was his... You know. Something."

"He never mentioned 'a something' to me, or a *someone*, come to that."

"Maybe I'm wrong," Jamila shrugged and picked up an empty glass that awaited collection on the bar. "But even if I am, you should ask yourself what you want, before you get lost in who wants you."

The pub door burst open with a theatrical flourish, and Big Maccie arrived, full of the cheer of a man who has fully regained his freedom. "Hello! Hello, one and all," he roared. "Who's buying?"

"Well, well. Look who's had a miraculous recovery." Jamila was already reaching for the tap to pour a pint of Guinness, adding a splash of blackcurrant. Dulcie paid for his drink before he could even pretend to go for his wallet. Maccie took the pint with a mock bow, admiring the creamy head forming at the top, and they moved together to a small table. Next to them, the pub's ageing fruit machine trilled and blinked to itself, aware that its best days were behind it.

Easing into the seat with a theatrical groan, Maccie cradled his pint like a priest with a sacred relic. "Now this," he held up the glass, "is medicine no doctor prescribes and no chemist stocks."

"It's great to see you properly back on your feet. How is Missy doing?"

"Alive, grumpy, and selectively affectionate. She only acknowledges me when I'm holding tuna."

"Sounds like nothing has changed. I'm glad her adventures have left her unscathed," Dulcie said. "Any thoughts on the Minet Road chaos?"

"I have had a lot of time to think it over."

"Do you think the man in the coat at the chip shop was the same person I sat next to at the council meeting?"

"I can't say, but I have thoughts. I have been building timelines. There is a theory forming."

"And you are not going to tell me more." Dulcie leaned back in her chair with a sense of resignation.

"Of course not." Maccie declared. "What kind of detective reveals their hand before the case is cracked?"

"The kind with a Netflix contract?"

"Tempting. But I don't have one, and anyway, I live by a code." He had no intention of sharing his ideas with Dulcie yet, or indeed the fact that he had turned his back bedroom into a full-blown investigation hub. Reminiscent of his detective days, the walls were covered with Post-it notes and bits of string crisscrossed between names, places, and dates, in a web of colourful chaos. He'd begun with the fragments of information Dulcie casually relayed, then added gossip collected from the pub, thoughts scribbled on envelopes, and the results of some discreet inquiries he made himself. Initially, he'd assumed it would all be a fool's errand, a bit of fun to keep his mind active. But now something was taking shape. Patterns were starting to form, and Big Maccie knew that patterns are never random. They point somewhere; you have to follow them.

"Well," said Dulcie, "consider this my official offer. I am ready to assist. I have a thing for true crime. Give me a trench coat, a notebook and a mystery to solve, and I am in."

"Would you settle for a shopping pad and an ink pen?"

"If I must."

"Do you have a note of all the crimes?"

"On my phone," she waved it over her half-filled glass.

"Then we have ourselves a deal. The best way forward is to finish our drinks and head to Bunce's: the sweet shop, the one that also sells groceries and is full of gossip. That place has seen more troubles than my health. If something strange is happening, it probably started there."

"Perfect. We need some more clues. Even if we don't find any, I need to get a packet of wine gums and a tin of soup."

"Then," Maccie downed the beer in his glass, "as Sherlock said to Dr Watson, we should consider the game to be afoot. Let's go."

And they did.

CHAPTER 21

Maccie and Dulcie entered the shop that bore the legend "Bunce's Sweet Shop and Licensed Convenience Store." The cheery jingle from the brass bell above the door added a nostalgic touch, complemented by old wooden floors, striped jars, and handwritten labels. Behind the counter, a woman looked up from a tray of fudge. She was in her mid-forties, full-figured, with a gravity-defying blonde topknot and flawless skin. She stood near a vibrant display of vapes and lottery tickets, keeping a watchful eye on the shop floor. When she saw them, her eyes narrowed. "Hello, Duncan," she said. His name dropped into the room like a stone through glass.

Big Maccie flinched, a slight twitch at the corner of his eye, just big enough for Dulcie to spot it. "Hello, Gillian," he said, voice strained through a smile that didn't reach his eyes. "How are you doing?" His eyes darting away from Gillian's face towards the door, the window, anywhere else. The tension between them was as thick and stifling as a summer storm; neither said anything more for a moment. Maccie's jaw was tight, his fingers drumming a restless rhythm against the counter.

"What can I do for you?" she asked, breaking the standoff but standing rigid, arms folded and expression blank.

"I came about the thefts. The chocolates. The expensive ones. I thought maybe I could help."

Gillian looked him up and down as if he needed instructions to open a door, let alone assist anyone. "You want to help track down some missing confectionery? I see. In that case, you'll want to speak to Mrs. Bunce. Not me." Without waiting for a reply, she turned away and slipped through the plastic strip curtain into the storeroom.

Maccie exhaled. Dulcie gazed up at him. "That went well," she murmured. "Why do I get the impression she thinks you made an excuse to come in here to see her, personally? Is there anything you need to share with the team?"

Before he could answer, the curtain stirred once more. A different woman stepped through, her hands in the pockets of a blue and white dress. A silver pendant glimmered at her throat.

"Hello. I'm Stella Bunce. How can I help you?" Her gaze shifted from Dulcie to Big Maccie. The smile froze, then disappeared. Almost imperceptibly, she shook her head, her short strawberry-blonde hair bouncing above an open face, with generous lips and deep brown eyes.

"I see." She folded her hands in front of her, as though bracing for bad weather. "I'm not sure you can be of any help here, Maccie," she said. "I think you've probably done enough."

"I know I'm as popular as a wasp at a picnic in this place. But I'd still like to try."

"Try what? To fix what you broke, or to make yourself feel better?"

Dulcie glanced back and forth between the two, her curiosity piqued. This was not at all how she had expected their collaboration to start. It seemed like she had walked into the middle of a conversation that began long before she arrived. She had expected polite formality, maybe a bit of resistance to their questions, but nothing like this. Whatever this was.

"I understand I might not be in your good graces," Maccie said. "But to be fair, I never made any promises to Gillian, and I'm not here to reopen old wounds. I've only come today because you and the other shops nearby are experiencing unusually high levels of theft. I know that can be par for the course, but local residents are being targeted too. I want to see if I can do something constructive to put a stop to it."

Dulcie cleared her throat. "We really do just want to get to the bottom of the mystery. Maybe we could start with the facts? Things like 'what's gone missing, when, who was on duty?'"

"And you are?" Stella asked.

"Dulcie Staples. I live up the road with Maccie."

"Good Lord!" exclaimed Stella, looking at them in horror, assuming Maccie had presented her with his child bride.

"No, no, not like that." Dulcie waved her hands apart and rushed to clarify the mistake. "I live at the same address, in the flat above Maccie's. I asked him to help investigate the goings-on, and we're looking into it together."

"Are you really? Well. How odd." Stella said, her expression easing just a little. "Alright. If you're both serious, I suppose I can fill you in on the facts. I may as well, given that no one else from your profession has taken any interest."

Maccie scanned the shelves filled with jars, tins, and neatly tied paper bags. The shop felt frozen in time, part grocery store, part museum, and a testament to sugar cravings. He nodded toward the discreet black dome on the ceiling. "You've got CCTV on the middle aisle. Does it cover the end display, where the Swiss chocolates are?"

"Yes, we installed it last year. Shoplifters were getting more and more brazen, particularly in that corner where the pick 'n' mix and pocket money sweets are. Since then, daily thefts have decreased, and my stock of sherbet fountains and liquorice wheels is steady."

"But not the chocolate?" Maccie asked.

"No," Stella replied, her mouth tight. "The thief goes straight for the high-end stuff. Lindt, Neuhaus, those imported Italian boxes we only get in for holidays. The ones with gold lettering."

"And you have footage of the thief?"

"I do," Stella said, crossing her arms. "Now, here's where it gets unusual. The video isn't perfect, but it clearly shows a specific person up to no good. My nephew Max was working that day, so I asked him about the customer. He got all awkward – not because he was involved, don't start getting any ideas like that," she added quickly, glancing at Maccie. "It's just that when I asked if he'd served a man or a woman, Max told me he preferred not to assume. He described them as having a feminine hairstyle, wearing a neck scarf, and he noticed a faint moustache on their upper lip. Based on their overall look, he wasn't sure whether it was a man or a woman. Maybe someone non-binary, he suggested. He's very respectful, bless him."

"You haven't seen them again?" Maccie frowned. "Max hasn't? I ask because I've heard you've had repeated thefts around the same time of day, which suggests it's likely the same person. Normally, you'd spot them easily."

Stella shook her head. "Not seen them before, and not since. We all keep watch now: me, Max, Gillian, and even Lilah, who only works Saturdays. We'd notice them if they turned up again, but they haven't. Yet the chocolate keeps vanishing."

"Is it possible they're sending someone else in?"

"You're suggesting a crime ring, dedicated to stealing chocolate? That's absurd." Gillian had returned quietly to the shop floor. "It's most likely one fixated nutcase if you ask me."

"Can I see the film?" Maccie asked. "It could be invaluable. As far as I know, it's the only time anyone has appeared on camera. They might be seen on someone's doorbell footage, but I've no authority to go knocking on doors.

"If you think it will help, then I don't see why not." Stella turned to Gillian. "Will you get the tablet from the office, please?"

Gillian vanished through the beaded curtain and returned with the tablet, her expression indicating that, as far as she was concerned, this was a waste of everyone's time. She returned promptly and handed the touchscreen over. "It's already cued to Wednesday evening's footage."

The grainy video came to life. The aisle appeared—canned goods to the left, confectionery to the right. A steady stream of locals passed through, buying bread and milk. "There," Stella said. "Look at the clock counter, it says 'twenty-one, fifty-two,' not far off closing time."

They huddled over the screen. A figure in a long coat appeared. Head down, hat low, scarf wrapped at the neck. A shoulder bag hung at their side. The person moved with intent. Not hurried, not browsing. "Walked straight to the chocolate display," Sheila narrated. "Took three Neuhaus boxes. Slipped them into the bag. Then—watch." The figure turned, glanced once toward the till, and walked out calmly with not a hint of hesitation at all.

"You said they weren't hiding their face?"

"Not really," Stella said. She tapped the screen, and a still image appeared. The figure was captured in the image mid-step. Eyes half-lowered. Lips pressed flat. The features were soft but not delicate, and the hair was neatly styled and tucked carefully beneath a cap.

"Hardly the face of a criminal mastermind," Maccie said, eyeing the suspect with wry scepticism. "Then again, we're talking about nicking sweeties.

Dulcie pointed. "That coat matches the one Barbara mentioned. But from what I can make out, the hair in this image is darker than she described."

"They've figured out how to get in and out without attracting any attention."

"You think they're sneaking in? Through the back?"

"Or the side door," Maccie suggested. "If they knew the

167

layout." He had seen enough over the years to know villains rarely used the front door. Amateurs often choose the easiest point of entry; professionals, on the other hand, study their target. If someone wanted to get inside and had the time and patience, they would approach the invisible access to the building as a puzzle to be solved. He suspected this particular trickster was relishing the challenge as much as the reward.

"We haven't used the side entrance in weeks. Not since the bins were moved." Stella looked thoughtful. "But I suppose it's possible."

"Mind if we take a look out back?"

"Help yourself. Just don't move the bins. The council won't take them unless they're placed exactly right."

"You have my word," Maccie said with mock solemnity.

Gillian made a noise halfway between a snort and a laugh. "That's reassuring."

Maccie regarded both shopkeepers with an inscrutable expression until Dulcie took his arm and guided him out of the door. They walked to the back of the shop, where a wispy swirl of steam rose from a vent and the hum of a generator filled the air. Hoping to discover something amiss, they both strained to catch any subtle sound or spot anything that seemed out of place in the shabby corridor that ran along the back of the buildings.

Above them, the sky was heavy and grey, gazing down on their endeavours. It provided no warmth or support, just a fine, misty drizzle that started to fall quietly, soaking the cracked pavement and, with studied indifference, sprinkled raindrops all over their possible crime scene.

CHAPTER 22

After an increasingly damp search behind Bunce's store, where they found only black plastic bags and cigarette butts, Dulcie and Big Maccie returned to the dry refuge of the pub to meet up with Uncle Les. The past couple of hours had been intriguing, but Dulcie wondered whether it had brought them any closer to an answer. Nevertheless, she remained optimistic that a swift drink might spark her brain into overdrive.

Les was already seated in his usual spot by the window, a man who understood the value of arriving early and ordering in bulk. A bottle of wine was opened and breathing; three empty flutes and two full pints sat before him, perfectly poured and glistening with condensation. "There you are!" he called out, raising his glass and gesturing for them to sit in the empty chairs reserved for their arrival. "I thought you must have fallen into a skip and decided to make it a home."

"We considered it." Maccie slid into the seat opposite. "Better company, fewer complications." His visit to the shop had been a disconcerting experience for several reasons.

"Drink up." Les slid a pint towards him like a benevolent landlord. "You look like you've been chasing down a wild goose."

Maccie took a grateful sip. "Close call. I had to visit my ex's workplace, and it wasn't friendly." He had always appreciated women, finding their company delightful. He briefly dated Gillian, ending it months ago. She was lovely, but Maccie wasn't built for emotional ties. For him, commitment meant returning library books on time.

"Ah," Les nodded sagely. "An encounter with an ex-girlfriend. That would explain the haunted expression."

"We were never really on boyfriend-girlfriend terms. At least, *I* didn't think it was like that."

"So," Dulcie said, grinning, "not exactly an amicable split?"

"Put it this way," Maccie said, "you saw how she greeted me like a gas leak. And honestly, I probably deserved it." He was a man who appreciated women, in all their fantastic shapes and sizes. He had liked Gillian and still did, feeling the kind fondness for her that could sneak up on a man. She was steady, fun and a fine-looking woman. But Maccie knew himself; he wasn't the type of man to turn up every evening asking about her day, exchange "good morning" texts or go curtain shopping with her. He was good for a night of passion and a great deal of entertainment, but strictly without strings attached.

"What'd you do? Forget her birthday? Leave the loo seat up?" asked Dulcie.

"No, it turns out that I can't manage more than one female at a time, and Missy-Mae is the one I'm best suited to," Maccie replied, finishing his pint. "Speaking of which, I should head off. If I'm late with her tin of tuna, she'll leave something in my shoe." He patted his stomach, which had started to rumble. "I'm famished for my dinner anyway. I'm treating myself to a full roast with all the trimmings."

"Beef?"

"Sausage," said Maccie. "I've got to build my strength up." He tipped an imaginary hat. "Try not to drink too much without me."

As he disappeared through the door, Les shook his head. "Poor soul. Romantic instincts of a Labrador and the attention span of a moth."

There's a lot of it around," Dulcie said, recalling the difficulties of her own romantic journey. The afternoon served as a pleasant distraction from her feelings about Tristan and the note he'd passed to a stranger while they were together. She was also concerned about the sudden coldness that had developed between her and Owen. Somehow, she couldn't get a grip on her mixed emotions, which stirred like currents under still water.

Les took a sip of his bitter and narrowed his eyes at Dulcie across the table. "Penny for your thoughts? You've got that look again."

"No, I haven't."

"Yes, you have, the one that says you're thinking too hard and not eating enough pie." Les was great at getting priorities right.

"I thought I'd have the soup," Dulcie replied, trying to put him off track.

"Soup is not food. Soup is something people apologise for at dinner parties. You need pastry." Uncle Les insisted.

Dulcie glanced around. The pub was mostly empty except for two retired gentlemen playing cards and a large bulldog snoring under the fruit machine. "I need to tell you something."

"Please don't say you're leaving, or voting for the other party, or cashing in the premium bond I bought for you on Millennium Eve."

She ignored him. "The complicated truth is that I like both of them"

"Both who?"

"Both of the boys upstairs."

Les leaned back, his pint paused halfway to his mouth. He frowned in a way that suggested he had already chosen his favourite and was now preparing his case like a barrister. "You mean Tristan and Owen?"

"Yes."

He took a slow sip of his drink. "Well, that's a recipe for chaos." He noticed that she had shared her dilemma without directly asking for advice or concealing her need for it. Her eyes examined his face, as if he had all the answers. However, when it came to sensitive topics like this, he felt completely out of his depth. "And by 'like' I assume you mean... not in the neighbourly sense."

"No," Dulcie said, then corrected herself. "Yes. I mean no, not just neighbourly. I mean, yes, romantically. Sort of." She slumped back in her seat. "It's complicated."

"In matters of the heart, my habit is to listen closely. Then, usually, I just nod. But I'm guessing you want my opinion?"

"Not really," Dulcie said. "But I know I'm going to get it anyway." She braced herself.

"Owen is a good man," Les stated firmly. "I think you already know that he has taken a shine to you. It was obvious before he locked himself out of his own home to prove it, subconsciously or not." He continued, warming to his theme. "That lad is steady. Thoughtful. Reads books with dragons in them. Does not wear two-tone shoes, dayglow cardigans and trousers that look painted on - you know who I mean by that."

"You make it sound like Tristan is a modern-day dandy."

"Because he is. There's no need to look like you've been dressed for the catwalk to buy milk." Les scratched his eyebrow. " On the other hand, Owen's the sort who would help you carry a sofa up the stairs and not even mention it afterwards. That's the kind of chap worth having around."

"I know, I do like Owen, very much."

"But? Come on, I know there's more to it."

"But Tristan is utterly irresistible," she sighed. "I realise it's shallow to be so swayed by looks, but I can't help myself. It's not as if either of them is unattractive, but Mother Nature hardwires some things in." She raised her hands in despair and sighed deeply. "For all I know, they could both be seeing other people anyway. At this rate, I'll end up with nothing but a bruised ego. Tristan is..." Dulcie struggled to find the perfect words. "Confident. Funny. He can make friends in an empty room. And he has this way of making you feel like you're the most interesting person in the place when he talks to you."

"He also poses as a wine buff and owns more hair products than sense."

"Those things don't count as red flags, just because he has a certain style. You're obviously biased."

"I'm practical," Les said, gesturing with his pint. "I've lived through real heartache. I can tell you right now, Tristan is the kind of man who leaves breadcrumbs but never brings bread."

"See? This is exactly why I didn't want to say anything." Dulcie had forgotten that she was the one who had opened up the conversation.

"Look, love. I'm not saying you shouldn't be drawn to him. But what matters is not who makes your heart flutter in a pub. It's who is still making you laugh when you're both wearing odd socks and trying to assemble flat-pack furniture with the wrong screws."

"You think Owen would do that?" She picked at the beer mat under her drink. "I guess he is the kind who would have read the instructions."

"If there's one thing I've learned in life," he said, "it's this: You can't make yourself love someone. And you can't make someone love you." Uncle Les regarded her with the solemnity of a soothsayer. "Both of are equally true, no matter how much you might want them *not* to be. I've seen folk wreck their lives because they wouldn't accept one or the other."

Love is such a mystery, isn't it?" Dulcie stared into her glass as though the wine were a crystal ball.

"No!" Les scoffed. "Nothing of the kind. I know exactly what love is, especially at the start. Love is feeling lucky.

That's it. That's all there is to it." He spread his fingers wide on the table. "If you feel lucky to have that person picking you as a partner, you fall for them. Keep them feeling lucky, and they'll keep coming back. Mark my words, it's a simple business." He reached across the table and gave her hand a firm squeeze. "You don't have to make a decision right now. Life has a way of deciding for you anyway. Remember: if you trust your gut, you won't go far wrong." He paused, then beamed. "You won't go far, but you won't go wrong."

They sat in comfortable silence for a moment, the sound of the fruit machine humming softly and the dog under it twitching in a dream. The low murmur of conversation drifted from the bar, mixing with the clink of glasses and the occasional crackle from the old fireplace. Les lifted his pint again. "Now. Can I interest you in something proper to eat, or are you planning to survive on fermented grapes?"

Dulcie raised her glass. "Fermented grapes sound about right for now."

Les grabbed the menu. "Not on my watch."

They reached a compromise, deciding on a Ploughman's lunch which, as Les said, was practically salad. The food was hearty and satisfying, and above them, the ceiling fan whirred softly, gently stirring the edges of the lettuce leaves on their plates. The fire crackled in the hearth, and the wine was full-bodied and soothing; they shared another bottle, and after a while, the world seemed like a better, more manageable place.

CHAPTER 23

The delivery van turned the corner, and Dulcie hugged herself with happiness. She had sent off two pieces of re-worked furniture to a seaside bistro, selling them online for a clear profit. Earlier that day, she had returned a restored footstool to a local customer, who paid in cash and gave her a generous tip. At lunchtime, she tried for the umpteenth time to hand over some of her profits to Uncle Les in lieu of rent.

"You really should take a cut." She offered him a neatly folded wad of notes. "After all, I couldn't do any of this without you."

"You keep your money," he batted the cash away like a moth. "I'm not short of a bob or two. I've been a fortunate man, and renting out these flats has made all the difference. I'm still paying off the conversions, mind. I'm not rolling in it. But what I've always said is, 'while I've got it, you can have it." He scratched the back of his neck. "When the day comes that I'm in my dotage, getting my face washed in an old folks' home, you can repay me with visits. Smuggle in a bit of whiskey and the Racing Post. Maybe a pork pie, if they allow solids."

That summed Les up, Dulcie thought. He was always deflecting generosity with humour. She pondered how different her life might have been if he hadn't stepped in to provide her with the space, the tools, and the firm encouragement she'd needed. Reluctantly, she tucked the money back into her pocket, overwhelmed by their lopsided relationship. "One day," she thought, "I will be arrested for smuggling a case of Scotch into a retirement home. And it'll be all his fault."

With bossy insistence, her phone started bleeping in her pocket, demanding she check the text it had just delivered. It was from Tristan and read:

Wine tasting gang 2nite @ 8:30. Run upstairs (crawl down :) Party!! C u later?

She felt a flutter of anticipation. Tristan had been elusive since the charity event, and while she saw Owen occasionally, he'd rush past her quickly, muttering a hello or giving a distracted nod. The relationship between them all hovered in a strange, undefined space, not quite something, not quite nothing. But this message meant she could at least hope for an evening of drinks, good company, and great music. The big dilemma was choosing what to wear. It had to be something casual enough for a house party, but with a touch of magic and a hint of décolletage.

By 8:15 p.m., after spending the entire afternoon planning her outfit, she was still struggling to choose between gold hoops and turquoise earrings to complement her denim jacket. The ring of the front doorbell, muffled greetings, and footsteps on the stairs stirred her into action. She finished her make-up like a contestant for a five-minute makeover, ran her fingers through her hair, and gave herself a quick once-over in the mirror. Not bad, she thought—maybe even verging on good. Grabbing a bottle of the very finest plonk that Bunce's had been able to offer, she headed upstairs to join the gathering.

The door to Flat 2 was already open, and rhythmic party music pulsed through the corridor like a heartbeat. Knocking felt pointless; no one would hear it over the bass, so she walked in unannounced. The flat was already buzzing. Owen was carrying two glasses of wine over to Ellie and Jessie, who perched on the windowsill with their legs tucked beneath them. Near the bookshelf, Tom was talking with Iden, the two of them nodding along to each other's words, a serene bubble in the middle of the noise. On the far side of the room, a young woman with a dark, feathered bob was examining the bookshelf. Her fingers glided along the edges, occasionally pausing to pull a book forward, read its spine and then slide it back into place.

Nestled in a corner, Tristan sat in a blue plastic bubble chair—an inflatable novelty wedged in to provide extra seating for the occasion. He was deeply engrossed in a lively conversation with two women Dulcie hadn't seen before. One woman had jet-black hair and almond-shaped eyes and wore a sunflower-yellow dress that shimmered as she moved. The other was a tall, willowy blonde dressed in a black shift, with the colouring and bone structure of a classic English rose. Tristan, wearing a snug rugby shirt with bold stripes that stretched slightly over his chest, seemed to be in his element.

"Dulcie!" he called out, spotting her across the room. "You made it here, all the way from downstairs." He grinned. "I think you know almost everyone, except Altheya here and her friend Natasha," he pointed at the two girls he had been chatting to. They nodded a hello. "Now, what delicious vino are we going to start you off with?" He stood and confidently moved toward her with an easy stride that caused her heart to race. "I know you've got a soft spot for Chardonnay," he said, wrapping his arm around her shoulders as he reached for the bottle in her hand.

"Pinot." She lifted it up to show the label. "But I'll take a glass of whatever's already opened, if you're pouring."

"You're in for a treat. We've ordered some delicious plonk, arriving any minute. We're hoping someone will appreciate the difference between a Sancerre and a Sauvignon Blanc."

"Well," Dulcie knew that her palate couldn't be described as discerning, "I'll do my best, but I may have to fake it."

Tristan laughed. "That's the spirit. I knew I could rely on you to join in the drinking with gusto."

"You make it sound like I never have a sober moment."

"Not at all. Though I am hoping you will sup enough to allow me to press my advantage." He put down his glass, lifted her empty hand and brushed the fingertips with his lips.

"Very gallant, but with everything and everyone crammed

into this room, we will *all* be pressing more than that." She pushed the bottle into his hand and squeezed further inside.

The revelry around them was beginning to pick up pace. Someone had started a playlist that swung energetically between disco and synth-pop. Altheya and her friend had made a space in the middle of the room and were already dancing. The brunette by the bookshelf had made her choice of book and was now browsing through it with one hand, while holding her wine in the other.

"Let me introduce you to Jennifer," Tristan said, guiding Dulcie gently through the crowd toward the woman, who was scanning the pages, oblivious to the dancers gyrating nearby.

"Dulcie, Jen. Jen, Dulcie," he announced with a grin. "Dulcie's our newest resident. She's just moved into the garden flat and she's making an absolute fortune off junk that all the neighbours are chucking out."

"Hardly a fortune, and never junk", Dulcie said, slightly offended on both fronts. "I'm just good at spotting what other people overlook."

"Nice to meet you," Jennifer said, her eyes bright, calmly assessing the newbie. "It's always intriguing to find value in overlooked places." There was something reserved and composed about her, but her aura was friendly. The wine glass hung loosely in her fingers like an afterthought, the book in her other hand already forgotten.

"Jen works with Owen," Tristan said. "I'm fairly certain she does most of the actual work, keeping him in line and oiling all the wheels. Honestly, I don't think he'd survive without her."

"Oh, I doubt that," Jennifer replied, though she didn't outright deny it. "He's capable enough, but sometimes forgets what day it is or where his emails are stored." There was a warmth in her tone that Dulcie believed hinted at something fonder, more complicated, and far less platonic than friendship.

The background song changed to a romantic ballad. Tristan clapped his hands and declared, "Right, I'm going to circulate. See if I can't get this music sorted so that you are irresistibly drawn to dance."

"If you get me dancing before glass number three, you're either a magician or I've met someone more persuasive than prosecco." Jennifer's eyes were twinkling.

At that point, Owen burst into the room, slightly breathless and wide-eyed.

"You won't believe this," he announced, loud enough to silence the music for a beat. "Somebody's only gone and nicked the case of wine."

Heads turned. Conversation faltered.

"What?" Tristan blinked, sitting forward. "How could they have done that? It has to be signed for."

Owen held his hands out in theatrical disbelief. " I guess somebody signed for it on our front doorstep, then had it away on their toes. It must have been the fastest heist in history. I'd only just got the delivery alert, ran downstairs, and by the time I opened the door, the van had driven off. Driver: gone. Wine: gone."

There was a stunned pause. Then Jessie gasped, clutching her chest with mock horror.

"No! I can't believe it. Our phantom thief has struck again."

A few of the guests murmured in agreement, half-joking, half-curious. Tom looked up from his conversation with Iden. "Wait, what do you mean, again?"

"I had a brand-new plant-pot pinched from my front step yesterday," said Megan, appearing from the hallway with a fresh glass in hand. "A succulent. Who steals a succulent?"

"Well, apparently," Owen rubbed his forehead in frustration, "someone with a fine wine palate, green fingers and zero shame."

"Was it the expensive case?" Tristan asked, eyes narrowing.

"The very expensive case. Twelve bottles of obscure, boutique whites from a vineyard I visited in the corner of the Loire Valley."

"So... what do we do now?"

"There are still a couple of bottles in the fridge. Not all hope is lost."

Jen raised her glass in his direction. "Then let's not waste it."

As the party resumed its chatter, someone switched the music to a more beat-driven, funkier tune. Guests began opening bottles of whatever was left, pouring liberally and with lowered expectations. Tom volunteered to pick up some beer from the shop and was roundly applauded.

Moving toward the kitchen, Dulcie spotted Owen already there, removing the cork from a single remaining bottle, a slender, sophisticated-looking white wine with a cursive French label, smug in its rarity.

"Should we put it to one side?" She asked, leaning

against the doorframe. "Or share it between us before it disappears?"

"The latter," Owen raised his glass in a toast. "To the bottle who saved the day." He poured her a generous measure and handed it over, their fingers touching briefly as he did so. They paused for a moment, removed from the noise and flickering lights of the living room.

"You look good," Owen said suddenly. He was fiddling with the corkscrew, absent-mindedly twisting the arms up and down.

"Oh." She blinked, surprised. "Thanks. You too."

"I mean, you always look good," he added, still casual, still not quite meeting her eyes. "It's really nice to see you."

"Are you saying that I scrub up well, out of my dungarees and clear of sawdust?"

"I wouldn't go that far," he grinned. They both stared at the floor, and a yawning gap filled their conversation. Taking a sip of wine, they let the moment settle between them.

"She's lovely," Dulcie stated, tipping her head towards the living room, where the party was back in full swing.

"Who?"

"Jennifer."

A pause. Then Owen gave a small snort through his nose. "Oh, Jen. Yes, she is, she really is. The absolute best," he agreed, but didn't say more. Which, for Dulcie, said plenty.

"Help yourself to food," Owen smoothly changed the subject. He turned to a selection of snacks on the counter, primarily cheese intended to complement the wine, and placed a generous chunk of cheddar, a spoonful of coleslaw and some salad onto a plate.

"I'm not hungry, thanks." The music thudded gently through the wall, voices rising and falling in the other room. "Shall we get back to the fray?" she asked, given that they seemed to have run out of things to say.

Rejoining the party, Owen sat down in the now-empty blue bubble chair, balancing a plate in one hand and cutlery in the other. Dulcie attached herself to Tristan and the others in the centre of the room, which had been transformed into a small, makeshift dance floor. They swayed with cheerful enthusiasm to the rhythm of the music, twisting and twirling with playful abandon. The mood was happy and full of fun, all of them singing along to the lyrics. Everyone was in high spirits until a new arrival stalked into the room.

That most dedicated of complainers, Gerald Waring, marched into the lounge clad in a dressing gown and slippers and positioned himself in front of the sofa. He planted his hands on his hips and glared, as if each bass note wounded him mortally.

Owen tried to stand up as a gesture of goodwill. Clumsily, he wriggled from side to side to extricate himself from the inflatable chair. Unfortunately, the hand he used to push up with, held a small, sharp knife - the one he had been using to cut cheese. The blade neatly punctured the seat, the chair gave a magnificent fart, and deflated like a hovercraft skirt. Owen hovered mid-squat, then he crumpled backwards, landing cross-legged like a startled yoga instructor.

There was a moment of surprised silence before the group erupted with glee. Shoulders shook, heads were thrown back, and hands clapped over mouths. Owen remained stuck in the wreckage, the remnants of the chair now a sad, squeaky puddle beneath him.

Gerald was appalled, as if the accident had been arranged for his benefit. "Is this a party or pandemonium?" he demanded, causing the room to fall silent. "Because the noise you are all making is thumping through my walls like a stampede, what with the leaping about and people falling all over the floor."

"It's a wine tasting, with a bit of dancing." Tristan offered brightly, standing beside Owen, who was being helped up from the carpet. "And if you ask me, the chair had it coming." He turned to face Gerald. "The whirling was impromptu, and the music merely provided a little ambience."

"We apologise for any disturbance, Mr. Waring," Dulcie said, attempting to pour oil on troubled waters. "Although it might not seem so now, this began as a very civilised gathering."

"Nevertheless, I strongly suggest you turn the volume down before I begin filing noise complaints with the council. Again." Gerald gave them all a hard stare to emphasise his point, tightened the cord of his dressing gown around his waist, and made a commanding exit, closing the door firmly behind him.

"That's my fault," declared Tom. "He slipped in the front door beside me when I brought back the beer."

"Never mind about him. That fellow loves to moan. I heard he once complained about the distant crashing of butterfly wings. Besides, I think it's about time to change the mood a little anyway." Tristan flipped through the music tracks. "Here are some classics to soothe our souls, something a bit smoother."

Jen made room next to her on the sofa for Owen. Their heads were close, knees angled inward, the low light softening their silhouettes. Jen was animated, apparently teasing Owen about his pratfall. He appeared to be taking it in good part, nudging her and leaning back, his expression open and amused.

Feeling hot from dancing and slightly giddy from wine, Dulcie welcomed the change of pace offered by the new melodies and flopped onto the vacant armchair.

"Hey, you." Tristan perched beside her. "I like that you came here tonight."

"I like it, too," she replied, looking steadily into his lovely eyes. Their faces were so close that their breaths mingled. Time seemed to stand still; the world shrinking to the space between them. He caught her eyes flickering upward, sensing her invitation to kiss, so he leaned down towards her upturned face. Her lips were warm and tentative, tasting of the last wine sip. His hand reached behind her shoulders, pulling her closer. Instinctively, her hand moved to his chest, fingers curling around his shirt fabric. After a moment of perfect indulgence, he opened his eyes and looked at her as if she were something delicate, something he'd been privileged to touch for the first time. His thumb brushed gently along her jaw.

"That..." he whispered, voice low and roughened by emotion, "calls for a celebration." He gently lifted the glass from her hand. "Stay there. I will be right back." He walked away with the confidence of someone who knew he'd soon be kissed again. Dulcie didn't move for a moment, then slowly, her fingers rose to her lips, touching the spot where his kiss still lingered. There was a softness in her expression, the look of someone tucking a memory away to be replayed many times.

Her thoughts were interrupted by the sudden buzz of her phone, vibrating with bossy insistence, regardless of the moment it was interrupting. Fishing the phone from her pocket, still half-lost in the echo of the kiss, she glanced at the screen.

Message from Jamila. She listened to the voicemail:

"Can you come to the pub, precious? Your Uncle has been enjoying the party, and now he's shouting, 'Home James, and don't spare the horses!' He tries to set off, but he's not seeing straight. Beer goggles. Can you walk him home?"

She tapped out a quick reply. "On my way," she wrote, sliding the phone back into her pocket.

Tristan's voice was drifting out from the kitchen, something about finally locating the corkscrew "in the drawer nobody ever uses." Then he reappeared, holding two clean but mismatched glasses and a half-open bottle with an old and tatty label.

"Right," he announced, "this one's supposed to taste like peaches and mountain ice."

"I have to go," Dulcie interrupted gently.

His smile faltered. "Go?"

"It's Les. He's been performing his version of Cirque du Soleil at the pub, and Jamila needs backup."

"Of course," Tristan let out a short laugh. "Your uncle

famously enjoys a karaoke night. It's uncanny, though, how he's managed to put a stop to my dishonourable intentions."

"I'm sorry," she said, twisting her lips. "I wish I could stay."

"Well then, we will have to consider this drink merely postponed. To be continued, right?"

She squeezed his arm and grabbed her jacket from the hook by the door. As she ran down the stairs and into the night, the cool air hit her like a reset button. There would be time to think later about the kiss, to mull over her feelings for Tristan, and the frisson between Owen and Jen. For now, she had someone to collect, someone who was probably under a pub table or hugging a fruit machine. She sighed. Uncle Les had done more for her than anyone else ever had. The least she could do was return the favour, one unsteady rescue at a time.

CHAPTER 24

The next morning, Dulcie stepped out of her flat to gather supplies. She had a shopping list tucked in her pocket and varnish on her mind. Wax, too, plus a new tin of dark oak stain, if she could find it. It was shaping up to be a practical sort of day, the kind that usually helped her feel grounded. The flump of bare footsteps padded down the stairwell in the hall.

Descending the stairs from Flat 2 was the English Rose girl from the party. Her blonde hair was slightly flattened on one side, her black dress crumpled in an unmistakable way, and she held her heels in one hand as if the walk home required a little less glamour and a lot more grip. Still, she looked composed. Pleased, even.

Dulcie offered a cautious, "Good morning."

The girl smiled without a flicker of embarrassment. "Morning," she called breezily, as though they were passing on the way to Pilates. She stepped past Dulcie, out of the front door and onto the pavement, disappearing down the street with the effortless composure of someone still basking in the glow of a memorable night.

Still holding the door, the cool air brushing against her skin, Dulcie let her gaze drift up to the landing above. Her mind was racing. After she'd left the party to collect Uncle Les, had Tristan hooked up with the English Rose? It was possible, she supposed. The girl had hovered close to him all night, laughing too easily, tilting her head in that way people do when they're angling for intimacy. The thought made her stomach churn. Had Tristan decided that their kiss last night was merely a fleeting, wine-induced moment? A shrug, a wink, and someone else in his bed an hour later?

Maybe the girl had crashed on the sofa? After a night of drinking, it wasn't unusual for someone to sleep wherever space allowed. The only other alternative was that Owen had enjoyed a tryst with Natasha. Was that her name? Perhaps that was the truth of the matter. Owen was hard to read, all closed-off glances and quiet intensity. The night before, he'd barely spoken to anyone, spending the evening tucked into a shadowy corner with Jen, like they were plotting the downfall of the Western World. But who knows what may have happened at midnight, if the party went into overdrive, as parties were wont to do? Yes. That must be what had happened. And besides, better Owen than Tristan.

She pulled on her jacket and puffed out her cheeks. There was no point standing there spinning stories like candyfloss. Romance was unpredictable, full of blurred lines and second-guessing. Work, on the other hand, was solid. Steady. It never let her down. She reached into her coat pocket and unfolded the crumpled shopping list. Her eyes landed on the first item: Varnish (matte).

She nodded to herself.

She'd start with that.

When she returned a couple of hours later, laden with heavy shopping bags, she found Les slouched at the table in his dressing gown, wearing sunglasses indoors like a hungover rock star, and poking half-heartedly at a piece of toast.

"Are you alright?" Dulcie asked, eyeing the untouched Marmite and the teaspoon floating in his tea like a tiny shipwreck.

"I'm tremendous," Les croaked. "I'm a one-man cautionary tale about overdoing beer and karaoke."

"So, just another Saturday night, then?"

He lifted his sunglasses and winced. "I got swept *away*, Dulcie. That crowd was electric. I'd barely started my rendition of 'Suspicious Minds' when Evie, you know, the girl from the band with those electric guitars?"

"*Tatu Tempo?*"

"That's the one! Velvet voice, attitude like a lioness. She joined me on stage. No warning. Just swooped in mid-verse like an angel in sequins."

"And you let her?"

"I *welcomed* her. Between us, we practically reinvented the duet. I mean, if Ant and Dec had been there, they'd have slapped a golden buzzer on the fruit machine."

"And how many pints had led up to this vision of greatness?"

"Three pints of Guinness, two gin chasers, and a Jaeger bomb I'm blaming on Jason behind the bar."

He rubbed his temples dramatically, then peered at her. "But never mind me. What about your evening? You were off to that wine thing upstairs, weren't you?"

"Yeah," Dulcie said, a little too quickly. "It was nice."

He squinted at her with the suspicion of a man who could read lies like creases in a well-worn map. "Just 'nice'?"

"Some wine, some chat. No fog machines or dramatic duets, unfortunately."

"Sounds like you should have come out with me instead. We had an absolute ball." Les groaned like a novice on a sailing ship, shifting carefully in his chair with one hand on his temple. Unmoved by his suffering, Dulcie stole one of his biscuits. He either didn't notice or decided not to say anything. Slumped against the table, he stirred the cold remnants of his tea, trying not to let the spoon click against the mug. Eventually, he looked up, his expression sheepish beneath his salt-and-pepper eyebrows.

"Listen," he said, "I'm sorry I got so blotto last night. You shouldn't have had to come and haul me home, like a tipsy pensioner back from a Jolly Boys outing."

"You were a tipsy pensioner."

"Fair point. Still, I hope I didn't ruin your night. I know you had plans upstairs. Wine and music and youthful hijinks."

"You didn't spoil anything. I'd had a good time. Things were starting to get... interesting." She said it lightly, but the word hung there with a faint shadow. Les didn't pick up on it.

"Well, that's what we like to hear," he said, trying to rally. "A good night all round, then." He leaned back with a groan that suggested his internal organs were still in recovery. "Can't say the morning's been as cheery, mind. I received a visit from Gerald this morning, bright and early. Apparently, our house has become a den of 'wild parties and disgraceful goings-on'. I told him if he was so shocked by the concept of merriment, he might try moving to a convent."

"What was he complaining about? We turned the music down when he asked us to."

"Oh, brace yourself," Les said, with mock gravitas. "He says he saw a man in a rugby jersey in a passionate clinch with a woman outside the house at midnight. Front garden, no less! Apparently, he recognised the very same woman leaving here this morning. Said it with all the outrage of someone witnessing a bank robbery."

"A... rugby jersey?" Dulcie felt a cold hand grip her heart.

Les nodded. "It's ridiculous. I don't know what he expected me to do about it. I'm a landlord, not the morality police."

A passionate clinch, witnessed by Gerald, the neighbourhood's surveillance watchdog. Dulcie's mind was racing, recalling images: the barefoot blonde girl descending the stairs this morning, like a cat that had got the cream... and a man in a rugby jersey. Well, she thought, that narrows down the suspects, given that Tristan was the only one wearing a top like that last night. "Gerald should start a neighbourhood newsletter," she said tartly. "The scandal would be thrilling."

Les snorted. "He'd call it The Moral Observer. And it'd be mostly photos of people parking slightly over the line." He took another sip of tea and muttered, "Honestly. The man acts like a bit of snogging will cause the collapse of the Western World."

Dulcie smiled but said nothing more. The smile didn't reach her eyes.

CHAPTER 25

Tristan answered the door with his usual charm, barefoot and bleary-eyed, the same rugby jersey he'd worn last night hanging off him, a visual reminder of everything she wasn't sure she wanted to know.

"Hey, stranger," he said. "Come to cure my hangover? I'm all alone," he said, his voice husky and suggestive. Stepping to one side, he gestured toward the lounge, inviting her in. "Owen and Jen arranged to meet someone from work, so the castle is empty and ours for the taking." Dulcie didn't move, her face set and unreadable, showing tightly controlled anger. He hesitated, eyes scanning her face, noticing the shift in her usual happy mood.

"Gerald had quite the report this morning," she said. "He saw a man in a rugby jersey kissing someone outside this house last night. Passionately, by all accounts. I believe I saw that same woman leaving the house this morning."

Tristan's smile faded. The mug in his hand hovered mid-air. "Right," he said, twisting his lips. "Yeah."

"Did she stay here, with you?"

A beat. He nodded.

"Okay," she shrugged. "Thanks for being straight with me." She had come prepared for a pointed interrogation, maybe even a full-blown argument, but his simple reply had thrown her. Her feelings were torn between approving of his honesty and despising the disappointment it caused.

"Natasha stayed over," he said quietly. "After you left the party, we got talking. Everyone had a bit too much wine, and one thing led to another. I'm not making excuses. She's a lovely person, but it was just a bit of fun. It was casual." He searched her face. "I know the timing is awful. Perhaps it doesn't look like it right now, but I'm serious about getting to know you. We could have something pretty great, I think, and I hope this doesn't stop us from finding out what that could be. I didn't mean to screw it up… whatever this is."

"You mean *was.*" Dulcie stared at her feet.

"You're not going to give me a chance? Not to redeem myself, not to show you there is potential for us to have a terrific time together?" He seemed astonished.

"No, I'm not." She shook her head gently. "I thought I could keep things casual. Go in with my eyes wide open and my heart firmly shut. Turns out, I'm more old-fashioned than I realised."

"But you and I, we've only just started. We haven't even got underway." A frown appeared under his tousled hair. "Natasha and I aren't an item; we had a fling. That's all it was, and it shouldn't stop *us* from progressing." Swallowing hard and taking a deep breath, he tried to make his case. "I told you the truth, I like you, Dulcie, I really like you, and I want to see where this could go."

I get that," she could see he was genuine. "You don't owe me anything. We're adults, and we're not even a couple. But that doesn't mean I have to follow you into a mess I didn't cause."

"It wasn't a *mess*," he said, a little sharper now. "It just happened."

"Even so, I'm not going to pretend it didn't shift something in the way I feel about you. I've been down this road before, and I promised myself not to go back." She measured her words. "I like you too, Tristan, but not enough to live on tenterhooks wondering if I'm the only girl in your world. Sometimes the light isn't worth the candle."

"Wow, you're saying no to getting to know me better? Just like that."

"I'm saying yes," she corrected, "to us being friends. Because I enjoy your company, I really do. But I'm not a backup plan or a second option. Turns out that I can't get into a relationship I didn't trust from the start."

He sighed, rubbing the back of his neck. "You're not what I expected."

"I get that a lot." She was glad she had said her piece, but her heart was in her boots. It was one thing to stand by her principles, which she knew without doubt was the right thing to do. But that didn't make it any easier when she looked up into that chiselled face and those seductive eyes.

"Right," Tristan cleared his throat. "Shall we toast the short, but heartfelt, golden age of our almost-romance with a coffee?"

She hesitated. "A coffee and some toast. Maybe with jam?"

"Friends who like jam. I can live with that. So does that mean you're coming in?" he asked. No hidden meaning this time. Just a simple, honest question.

She hesitated only a second. "Sure," she said. "If it's still okay."

"Of course. Always." He led the way back into the flat.

The rooms bore unmistakable signs of the previous night. The coffee table and side surfaces were scattered with empty glasses, some of which still had dregs of wine at the bottom. Plates with leftover snacks rested next to used napkins and crumpled paper cups. Everywhere was disordered and messy, cluttered with typical party debris —a place waiting to be put back together. Moving into the kitchen, they saw a row of empty bottles along one wall, which stood in testament to the revelry of the evening. "I think I drank most of that Pinot Grigio." Dulcie pointed to the one which had been her contribution.

"Impressive." Tristan grinned, flicking on the kettle with one hand and reaching for a clean mug with the next. He held it up like a peace offering. She rolled her eyes but nodded her acceptance.

"Would it make any difference," he asked, "if I said that Natasha isn't a patch on you?" He sat at the kitchen table, busying himself by collecting the bowls from last night's buffet into a heap at one end.

"No, it wouldn't. And honestly, that's a horrible thing to say." Her fierce words splashed like cold water. "Don't drag another woman down because you still fancy your chances with me. You couldn't be more wrong." The connection that had once linked them was now an echo in the wrong key.

"I am in the bad books, aren't I?" Tristan slumped back. "I don't suppose there is anything I can do to redeem myself?"

"We are past all that now. I meant what I said. From now on, we are strictly in the friend zone."

"I think you've made that pretty clear." The kettle boiled, and Tristan poured steaming water into mugs, stirring the coffee as they filled to the brim. He appeared to be thinking over their conversation and seemed to come to a decision. "Perhaps there is one thing I can share, something that you might be interested in." He made a show of fetching milk from the fridge and adding a splash to the mug he now held out. "Given that I'm now only a friend, I could reveal a bit of insider information to you."

"Go on."

"Owen and Jen are not a couple," he said. "They get along brilliantly and are practically glued at the hip, but they're colleagues when all's said and done. They work together really closely, but there's nothing more to it."

"Really?" Dulcie realised that she was genuinely surprised. "They seem so well-suited."

"Not at all. I know for certain that he's not her type. Not in the least."

"Are you trying to tell me that she's gay?"

"Only in my dreams," Tristan said with a lecherous smirk. "No, she's into the high-powered, big-city, jet-setting type. She's been dating the CEO of a top 100 company for the past couple of years. He travels the world doing heroic, Bond-like things. With Owen, she gets her academic and business fix; it's all intellectual stimulation and project collaboration, but absolutely no sparks of the romantic kind."

"Why are you telling me this now?"

"Because you would have found out eventually, whatever happened. I wanted to get a head start. Before our status changed to that of strictly pals." Tristan popped bread into the toaster.

"What do you mean by that? Why would you need a head start?"

"When it comes to impressing women, Owen thinks I have all the advantages. He says, 'I am to his ego, what a hole is to a balloon.' Tells people that when we go out clubbing, he gets trampled in the rush. Like I'm some kind of babe magnet."

"And that isn't the case?"

"I suppose it might be, in some ways." Modesty didn't suit Tristan. "But none of my relationships stick. Owen is great at listening to everyone he meets. He makes a real effort to get to know them. He is terrific company, and he always makes them laugh. The only reason he's single is that he chooses to be." He shrugged his shoulders. "I thought I would make a play for you before he got the chance."

"Do you think he *wants* to take a chance on me?" asked Dulcie. It was a strange situation, asking for details of one man's fancy, from your fancy man, which was how Auntie Margaret would have put it.

"He hasn't said a word, but I recognise the signs," he replied. "When he's into someone, it's like his brain's got twelve tabs open. And it's fair to say that he's all over the place at the moment. Ever since I took you to that Birds and Bees charity do, he's been acting weird. You must have noticed he's been avoiding you, scuttling away as soon as you come into sight. If he weren't bothered, he'd be chatting your ear off. That's his default setting; he's always friendly."

Tristan shrugged, more to himself than to her. Technically, he was committing a bro-code foul by hinting to Dulcie that Owen was besotted, but it wasn't a total breach of the unwritten rules. "I could be wrong. But don't be surprised if he accidentally confesses undying love while asking if you've found the bottle bank, or the library, or any other flimsy excuse he makes to talk to you. And when he does, do me a favour... pretend I never said a word."

Tristan leaned back on the kitchen stool, stretching his arms behind his head. Since his chances with Dulcie were scuppered, he'd had nothing to lose by casting a vote for Owen, who was, after all, a good friend. Sometimes fate needs a little push in the right direction. As for himself, there were always nightclubs to visit, Natasha's number saved in his phone, and if all else failed, somewhere in his room, he still had the contact details of a charming stranger written down on a paper napkin.

CHAPTER 26

It was well known that the Witch & Stable pub had existed for many years before its current regulars were a twinkle in the eye of its previous ones. Like a crooked-backed troll, its ceilings sloped at strange angles, and the entrance leaned to one side, as tipsy as its patrons. It wasn't trendy or spotlessly clean, but it offered warmth, darts, and crisps that tasted of something you'd once eaten in a caravan.

Big Maccie sat hunched at the middle table, nursing his pint as if he hoped it might reproduce before he had to buy another. Beside him, Les was already three-quarters through his first drink, immersed in the self-satisfaction that came from mild intoxication and good company. He raised his glass in a salute: "May you live to be a hundred, with a year to repent."

Maccie clinked his tankard against Les's beer mug. "Thanks, but I don't think I'll get that far. My health record has dropped out of the top twenty."

"Nonsense. You're nothing but a shirker," Les declared, tapping the table for emphasis. "A professional malingerer. It's your civic duty to bounce back with all the vigour of your rusty-haired ancestors. I, myself, was climbing a stepladder only ten days after my hip replacement."

"You were high on codeine and painting the ceiling with limewash," Maccie muttered, without looking up.

"I'm only pointing out that you need to get out and about, further than the bookies, Bunce's and this pub. Come out with me tomorrow morning. I'm off on a jaunt with friends from my U3A class to visit the last working windmill in London."

"I had surgery, Les."

"You had a nap and some nurses mopping your brow. And now you're loafing around your flat in a robe like the Queen of Sheba. Anyway, it's only up the road a mile or two. It'll do you good to get out." Les leaned back, pleased with himself, and took a hearty swig of bitter.

Opposite him, Jamila was gently swirling her gin and tonic. It was her night off, and she planned to enjoy it, ideally without listening to Les talk about medical stories. "You're on form tonight," she said, looking up at him.

Les gave her a lopsided grin. "Must be the thrill of losing another tenner. I bet on a bob-tailed nag called 'Chase the Ace,' - a horse so slow it's probably still running. Lovely little grey who looked *so* promising in the paddock, but she was deaf to the starter's pistol and I think she spent the rest of the race admiring the hedge."

"You always choose with your heart, not your head. That's why I never let you near a wine list."

"Touché," Les said, raising his glass. "Though you could soften the blow with a sympathetic dinner sometime."

"That sounds dangerously close to flirting, Les."

"If it sounds dangerous, I must be doing it right."

"I don't know how to take you sometimes." Jamila bit into a twiglet taken from a packet that lay between them. "I can't tell if you are serious."

"Could be serious, you never know with me." He tapped the side of his nose. "You can't blame me for trying when the alternative to one of your delicious stews is a poor existence, littered with betting slips and bar snacks," Les said, stuffing a few of the latter into his mouth.

Maccie pulled a crumpled racing paper from his coat pocket. "That reminds me, thanks for nothing, Les," he said glumly. "The tips you give me are about as useful as the ones I've picked up from the shop owners in the street."

"In what way?" Jamila asked.

"Despite what he would have you believe, I've been busy during the past week, holed up in my flat. And I haven't been talking to the walls. As a matter of fact, I've been investigating a rash of peculiar crimes. That famous detective, Hercule Poirot, relied on his 'little grey cells' to solve mysteries from his armchair. If it's good enough for him, it's good enough for me."

"What's the latest?" Les hadn't heard much from Dulcie on the subject recently. She had other things on her mind.

"I've got details of packages swiped, windchimes stolen, more shoplifting. Nothing which stands out on its own, but it's building up a picture."

"Very good, Inspector Maccie." Les gave him a quick salute.

"Dulcie will be chuffed to hear you are fully on the case. She needs a distraction, since things fizzled with that streak of sunshine in flat two."

"Nice enough lad," Maccie countered.

"Too keen on mirrors for my taste. I know I'm biased, but I want what's best for her. She's had a rough year—new job, new home, odd neighbours, present company included. I've tried to give her some advice, but the only rule I've ever lived by is 'never fly a kite in a thunderstorm,' and that's no help in matters of the heart."

"Don't worry so much. She's a smart girl. Heart's too big for her own good, but she'll sort herself out."

"That's right," Jamila agreed. "Whatever happens, I'm sure she won't steer back to Tristan. Unfortunately, he strikes me as the type who gets a lot of rebounds.

"Don't say that. I'd rather she dated whoever swiped the windchimes."

The clock behind the bar ticked through the lull in their conversation. In the corner, a couple argued politely over dominoes. The pub felt, as ever, like a place happy with its history. It had been updated with Wi-Fi, but still offered pickled eggs, pork scratchings and dry-roasted peanuts for the more discerning palate. Jason, a relief barman who worked alternate shifts, lifted the service flap and strolled toward their table. He gathered empty glasses along the way, grabbing several with one hand while he scrolled through his phone with the other, his thumb flicking over the screen.

"You lot alright?" he asked, without glancing up.

"Just about, thank you," Jamila replied, raising her drink.

Jason grunted in vague acknowledgement and wandered off again, trailing the clink of glassware and the tinny noise of a video playing on his phone.

"Top-tier service," Maccie muttered, watching him go. "You could keel over in here, and he'd wipe around you."

"He's usually quite chatty," Jamila said. "Customers love him. He's got the gift of the gab, and he knows how to put down any bar-stool hecklers. Honestly, his only real flaw is showing up late for his shift. He's usually right in the centre of any goings-on."

Les knew what she meant. He blamed Jason for urging him to drink shots on Saturday night, and he was still feeling the effects. He looked over at the lad, who had a stocky build and broad shoulders, with a tuft of hair curled at the nape of his neck. Jason moved around the pub with practised skill, doing just enough to look busy without attracting attention. Les wasn't sure if he would fit on the spectrum of Dulcie's type, but it was tempting to give matchmaking a go. He probably wouldn't interfere on balance - she'd only accuse him of playing Cupid in beer goggles.

Jamila pushed her chair back and stood, stretching with a soft groan. She reached for her coat, shaking it out before sliding into it. "I'm off to enjoy a bubble bath and a good book," she looped her handbag onto her shoulder. "Let me know if I can be of any help, Maccie. I'm always happy to keep my ear to the ground."

Les gave a vague wave. "If you fancy helping me to make casseroles, I'm willing to give it a go...even with peanut butter and no chips."

"Good things come to those who wait, Les." She gave him a

wink that could've powered the jukebox, then moved away, heels clicking toward the door.

"Ever hopeful, eh mate?" Maccie watched the glamorous figure of Jamila disappear past the tables on the far side of the bar.

"I may be over, but I'm not out," Les sighed, looking increasingly glum as the door closed behind the object of his affections. "Well. That's me back to microwave shepherd's pie tonight and tiptoeing around Dulcie. Advising the lovesick is not one of the things I do best."

"She'll be alright. She's got you to lift her spirits. Even if you are a sentimental old goat."

"Right back at you, you cantankerous beggar. I'm relying on you to distract her with all this talk of fish and crooks."

The pub had thinned out by the time Les and Maccie nursed the last of their drinks. Les drained the final mouthful of his beer with a satisfied sigh, smacked his lips, and gave the table a brisk tap. "That's your lot," he said, pushing himself up. His knees popped audibly, and he gave them a disdainful glance. "They should employ me to stand up at the start of every horse race; that noise is loud enough to set them all off running."

"I couldn't even finish my drink." Maccie glanced mournfully at the quarter-pint left untouched.

"I may have misjudged you. A man must be properly under the weather if he can't get to the bottom of his glass. Let's get you home, and you can rest up before our little outing in the morning."

The two men ambled toward the door, their footsteps echoing off the pub's old wood floor. Les paused at the threshold to fumble with his cap, pulling it low over his thinning hair. Outside, the evening air was cool and damp, tinged with the smell of rain on concrete. "Tomorrow, then?" Les said, jabbing a finger toward Maccie's chest. "Nine o'clock sharp. Brixton Windmill is two hundred years old. If that doesn't make us feel young, I don't know what will."

Maccie buried his hands deep in his coat pockets. "Nine it is."

They walked along Minet Road, side by side. Fat raindrops started to splash erratically on the pavement ahead, and, in the cool, moist breeze, they could hear a jingle of random notes coming from windchimes that were haunting, melodic, and very likely stolen.

CHAPTER 27

Repeat custom is always welcome, so Dulcie was pleased to receive a summons back to the home of Marjorie Donaldson, the same sharp-witted old lady who had given her a cabinet, now transformed into a sage green and brass-knobbed thing of beauty.

She reached number 52 Gordon Grove, a little out of breath, dragging her battered parcel trolley behind her. The front door was already ajar, sunshine spilling over the patterned hallway carpet. Somewhere inside, she heard the distinctive whirr of Marjorie's electric wheelchair.

"Come in, dear!" called out a bright voice from within.

Stepping inside, Dulcie was enveloped by the familiar scent of lavender furniture polish and something slightly scorched, which was probably toast. The hallway had an old-fashioned charm with an original, tessellated floor. Family photos lined the walls, knitted dolls guarded doorways, and a radio tuned slightly off station hummed away to itself. Marjorie rolled into view from the lounge, cheerful as ever. On her lap were two knitting needles and the beginnings of what looked like a very small, very orange hat.

"There you are," she beamed. "I've emptied the shrank. It's all yours for the taking."

"The… shrank?"

"Yes, yes—the wall unit. It's German; that's what they call them. Practical but solid, my daughter brought it back from her travels. I thought of you straightaway." Marjorie turned smoothly on the spot and led her into the lounge, which was dominated by a vast and unapologetic piece of furniture running the full length of the wall. Polished walnut, smoked glass, ornate handles—enough shelving to store every book Dulcie had ever owned.

"Oh. Wow," Dulcie managed.

"Isn't it marvellous?"

"It's…magnificent," Dulcie offered. "But there's no way I could transport it on my trolley, even if it could be broken down. I'm so sorry, Marjorie, but I don't think I can make use of it."

"Oh dear, you too? Nobody seems to want it. Too big for most modern houses, I suppose." She ran her hand fondly over the wood. "I rather suspected you might say no. But it's been such a miserable week, I thought a miracle might happen."

Marjorie was about to elucidate further about her trials and tribulations when someone else appeared in the doorway, drying his hands on a tea towel.

"Oh!" Dulcie was astonished. "It's *you*."

"Fancy meeting you here." Owen looked up and smiled, surprised but pleased to see her. He was wearing a faded hoodie, grey joggers, and a pair of canary-yellow washing-up gloves that clung to his forearms.

Dulcie pointed at the shrank. "Marjorie wants me to take this off her hands, but I only have my trolley. It's great for bedside tables and magazine racks, but not massive Bavarian cabinet, so unfortunately I won't be able to take it on," she explained. "I don't suppose you're here for the same reason?"

"She's one of ours," Owen said, peeling off the gloves with a snap. "One of the clients from the care agency I co-run with Jennifer. Jen's my business partner. I'm the practical one, and she handles the marketing. Today, one of our carers called in sick, so I offered to step in."

"But you're a lecturer, aren't you?" Dulcie was confused. She felt like she had slipped into a parallel universe.

"Part-time," Owen replied. "Ancient civilisations one day, helping Marjorie pack knitted hats for premature babies the next."

Marjorie waved her hand. "He makes an excellent sandwich but he is *not* very good with the Hoover. I like him better than the last one, though."

Dulcie paused to take in this surprising aspect of her housemate. She'd been talking for weeks about her venture, yet he had never once mentioned running a side hustle of his own. How extraordinary. How modest. How oddly *annoying*.

Owen offered to tune the radio, hoping to change the subject. "Shall I tweak it a little, and then you'll be able to hear it better, Marjorie?"

"I'm ninety-three years old and I've heard enough," Marjorie snapped back irritably. She gave a small, dramatic sigh and leaned slightly back in her chair. "Nothing is going right; I can't get a new carpet fitted until someone removes this huge piece of furniture, and yesterday two of my friends cancelled our trip to a recording of Gardeners' Question Corner. I was so looking forward to it." She slumped back, her face a picture of misery and her eyes beginning to glisten with frustrated tears.

"Added to that, I've run out of two-ply wool, I take so many tablets that I rattle, and my only remaining relative has moved to a rest home miles away. I can only visit her once a fortnight, and I sometimes wonder if it's worth getting a return ticket. Might as well check myself in and be done with it."

Her palpable misery clouded the air. Owen shot Dulcie a glance, the unspoken question between them: *Should we do something?*

She gave the tiniest shrug. Maybe.

"It's getting lonely here anyway," Marjorie said, gloomily. No one's left on my team. My family and friends have all gone away, some for good. I keep myself busy, I always have done, but it's not the same."

The room was quiet, other than the buzzing of the radio, still manfully pouring out a melody, despite the buttons being a little off-kilter. Then Dulcie cleared her throat. "With the best will in the world, I can't take the shrank away. But I can take you to Gardener's Question Corner."

Marjorie blinked. "Don't be silly."

"I'm not. We could both take you." Dulcie insisted. "You've got three tickets, haven't you? I like plants. I'm sure Owen likes plants."

"I do." Owen slowly removed the gloves. "I haven't had much experience, and I'm not much of a one for digging. I like my leaves green and my hands clean. But I love flowers, especially when someone else has watered them, potted them, and made them thrive like you do with your window boxes."

Marjorie looked between them with a wily expression that suggested she was several steps ahead of both. "Goodness me," she said, lips pursed in delight. "Now I come to think of it, Jamila mentioned you used to work as a gardener in a stately home, Dulcie." She was warming to the idea. "My very own expert to accompany me, how exciting!"

"I really don't know that much. I mainly worked in the greenhouse and on the till."

"Wait a moment. Marjorie gave a theatrical little gasp and leaned forward in her chair, eyes twinkling. Are you two trying to cheer me up, or is this an excuse to gallivant around together, while I play the role of giant gooseberry?"

Dulcie felt the tips of her ears warm. "Marjorie!"

Owen jumped in. "I mean…I don't usually take my clients out with me when I go on dates to impress young ladies, but if I did, you'd definitely be my first choice."

"Well, I'm happy to be a third wheel, as long as we finish the evening with a frothy coffee in a posh cafe." Marjorie confided, "Back in my day, that's exactly what a rendezvous called for."

"It's a deal," Owen stated. "We will collect you on the way

and celebrate the occasion in style."

Invigorated by this unexpected turn of events, Marjorie burst into action like a general marshalling her troops. Within minutes, she had proposed departure times, argued the merits of taking the train rather than the bus, and strongly hinted that they should all wear something floral to suit the occasion.

Caught in the gentle whirlwind of her enthusiasm, Dulcie and Owen found themselves swept along with the plans. Fate had thrown them together in a ridiculous way, and this time, neither was pretending not to notice. Dulcie caught herself glancing at Owen more than once, and he, for his part, kept adjusting his hair when he thought she wasn't looking. Despite their false starts and awkward conversations in the stairwell, it was beginning to feel like something special might grow between them. A solid, lasting friendship, possibly even a romance. Albeit one chaperoned by a woman who could parallel park a wheelchair better than either of them could handle a first date.

CHAPTER 28

Kay Kenneths let herself into her home with the kind of grace that came from decades of entering stage left. She unfastened a silk scarf from her neck, removed her shoes, and silently padded barefoot across the bedroom rug, a remnant from a long-forgotten film set. Pouring a large glass of Sancerre from one of several identical bottles on her dressing table, she sipped the wine, let out a long sigh, and reclined on her padded chair with the dramatic flair of a woman who often died nightly in front of a paying audience.

The wine was superb. Light, crisp, with hints of elderberry. She swirled it in the glass and gazed up at the ceiling. "Les is probably drinking something called 'ale'," she murmured. "That beast in their basement no doubt favours whisky that smells like peat. And the girl, Dulcie. She's probably halfway through a box of supermarket rosé."

She smiled serenely.

Of course, none of them realised they were living next door to a criminal.

Perhaps that was going too far. It depended on how you defined "criminal." Petty theft, light trespassing, the occasional reallocation of parcels... nothing violent. Nothing *personal*. Certainly, no weapons, aside from charm. Kay Kenneths, once darling of stage and screen, had become someone altogether more electrifying: a woman of disguise. A shadow in the hedgerows. A whisper at the post-box. A spectre who could steal your Amazon delivery and vanish before you'd finished scrolling TikTok.

She was invisible. That was the truth of it. Auditions no longer came her way, and when the new roles had disappeared, so did the men, the money, and the press mentions. She had acquired a peculiar, intangible cloak that comes with ageing and irrelevance. People had stopped noticing her. Not just metaphorically, but actually. They would walk past her in the supermarket as if she weren't there. Neighbours nodded politely but never remembered her name. Children, the cruellest mirrors of all, looked through her like she was made of glass.

And so, one afternoon, alone and bored to sobs, she'd thought: Why not? Why not make use of this accidental gift of invisibility? Why not change the script, combine her skills and have a little fun?

On the other side of the room, her wardrobe was slightly open. Inside, chaos reigned with fabrics and wigs packed into garment bags, hatboxes, and labelled costumes, including a well-used beige trench coat and a football scarf. Blonde bombshells. Greying matriarchs. One bold costume sported elbow pads and yellowed teeth; another had orthopaedic shoes and body padding. Each costume was carefully folded, ready to be part of the next performance.

Her pièce de résistance had been the sweet shop disguise. She grinned, stretching like a cat basking in the late afternoon sun. To steal her favourite chocolates, she had dressed as a woman disguised as a man who might, again, be cross-dressing. Who could recognise someone who didn't exist, dressed in a wispy scarf, a faint moustache, and pearls? Especially when her next incarnation had been a silver-haired pensioner in a tweed skirt.

On the day of the party at number 67, it had been sheer luck that she was already wearing her brunette wig and the pink shell suit when a delivery van had come to a halt outside their door. The logo on the side of the truck indicated a cargo of wine. Adopting the expression of someone expecting a package that had *definitely* been paid for, she'd trotted up their stone steps just as the driver stepped out. He'd barely glanced at her; thrusting the box forward, desperate to be back in the cab before anyone asked questions or made him carry anything. One flamboyant squiggle on his iPad and the wine was hers. Fair game, she reasoned. If the universe put a parcel in your hands and no one asked for ID, it was practically a gift. Timing, outfit, and attitude—flawless. It wasn't theft. It was theatre.

"Here's to you," she toasted the dividing wall of the terraced house. "Thank you, boys, for supplying drinkies for the interval"

Turning her head slightly, her gaze drifted to the garden outside her window. The moonlight caught on the blooms of the begonias—stolen, of course, from the planters along the road. They were thriving, radiant and defiant in foreign soil. Kay stared at them, pleased by the colours in the display, more results of her derring-do. Sadly, nobody else would see the flowers because no one ever came to see her. Not her agent, not Les, not even next-door's cat. She'd stolen that too, Maccie's cat, Missy-Mae. It wasn't planned, but the wretched thing had appeared on her windowsill one afternoon, all entitlement and twitching whiskers, presenting a crime of opportunity. One open tin of tuna, and she had captured an unexpected hostage. Several days later, Dulcie had been invited in to admire the chaise lounge, and they'd both frozen at the sound of Missy causing havoc in the kitchen. "The plumbing," Kay had said, cold sweat dripping down her spine. The girl had accepted the lie, but it had been a narrow escape, and she let the cat out soon afterwards. Not that one mistake had stopped her. Oh *no*. If anything, it had confirmed something essential: there was still a way for her to live a life of thrills and spills.

Through her window, Kay could see the glow of light coming from Dulcie's room next door, illuminating the edge of their shared fencing. That young lady had promise, she thought. Nervous energy, odd romantic ideals, but a decent eye for detail. Might even grow into a worthy adversary one day.

But not yet. For now, Kay was ahead of the game. She had many secretive plots and wicked schemes to look forward to, and that, she decided, was worthy of a toast. "To the victor, the spoils," she said, pouring another glass. Which reminded her - she had delicious, illicit haddock to look forward to for supper. Again.

CHAPTER 29

The sun was past its hottest hour when Dulcie arrived at Number 52 with a thermos of tea, a tin of homemade Viennese whirls made from her mum's favourite recipe, and a sense of excited anticipation. Owen was already there, coaxing Marjorie's wheelchair over the front step with the kind of precision usually seen in people untangling fairy lights.

"I've changed my mind," Marjorie announced as Dulcie approached. "You're both too punctual. It unnerves me."

"We're here on time because we're looking forward to our evening out," Dulcie assured her.

"That's all very well, but we don't want to cut it too fine," said Marjorie, changing her mind again. "The train won't wait," she checked her watch with increasing urgency.

Owen, still grappling with manoeuvres, grunted. "Blame the step, not me. It's a medieval obstacle."

"If this were a siege, I'd be the battering ram." Marjorie

quipped, perched in her wheelchair with regal poise.

"Less drama, more speed." With one final heave, Owen cleared the step and straightened up, breathless. "Right. Next stop: platform. Preferably before departure." They set off at a brisk pace, wheels rattling and nerves fraying in sync.

Getting to Carshalton, as Marjorie had predicted, was less a simple journey and more a series of increasingly tough challenges. The brief walk to the station was harmless enough— a pleasant city stroll that lulled them into thinking the rest of the trip would be smooth sailing. However, there was also the queue for the station lift and the wheelchair ramp into the train to navigate. Once onboard, Owen had to function as a mix of travel buddy and bodyguard, stepping between Marjorie and a commuter who had no concept of personal space. Dulcie stood in front of the wheelchair like a diminutive nightclub bouncer. By the time they emerged into the twilight of the town, everyone was dishevelled and slightly sticky.

"I don't wish to alarm anyone," Marjorie said, fanning herself with an ancient folded map of the town, "but I've started sweating in parts of my body I thought had shut down in 1983."

"Should we go to the park and find you a bit of breeze?" Owen asked, gently pushing her along the pavement.

"Certainly not. I want to get front row seats and a clear line of sight to Simon Broughton's moustache."

The recording was to be held in a small community centre, with floor-to-ceiling curtains and a smell of disinfectant. When they arrived, they were offered refreshments from a trestle table laden with cakes and teacups. Marjorie, newly rehydrated and embracing the spirit of the occasion, guided them through the corridors like a sea captain steering her ship to port. In the main hall, a young woman with a walkie-talkie collected their ticket slips and led them to a wheelchair area at the end of a row of seats, facing a modest stage. A long table, several microphones, and two pop-up banners displaying the title 'Gardener's Question Corner' had been set up. Gradually, the room filled with people chatting about slug deterrents, compost ratios, and the virtues of padded kneepads.

Just before the show began, the girl who had shown them to their seats walked to the front of the room and introduced herself.

"Hello, everyone. I'm Claire Bedgrove, the team's assistant. I want to welcome you and thank those who submitted a question for the panel, which will be led today by our experts, Simon Broughton and Maisy Lynton. We have selected several queries which we would like to answer during the program, so if your name is called, please join me here down at the front." She picked up her clipboard and began to read from a list. Somewhere in the middle, she called out, "Mrs Donaldson."

Marjorie raised her hand, was overcome with stage fright, and snatched her hand down again. "I can't do it," she hissed to Dulcie. "You'll have to step up and do it for me."

"No problem," Dulcie assured her, as delighted as a TV wannabe smelling a whiff of fame. She was up and off to the reserved seats in a flash. Owen, who had already spotted the flaw in this plan, had no chance to stop her.

The assistant producer looked up at Dulcie and asked if she was Marjorie Donaldson. "Yes. Yes, indeed I am," she firmly declared. The young woman looked at her doubtfully, but handed over the ticket with the relevant question. Dulcie read it and saw that, for unfathomable reasons, her friend had written in the name column 'Marjorie Donaldson... Aged 93.' This was the first indication that she had bitten off more than she could chew... But it was too late now, and she was led to the front row alongside the other questioners. There, she listened carefully as the show began, the recording started, and the compère announced that Gardeners' Question Corner was the radio station's most popular programme, attracting a steady audience of two *million* eager listeners. Counting down without words, by holding up her fingers, the assistant indicated that the broadcast was going out live in three, two, one...

The programme got underway and the first six questioners took their turns. Her fellow enquirers appeared to be members of elite gardening clubs, posing challenging, technical questions. Then, it became apparent that the panel had questions of their *own* in return. A trickle of cold sweat ran down Dulcie's neck. She hadn't expected to have to participate. Aghast, a yawning chasm of horticultural ignorance opened up in her head.

Meanwhile, Owen, seated six rows away, was acutely aware that Dulcie knew about actual gardening could be written on the back of a seed packet, leaving space for a shopping list. He wondered if telepathy ever actually worked—or, failing that, if he should crawl into his own rucksack to avoid witnessing her downfall.

With rising panic, Dulcie listened to the gardening experts bantering back and forth. Her imagination ran wild. What if they asked her for facts about Dahlia's? Or how tall her Rusty Mintons grew? Should she startle the listening nation with a total guess?

"Four centimetres?" or *"Ten feet?"*

There were so many questions that she didn't know the answer to:

"Do you have honey fungus in your garden?"

"Yes, delicious!"

"How loamy is your soil?"

"About 90 per cent?"

The horror of her predicament hit her and, as her old grandad once said, after she'd taken him for a motorbike ride, 'Smell it? I'm *sittin'* in it.'

Her turn drew closer, and she started to shake, imploring the heavens for divine intervention. Suddenly, the boom microphone hovered near her head. With seconds to go, she decided to state her own name but confess that her question, about the best way to re-pot bi-annuals, was being asked on behalf of an elderly neighbour.

World-famous garden expert Maisy Lynton, who could doubtless spot a duffer at thirty paces, asked her to elaborate. Taking a deep breath, Dulcie launched into a speech about daffodils and mentioned nutrients for root balls, frantically throwing in half-remembered facts from her holiday job. Mercifully, Simon Broughton picked up the thread and shared plenty of good advice, which largely went over her head. But she nodded, smiled and looked enlightened, and to her overwhelming relief, they moved on.

The rest of the program passed in a blur for Dulcie, who sat in a puddle of perspiration and relief. At last, it was all over, and they joined the happy, bustling crowd making for the exit. As they stepped back into the street, she realised she was physically shaking.

"That was one of the worst experiences of my life," she said. "I'm not sure how we managed it, but we seem to have survived."

"Barely," Owen replied. "I've never had to witness someone actually fly by the seat of their pants. I nearly passed out."

"For a moment there, I felt my ancestors running about in the sky panicking that I was about to shame them forever, giving bad advice to a grateful nation." Dulcie displayed her trembling hands. "I always thought I would mess up big time one day, and I could hear them shouting, 'This is not a drill, people. It's not a *drill!*"

"I think you did very well," Marjorie said. "No one would have guessed that you were so nervous." She looked at the pad and paper in her lap. "They answered your question and more. I've made lots of notes, and my window boxes should be magnificent next year."

"Yes, I've got to hand it to you, Dulcie," Owen said, admiration flowing from every pore. "How did you pull it out of the bag like that?"

"My cousin Paul once told me, 'People will accept anything you say, as long as you say it with confidence," she confided. "I wasn't sure what he meant at the time, but never was a truer word spoken."

"I'll bear that in mind, next time I'm in a tight spot."

The evening breeze calmed their nerves as they walked together alongside Marjorie toward the nearest pub. Giddy with relief, neither of them said much more, but there's nothing like surviving a narrow squeak to pull two people together. This extraordinary trip had formed a tacit bond between them. In the future, Dulcie hoped they would all look back and laugh about today. In the meantime, however, she would be spending a great deal of time with a cool pack on her head, lying down in a darkened room...

CHAPTER 30

Detective Sergeant Maccie had never particularly wanted to be a detective. His early ambition had been to become an artist or a sculptor, preferably in bronze, something weighty and with gravitas. But ambition didn't pay council tax, and when his mother handed him a police recruitment leaflet with a Post-it on it reading 'Final Salary Pension,' he understood his future had been decided.

Still, over the years, he'd come to find a kind of art in his work: the slow carving of truths from stone-faced lies, the soft chiselling of an alibi until it crumbled. Following a pattern until a result was achieved.

In the end, it hadn't been hard to work out who had been plaguing Minet Road. The petty thefts had begun to fit together like pieces from mismatched jigsaws that, strangely, still formed a picture. A box of wine here. Wind chimes there. A full-grown begonia. A stash of chocolates. Odd things. Pointless, until you considered the mind of the collector. And Maccie, for all his weariness, had an excellent eye for collectors.

Knowing the identity of the crook was one thing. Acting on it—that was the part that had kept him confined to his flat, pacing from room to room. The question of what to do had weighed down on him, gnawing at the edges of his sleep. Once upon a time, he would have simply made an arrest and passed the problem to the custody sergeant. That was long, long ago.

Then came his day out with Les. They'd taken the bus and explored a small museum tucked away behind modern flats. For a few quiet hours, they stepped into a different century—London as it once was: green fields at the edges, the smell of horse-drawn trade, and the business milling of flour, crucial for the daily bread of life. Between the reconstructed grindstones and worn maps on the walls, he'd stopped turning his thoughts over like a stuck record. As they headed back to the bus stop, Les chatted about rye bread and sawdust floors, and Maccie decided what to do. The past had offered him perspective; now he was ready to face the present.

With the wind pressing into every crease and fold of his clothing, he stood on the shiny doorstep of Number 65. He was dressed in his usual civvies: a plain knit jumper, creased chinos that had seen better days, and a pair of worn basketball trainers that squeaked slightly on the polished stone beneath his feet. Shifting his weight, he looked once at the brass numbers neatly screwed into the red brick, then reached out and rang the doorbell of Kay Kenneths. The chime inside sounded polite, distant, and slightly flat. The

228

front door opened, and she appeared in a silk dressing gown patterned with tropical birds. "Well, if it isn't your good self, Duncan McCallie. An unexpected visitor. How nice." Kay's expression was less than friendly. "You haven't arrived bearing whiskey. Should I be worried, or are you redirecting post?"

"I've not bought anything with me, but I'd like a few minutes of your time, if you can spare them." He'd dealt with others like her before. They responded best to flattery and gracious requests, at least at first. "May I come in?"

"Of course. Any man of my acquaintance who knocks and asks politely is welcome, provided he wipes his feet." She turned and led him inside, the dressing gown flowing behind her like a stage curtain. The house was immaculate in the way lonely places often are.

"Do sit down. I'll make us both a little drink."

"No need," said Maccie, remaining standing. "This won't take long."

Kay ignored him and picked up a crystal decanter, pouring a generous measure into a brandy glass. She swirled the liquid, took a sip, and sat on the edge of the chaise longue with the composure of someone responding to an unexpected admirer.

Maccie took a deep breath, hands in his pockets. "I know it's you."

She tilted her head, amused. "I'm afraid you'll have to be more specific. I've played many roles."

"You're the one who's been taking parcels. The wine. The fish. The chocolate from the corner shop. You've been destroying window boxes, and I suspect you're behind the incident with the missing bicycle, though I admit that's outside of your modus operandi."

"Petty theft? Me? Why on earth would I indulge in such a thing?" Kay was unmoved. "I'm loath to point this out, Maccie, but we all know your role as Detective was over some time ago." She pulled the belt around her kimono tighter. "Which is just as well if this is the quality of your conclusions."

"Nevertheless, you're guilty"

"Now look here," Kay stood up dramatically and raised herself to her full height, channelling every indignant character she had ever played. "You can't come into my home and make baseless accusations. There are laws against slander, and I shall…"

"I know about the scratches on your skin," Maccie said, cutting in. "Dulcie mentioned them, in passing. She told me you claimed the grazes happened when you were trimming your roses."

Her eyes narrowed. She drew her arms closer to her body. Faint marks remained on her pale skin, healed yet still visible.

"Your shrubs are the Maid Marion variety, just like my dear old granny used to grow." Said Maccie. "She loved them for their pretty, pink petals and, as she was fond of pointing out, they have hardly any thorns. Not that those were bramble scratches that you had, anyway. I should know, I've seen that pattern many times before. On my own hands, in fact."

Kay looked at him defiantly.

"Missy made those marks on you," he said evenly. "I

recognise her work. You catnapped her. Then you made a big display of pruning your plants as a kind of alibi, a reason why your arms would be covered in scrapes. I'm guessing that Missy made her feelings clear before she made her escape."

Standing firm, Kay raised her chin, her eyes flickering with stage confidence. She made a brittle, theatrical sound and waved dismissively as if swatting away a ridiculous script note. "Honestly, darling, this is ridiculous," she said, her voice still polished from years under the spotlight. Maccie held her with his icy gaze, and as the minutes passed, her bravado faded away. Glamour peeled away from her in layers. She put down her glass, rested her elbows on her knees, and buried her face in her hands.

"Why don't you tell me about what's been going on here? You'll feel better if you get it off your chest," Maccie stated.

"Missy didn't escape," Kay said quietly. "I let her out. She made it clear we would never be friends." Her voice quivered. "If you tell anyone, if this gets out to the wider world, do you understand what would happen?" Suddenly restless, she jumped up and paced in circles around the room, wrapping her arms around herself.

"Why should that matter to the rest of us?"

"It shouldn't. But I didn't mean to hurt anybody. My life has been so empty in recent years. I got caught up in the excitement of the moment. It was an irresistible urge to be *someone* again, someone who made an impact, even a very bad one." Her eyes pleaded with him. "You must understand, theatre's the only avenue that still calls on me occasionally. Bit roles, touring jobs. A radio play now and then. If it's known I've been... shoplifting and tampering with deliveries, I'll be done. Finished. Not just professionally, but publicly. Please don't report me, Maccie."

"I've dedicated my whole life to the law. Tell me, why should I make an exception for you?" His jaw was set firm.

"Because," she said, with raw honesty, "I'm begging for a measure of mercy. In the past, I have misjudged you, but I believe you are a compassionate man; otherwise, you wouldn't have come to me first, before informing anyone else." She scanned his face. "And you have that look. The one that means you might not want to crush someone unless you have to."

There was a long, tense standoff. Neither of them moved. Kay hardly breathed.

"I gave all this a lot of thought before tonight." Maccie dropped his gaze to his shoes. "And, considering I'm no longer with the force, I'm not obliged to make any arrest. Citizens' or otherwise."

"You're not?" Kay sounded hopeful.

"As you said, I retired a while ago," he said. "Bit of a health thing. Also: burnout."

"Thank you, Maccie. I mean that. Oh, you don't know what this means to me...

"But," Maccie continued quickly, "I can't just let this lie. What you've done—many have noticed. People have been upset, and they've all suffered losses. You've shaken trust in a community that barely holds itself together as it is. So, action has to be taken."

Kay closed her eyes. "Oh god."

"I think," he said carefully, "you need to make restitution.

Return what you can. Replace what you can't. Maybe slide a few anonymous notes through some letterboxes."

"Notes? You mean letters of apology?"

"You want this to stay quiet?" Maccie asked. "Fine. I will help you keep it all under wraps as long as it all stops here— no more costumes. No more parcel pinching. And no more imprisoning cats, for pity's sake."

"I didn't imprison her," Kay said weakly. "She came in of her own accord. I just didn't...let her out. And you are right about Owen's bicycle. That wasn't me. I'm not the *only* person in this city who's been up to no good."

"No one is accusing you of every misdemeanour in London." He stood up. "But you have been something of a one-woman crime wave. Let's try for redemption, before a scandal breaks, shall we?"

"I don't think I can fix it." Kay looked up at Maccie, her eyes pools of remorse. "If I send apology notes, they'll know it was me. My handwriting is too recognisable, and a typed one with no name would be pointless. And if I try slipping envelopes of cash through letterboxes, it'll just make things worse, inflame the situation. No doubt they'd wonder where the money came from, and whether it was from an honest source or some scam. It wouldn't make sense." She paused, pulling her wrap tighter around her. "Besides, now that you've caught me, I don't think I could go out there again, not in disguise." She shrank into herself. "I've lost my nerve. It used to feel like a wonderful game. Something daring. But now it just feels... frightening."

Maccie nodded slowly, rubbing his chin. "Let me give it some thought," he said. "There will be a way through this, but I can see that it has to be the right one. As long as you promise this will be the end of all your mischief, I'll come up with some way of undoing all that's been done." He moved towards the hall, turning at the doorway. "I'll let myself out."

She nodded; her posture still regal despite the hollow under her eyes. Before he could open the front door, she called after him, "Duncan, would you... Perhaps you could stay for a cup of tea when you come back? Or a glass of whiskey? No tricks. Just...a few extra 'minutes of your time', as you say?"

Maccie turned back and offered a small, kind smile. "We'll see, Miss Kenneths."

He left, the door clicking gently behind him.

Curtain down. But she knew the second act was pending.

CHAPTER 31

There was a knock at the door of the garden flat —
sharp, then softer, like someone trying to sound confident
but losing their nerve halfway through, like a question,
wrapped in wood, waiting for an answer.

Sitting on the sofa, Dulcie was holding a book that she
hadn't glanced at in half an hour, sipping tea that had
been reheated multiple times, turning it into weak warm
water. She hadn't heard from Owen for three days, not since
the so-called 'Mad Outing' with Marjorie. That afternoon
had strangely bonded the three of them, as survivors of
an extraordinary, exciting, but mildly traumatic encounter
with fame. They all took a drink afterwards to calm their
nerves, with Marjorie enjoying a Bailey's so large that it
made her cheeks glow pinker than a garden rose. But, while
she liked Marjorie and was impressed by her appreciation of
creamy liqueurs, Dulcie wasn't daydreaming about getting
closer to *her* after the strange outing. There was only

one person from that escapade that Dulcie wouldn't mind getting stranded on a desert island with.

She opened the door. And there he was.

Owen.

"Hi." He gave her an adorable, cheeky smile. "If you can spare the time from your new broadcasting career and signing autographs for fans of gardening, I was wondering if you'd come along with me somewhere?"

"Right now?"

He nodded. "I've got something planned. Nothing wild. Just... something I want to share with you." He lifted a wicker basket that looked like it belonged in a Beatrix Potter illustration. "Picnic," he announced. "You. Me. Somewhere nearby, very cool and slightly perilous."

"Sounds risky? Are we robbing a bank?"

"Only if they have hummus." He scanned her outfit. If you're free, then grab a jacket."

"I'm not ready," she hesitated. She was wearing joggers and one of Les's old cardigans, her hair falling in the untidy waves it took on when she skipped the blow-dry. "I look like a deranged librarian."

He gave the smallest smile. "You look exactly like you. Only wrapped in scruffy packaging."

"I find it helps keep the paparazzi at bay, now that my radio profile is so high," she joked. Where are we going?"

"The roof. Les gave me the key." He lifted his hand and waved it happily.

"The roof?" she repeated. "Here? There's access to the actual roof?"

Owen laughed. "I know, it surprised me too. There's a door

on the landing next to Jamila's flat which leads to a tiny staircase. Most people don't notice it. I never did. But Les swears it's like the entrance to Narnia. It used to be his 'thinking spot' back in the seventies."

She pulled the cardigan tighter around herself. This was an opportunity not to be missed. "Give me five minutes?"

"Take as long as you like." He stepped back, hands in his pockets.

When she reappeared, her hair was loose, she was slightly out of breath, and she was now wearing jeans and a fleece. He looked at her as if she were sunlight itself.

They ascended the stairs together, passing the worn wooden main staircase and Jamila's closed door, to the small door beside it. Owen unlocked it, and with a bit of shoulder effort and a groan from the door, it swung open to reveal a set of tapered stairs leading to another entrance. They stepped out into the fading sky.

The rooftop was bordered by a narrow, slightly uneven path that showed signs of discolouration and had patches of moss sprouting in spots. Below, Brixton stretched out its cosmopolitan landscape for inspection: chimney pots, train tracks, neon-lit shops, and trees shaded dark against the evening sky. At one point, the narrow track widened into a small, flat area beneath a loft window ridge. Earlier that evening, Owen had cleaned the eaves and spread a thick blanket, weighted at the corners with jam jars holding flickering tealights. Above their heads, the last hints of twilight melted into black.

Dulcie turned, wide-eyed.

"You did all this?"

"With Les's help. He provided the key and the jars and told me to 'stop dithering around like a moon-struck cabbage." He put down the basket and lifted her hand by the fingers. "Your table awaits, m'lady. Shall we?" They sat side by side and Owen began unpacking: a small punnet of cherry tomatoes, a pack of crackers, some sliced cheese, a jar of chutney and moist squares of lemon drizzle cake. "I didn't know what you liked," he said. "This is my best guess."

She picked up a tomato and rolled it between her fingers. "It's a good guess."

"Then we should make a toast to our sumptuous banquet." Owen opened the bottle and poured the wine, which fizzed and sparkled in the candlelight. The prosecco bubbled softly as they drank to each other, comfortable in the brief silence that followed. Dulcie leaned back on her elbows, sleeves sliding down her forearms as the breeze teased strands of her hair. She glanced over at him. He was watching the wind ripple through the branches of the London Plane trees lining the road, his hands resting loosely on his knees.

"Why'd you move here? This building? This part of town?"

Owen looked up at the sky for a long moment. "Because it felt unfinished."

"What did?"

"Everything." He turned to her. "The work I was doing before. The city I left. Me. I'm not sure if I can put it into words, but for some time, I felt like I was living the wrong life. That I'd skipped onto the wrong track and was heading the wrong way." He pulled the stalk from another tomato. "So, I picked a new path for myself and applied for the job at the university. The rest is history. Or in my case, historical folklore."

Dulcie hesitated, then set her glass down carefully. "Can I ask you something else?"

"Of course. Ask me anything you like."

"What made you set up the care agency with Jen? Juggling a business with your work as a lecturer must be a challenge every day. Do you like the contrast?"

"I suppose," he said, "it's because I spent much time with my grandfather when he was in his final illness. He had a caregiver who was terrific at looking after him. Kept him dignified, laughing, and able to enjoy his good days. Even taught him how to use emojis, which... we all regretted."

She snorted.

"It stuck with me," he continued. "Plus, I was lucky enough to work with Jen, and she has her fingers in all sorts of pies. We inspired each other. Together we are greater than the sum of the parts, as they say. Besides, so many people who need care tell great stories and are way better at one-liners than anyone. Most of them are legends, and lots of them make me laugh like nothing else."

"That's a lovely way of looking at it. It's so ... decent of you."

"It's funny, I get the feeling you don't trust decent people. Like you're waiting for them to drop the act."

"I suppose I put my walls up."

"It's okay," he said quickly. "I get it. I've got my alarms too. You've been burned. And now you double-check for smoke."

He reached across and touched her hand, intertwining his fingers with hers. Dulcie didn't pull away. There was a magical moment as they drew closer, and she rested her head on his shoulder, leaving it there, both of them gazing at the rooftops and the glowing lamplights.

Then he said, quietly, "You liked Tristan first." It wasn't bitter. Just a fact being placed gently in the space between them. "I always thought he'd be the one you'd match with. He goes in guns blazing. Says the right thing. Makes the first move. He's the human version of a highlight reel," Owen went on. "Meanwhile, I'm... more of a behind-the-scenes documentary."

"Tristan made himself hard to ignore. He flirted with me the moment you introduced us. And he was bold. Charismatic. For a while, I thought... maybe that was what I was looking for."

"And I guess I'm more of a 'slow-burn, emotionally available, knows-your-dogs-birthday' type?"

"You are, which turns out to be exactly what I want." She smiled. "I like you, Owen. Don't assume you're the second choice, because you're not. You make people feel like they matter." She brushed her hair from her face. "With you," she said, "I feel... understood, connected, steady"

"Wow, damned with faint praise." Owen sipped from his glass. "Who knew it was sexy to be so dull?"

"I never said you were sexy." She thumped his arm gently. "But you are. You are also funny, caring, and on the same wavelength as me. Turns out that's all I ever needed, to get hot under the collar.

"That's promising." He turned his gaze to the flickering candles around them. "I'd love to take you on a proper date." Owen looked searchingly over her face. "Somewhere special, without this wheelchair-chaperoned, petty-theft-adjacent, bookcase-bonding stuff we seem to have been caught up in. What I'd really like to do is something daft like buy flowers and try to sweep you off your feet."

"Interesting. And what makes you so sure I'd say yes?"

"I'm not. But I'd like to try." He hugged her closer. "I've wanted this, wanted you, since the moment you overbalanced my bike and trod all over my books."

"It's my go-to method for attracting men."

"It works." Slowly, Owen leaned in. And when their lips met, it was soft, warm, and slow, like the end of a long winter. The city spread out below them, bustling, thriving and full of others meeting up, making up, breaking up — but at that moment, only a few young lovers such as they were sharing their very first, tender kiss.

CHAPTER 32

Sunlight filtered through the kitchen window of the garden flat, casting lazy patches over the scratched table where Dulcie was attempting to do her accounts. A calculator, an open notebook, and a stack of receipts sat there, looking as though they were involved in something terribly important. In reality, the numbers refused to behave. She was meant to be calculating the cost of salvaged wood from her trip to the Peckham warehouse, or checking if that Camden couple had haggled too hard over her upcycled dresser. But her mind kept wandering in sideways shuffles, back to last night. Owen's hand on her cheek, his fingers gently tracing the edge of her mouth as if trying to memorise it. Last night ended without further romantic gestures. It hadn't led to tangled sheets or shouted declarations. There was just a kiss, then another, followed by talking and laughter. They had walked back down the stairs, Owen's fingers interlocked with hers, as if he'd been longing to hold her hand forever. At the door, he gently held her close with a light touch before saying goodnight.

The kettle clicked off unexpectedly, catching her by surprise as she'd forgotten that she'd switched it on. As she reached for a fresh cup, Uncle Les entered the kitchen, drawn by the aroma of coffee and the prospect of breakfast. He was dressed in a tiger-print silk robe and comfortable brown moccasins, giving him the appearance of a Las Vegas illusionist. Pausing at the doorway, he looked at her. "Well, if that isn't the dreamy look of a woman who's been properly kissed, then I'm a monkey's uncle."

"Thanks! You *are* my uncle, so guess what that makes me?"

Les moved swiftly on. "I take it that the rooftop was sufficiently romantic? Did it do the trick?" He wandered over to the biscuit tin and began rattling it like a maraca. "I felt the time was coming when you two needed to sink or swim."

"So you gave him the rooftop key?"

"Of course I did," Les chirped. "It's never been known to fail. Besides, I told him if he didn't act soon, my only alternative was to trap the pair of you in a lift and cut the power." He took a seat opposite, holding a ginger snap as if it were a microphone. "Come on. Spill the beans. Did Prince Charming wake the sleeping Princess with his kiss?"

"Yes." She knew he wouldn't give up, so it was best to cut him off at the pass, before he wandered into more dangerous territory. "We're taking it slow, but it feels like it could be the start of something."

"That's the best way. Besides, he's the fairy tale expert, and they always end happily ever after. Did he ask for a date?"

Before she could answer, a knock at the door interrupted

them.

"Speak of the devil. I bet that's him, drawn back for seconds." Les reached across the table and gave her hand a brief, affectionate squeeze.

Dulcie rose and rushed into the hallway, her heart beating a little faster. She opened the door to find Owen standing there as she had hoped, although to be honest, in that moment, he looked more like an errand boy than a knight in shining armour. His hair was windswept, and he was carrying a greasy paper bag that filled the air with the warm, inviting smell of freshly baked bread.

"I thought you might not have had anything to eat yet," he said.

"Come in. But fair warning—Uncle Les is in full investigative mode."

Halfway through his second biscuit, Les raised his mug in salute. "Welcome to the pleasure dome, son. Come to return my key, eh?" He gave Owen a wink so theatrical it could've had first billing. "I always say, one good turn deserves another, and by sheer coincidence, you're exactly the kind of able-bodied young chap I need right now." He heaved himself upright, brushing crumbs off his robe and smiling like a Cheshire cat. "I want to shift the sofa, and it'll take a bit of muscle. I thought I'd move it so Dulcie can watch the telly properly. With a friend, if you catch my drift." He gave Owen a nudge, "Given that such an occasion might soon be on the cards."

Owen shot her a look that said, 'It's probably best to humour him,' and followed Les into the next room. Dulcie grabbed a couple of plates from the cupboard for the mystery food in the bag. Croissants? A Danish? Either way, it was a typically thoughtful gesture, the kind that made her think this man was a keeper. She heard the sounds of furniture being moved—Owen's grunts and Les's shouted instructions: "Pull to the right. Lift your arm. Not *that* arm, the other arm. And mind the skirting board!" Amused, she shook her head and laid the table, placing forks beside her phone, which began to ring. Wiping her hands on a tea towel, she glanced at the screen and frowned slightly at the caller ID.

Tristan.

Not wanting the ringing to go on too long, she picked up and accepted the call.

"Dulcie," came Tristan's voice, "I know I'm probably the last person you want to hear from."

"That's not exactly true. I haven't banished you forever from my sight, Tristan."

"True, but you did shove me as hard as you could into the friend zone. The thing is, I think that we, that is to say, I, may have made a huge mistake."

She sighed. "Go on, then."

"It's Natasha."

"Let me guess. She's not as casual as you pretended?"

"No. I mean—yes. Sort of. She's bombarding me with texts."

Dulcie leaned against the counter. "And this is... shocking to you?"

"She's not the issue. The issue is... and I admit this is as much of a surprise to me as it is to you...it turns out that I have strong feelings for someone else."

Silence stretched like elastic.

"Tristan," she said carefully, "please don't say what I think you're about to say."

"It's you," he said, voice cracking. "I can't get over the fact that we never really got the chance to find out how good we could be together."

She pinched the bridge of her nose. "This is so badly timed that I'm almost impressed."

"I know I messed up. And maybe I ruined our perfect start. But I can't just stand back while you ride off into the sunset."

"Tristan," she said, looking out the window as clouds began to gather. "You're charming, you're fun, and great company. But I can't be the person you want when someone else beats you to it."

"But I do want you," he insisted. "Not as a fling. For real. I've been thinking about you since the moment you kicked me into touch."

"That's the problem. You started thinking about it too late. Anyway, there's no going back, even if I wanted to, which I don't."

"Are you sure about that? I know you felt that moment of magic we shared at the party." His voice was husky.

"Briefly. Looking back on it, our connection was as shallow as a puddle, and besides, I've already moved on."

"Can I move adjacent to where you're moving?"

"Goodbye, Tristan."

She hung up.

Slightly flushed from helping Les rearrange the front room, Owen returned to the kitchen, retrieved the paper bag and handed it to her. "From that bakery at Camden Farm," he said. "Bread rolls and doughnuts. One of them is rhubarb and custard. I picked it because it sounded ridiculous. But also... it reminded me of you."

"Rhubarb and custard? How do you work that out?"

"Unexpected. Classic. A little sharp. Surprisingly sweet."

"You're pretty good at this."

"I'll ruin it eventually, watch this space." He grinned up at her from his seat.

She settled beside him, their shoulders brushing. "I should probably tell you," she said cautiously, "Tristan just called me. He was making a last-minute bid for redemption." She hurried on. "I want you to know that I shut him down straightaway. It didn't matter to me what he said. In fact, I don't know why it ever *did* matter to me."

Owen was quiet for a beat, then said, "I guess that means you choose me."

"I do. I'd rather eat rhubarb doughnuts with you than be serenaded by anyone else."

He laughed softly. And then she kissed him—slow, sweet, and sure.

"I think," Owen murmured, "this might be the moment to sort out going on that proper date. Away from Brixton, away from Les, and away from my amorous flatmate."

"Sounds like a plan. What did you have in mind?"

Les chose that moment to stride back in, phone in hand. "Hold that thought. I've had a message from Maccie. He says he's summoned us all to his flat tonight. Emergency meeting. He doesn't say what it's all about, but he's putting together a buffet, which is just as well. I can't solve problems on an empty stomach."

"Should we go?" Owen asked her. "It isn't exactly dinner

and a show."

"No, it's sandwiches and a surprise." Dulcie sighed, smiling. "Not the most romantic venue I've ever heard of, but then, nothing about us has been ordinary so far. So why not?"

CHAPTER 33

In the basement flat, Maccie set up six mismatched chairs in a circle. Each chair came from different parts of his life, from his favourite recliner with a permanent indentation to an old dining chair with a shaky leg that made sitting slightly risky. He arranged them thoughtfully, as if the precise placement was essential, allowing him to size up the group that would soon assemble there.

On the sideboard, a buffet was arranged with the casual hospitality of a lifelong bachelor: sweating cubes of cheddar, a cracked bowl of olives, sandwiches still wrapped in plastic, and a tray of cupcakes with glossy frosting that betrayed their supermarket origins. A bottle of whiskey sat close by, open and breathing into the expectant atmosphere. Dulcie and Owen arrived first, hand in hand, as if stepping out of a secret they'd decided to share. Although slightly surprised, Maccie said nothing and accepted the bottle of wine they offered without comment.

Les arrived soon after, cheerfully setting a packet of Hobnobs and another of cakes on the sideboard as if it were a rare treat. No one questioned it, since biscuits had a way of making themselves welcome. Jamila appeared behind him, shaking a little drizzle from her coat and saying that Tristan had sent his apologies. "Work," she explained, with a shrug that hinted at scepticism. They all nodded, accepting the excuse without comment.

Missy brushed against Dulcie's legs with the imperious air of a cat who believed guests should announce themselves properly, then vanished beneath a chair without a sound. Once everyone was seated, drinks in hand and cushions claimed, Maccie stepped forward. He adjusted his collar with the solemnity of someone about to give a toast, then cleared his throat—a trumpet call to attention.

"Right," Maccie announced. "I've asked you here because I need to talk to you about something that, if handled poorly, could go public in a rather unpleasant way." He eyed their expectant faces. "I've got some difficult news to share with you. It's about Kay Kenneths."

"She dead?" Jamila interjected in alarm.

"No," said Maccie. "Worse. She's been robbing us."

There was a collective intake of breath. Les gasped and dropped a Jaffa cake into his tea.

"She's been nicking parcels, food, flowers," Maccie continued. "Begonias, chocolate, wine."

"Oh! You mean my special case of wine for the party?" Owen was half-outraged, half-relieved to solve the mystery.

"She even catnapped Missy," added Maccie, looking at the well-rounded, purring victim. "Actually, I think 'detained under false pretences' is more accurate." Either way, I confronted her. She admitted everything."

"What did she do with my bike?"

"As a matter of fact, she isn't responsible for that, Owen. She's an opportunist, make no mistake, but it seems she has standards."

"Charming. A discriminating thief."

"Crikey." Les shook his head. "I never would have believed it of her. She's so posh. She struck me as the type who would take a silver teapot on a camping trip. You surely aren't telling us that she's skint?

"She says she did it because... well, because no one sees her anymore," Maccie said. "She's a bit of a has-been, largely forgotten by people who once worshipped her. I think stealing made her feel alive again, a way of being centre stage. Slipping through the dark, playing the part of a thief in the night—it thrilled her.

"She might be unwell," Jamila said, looking pensive. "Not in a dangerous way. But lonely people can do some very odd things."

"I had no idea someone like her could feel so isolated," Dulcie mused. "I got the impression she had swathes of friends."

"Which proves her point in a way." Owen was sympathetic. "My care team come across a lot of her generation who put on a good front, when they are struggling behind the scenes. Given the old 'stiff upper lip' mantra, it's unsurprising."

"No," said Maccie, "but what else is unsurprising is that she's asked me not to turn her in. Begged. Said it would destroy what little she has left of a career."

"She's not wrong. The Echo would go nuts over this. 'Washed-Up Actress Turns Cat Burglar' practically writes itself," said Les

"So, what do we do?" asked Dulcie, looking around with saucer eyes.

"I've offered to help her make things right. Quietly. Anonymously. No police, no papers. But I can't do it alone," said Maccie. "I'm still not firing on all cylinders. I need help, and I need secrecy, which is why it's just the five of us here, a small, trusted crew. I want to return what we can," he continued. "Replace what's gone missing. She'll have to cover the cost of goods and gift cards, that sort of thing, but she can't be the one delivering them. The illusion that she'd never be caught out is shattered, and she's lost her nerve completely"

He looked around. "So I'm asking: will you lot help me? Bit of undercover restitution. Community compensation on the quiet?"

"Can I wear a hat with earflaps when we do it?" Asked Les. "Because I've got a deer-stalker and I'm never going to stalk a deer this side of Brockwell Park. It makes me look like a proper detective, so folk will know I'm on the right side of the law."

Owen raised his hand. "You can count on me. I've got a torch and a face people don't remember."

"I'm in." Jamila shrugged. "I don't see how we can get into trouble for *giving* people things, and I like the idea of righting the wrongs."

"I'll help too," agreed Dulcie. "I think I owe her that. "In all honesty, what thrilled me most about Kay when I met her was the hope that a little of her stardust might rub off on me. That it might boost my business if she used my services. And that feels... a bit shameful now."

"Perfect," said Maccie. "We're a team, then."

"Code name?" Les asked eagerly. "We should have a code name."

"No. We're not the A-Team."

"How about the K-Team?" Les offered, with a hopeful grin.

Everyone groaned loudly, releasing the tension in the room like a burst balloon. They continued discussing the plan, exchanging ideas like pebbles skimming across a pond. It was agreed they would meet the following evening at Kay's house to plan how to undo the trouble caused by the infamous Minet Road felon. With that, they fell upon the buffet, appetites sharpened by the extraordinary change in their circumstances, from fond neighbours to suburban superheroes, a band of benevolence and Maccie's appointed righters of wrongs.

CHAPTER 34

Kay had lit candles. Not to create atmosphere, but because the overhead bulb was exceptionally bright. "A woman of a certain age deserves flattering illumination," she insisted. The flickering candlelight cast long shadows across her cluttered lounge, making it look as if it were set for a séance rather than a meeting of gracious conspirators.

The group was tightly packed together, like a jury debating stolen goods, which in many ways, they were. Les sank into a plush pink armchair, its buttons strained and almost ready to pop from the tension. Owen stood uncomfortably near the window, partly hidden behind heavy curtains, clutching the clipboard Kay had given him with exaggerated seriousness. She said it was necessary for 'mapping stage directions for all the cast,' but he had no idea what she meant. He held it loosely until he found a moment to set it down on a sideboard.

Dulcie sat cross-legged on the floor, poised and practical,

while beside her stood the chartreuse chaise longue. Jamila perched at its edge, spine rigid, knees locked together. She looked like someone enduring a hostage situation, waiting for her chance to bolt.

"I must say," Kay began, swirling a glass of pale sherry as though conducting an overture, "this is rather exhilarating. Once it's all over, I have half a mind to write it all down into a script. I can see this story going down marvellously with a West End audience. It's such a fantastic plot."

You've *lost* the plot, more like." Les wasn't in the mood for theatrics. "We're here trying to keep your name off the front pages, not hand-deliver the story to the tabloids."

"That's the wonderful part!" Kay pressed on, eyes twinkling. "The marvellous brilliance of it! Who would ever suspect me, playing the lead in the story of my own cover-up? It's positively Christiesque! I'm sure Agatha would've adored it. Guaranteed to be a sure-fire hit!"

"Guaranteed to alert the authorities more like."

Jamila leaned sideways and whispered to Dulcie, "I told you she was unbalanced. But I underestimated. She's revelling in this madcap scheme."

"We discussed what needs to happen, Kay," Maccie said, his tone firm. "Your friends here are going to put right your misdemeanours, and you'll get professional help to ensure this doesn't happen again. This isn't a game."

"Yes, yes," Kay said with exaggerated contrition, her sherry poised mid-air. "I am profoundly grateful to each one of you for aiding me in this most unfortunate... pickle. Your loyalty is truly touching." She smiled at them as a monarch might smile at her most favoured courtiers. "Magnanimity, darlings, I call it food for the soul."

"I've no idea what that is," said Les, "but if we don't get on with the job in hand, we will be here all night. What's the next step?

On the coffee table lay a collection of stolen items: three boxes of fancy chocolates, a decorative peacock-shaped wind chime, a small potted bay tree, a tiny succulent, and a catering pack of vinegar bottles. Nearby, a few unopened parcels still sealed and addressed rested, collected from doorsteps during Kay's short but intense theft spree. It was never really about the items—just the thrill of misappropriating them from their rightful owners.

"Kay's already given me a replacement crate of artisan wine," Owen acknowledged. "We've accounted for nearly everything else," he reported, peering at the clipboard. "The vacuum-sealed haddock is in the freezer. We'll pack it in the picnic box when it's time."

"The little bay tree is for Marjorie," Dulcie added, pointing to the plant. "It's compensation for losing all of the plants in her window boxes, which she's already replanted. The tag says, 'In appreciation of your wonderful window box displays.' She'll probably think it's from a secret gardening fan.

"Her begonias are thriving in my back garden anyway," said Kay, unapologetic about the flower-knapping escapade.

"Right then." Maccie clapped his hands together. "Tonight's the night. One sweep and it's done. We return the goods, restore the peace, and keep Kay off the evening news," he continued. "I'll drop the parcels back at their addresses and, as I'm the tallest, I think I can put the windchimes back in place without a ladder. Back garden at Number 12," he said, consulting his notebook.

"Owen and I will return to the fish shop around eight, when it's busiest," Dulcie said. "I know Mrs. Martins leaves the back door unlatched for the delivery guy. He's always punctual—7:50pm on the dot. We nip in right after."

"That leaves me pushing chocolate onto a shelf like a reverse burglar," Les grumbled. "But fine. I've the figure of a racing snake and the fingers of a royal harpist, so it shouldn't pose much of a problem.

"I'll distract Mrs. Bunce for you," offered Jamila. "She loves a chat, and I happen to know her nephew is in the rowing trials. Boasting about that should buy you five minutes."

"Alright, team. Rendezvous back here after. Confirm all's done." Maccie checked his watch. "Everyone knows what they're doing. Let's go and return some dignity to this street. *Quietly.*"

"You can't tell me this isn't absolutely thrilling." Kay was happier than she could remember. "This feels like opening night, with no dress rehearsal. You'll see. There's nothing like the adrenaline rush of a seamless performance."

The group exchanged cautious glances. Some sceptical, some resigned, some secretly energised. They gathered their assigned goods and prepared themselves for their peculiar mission of redemption.

Somewhere in the twilight, the invisible curtain rose.

CHAPTER 35

At exactly 7:45, Dulcie and Owen arrived in the alley behind *Absolutely Battered*. The spot was not named on any map, nor would it be, unless someone published 'The Forgotten Passages of Urban Britain.' It was narrow, cluttered with crates, and smelled of last week's cooking oil. A flickering bulb above the chip shop's back door buzzed intermittently, like an anxious fly searching for the exit.

Dulcie held the picnic box close to her chest like a relic from a spy movie. "I feel like someone's going to leap out and frisk me for haddock."

"This has got to be the craziest first date in history," Owen crouched beside her, holding the vinegar bottles. "Why do I get the impression that time spent with you will always end up in some kind of mad escapade?"

"I mean, it's possible," she grinned. "It might even get crazier than this, after all, I wouldn't want us to peak too soon."

At 7:50 pm, a white van pulled into the alley, reversing with a grating beep, beep, beep. The delivery man got out, humming to himself, and unloaded a stack of boxes onto his trolley. He glanced their way with the blank indifference of someone whose job had long since desensitised him to anything suspicious. Without a nod, he wheeled his load inside and propped the back door open with one of the boxes.

"He didn't even blink," Dulcie whispered. "We could've been robbers. Or flash mob performers. Nothing."

"He's seen worse than a couple of loiterers. This is probably the least weird thing that's happened to him today."

The man returned a minute later, hands empty, hopped into the van, and drove off with a grunt and a rattle. The door remained invitingly ajar.

"Alright," Owen said, straightening his shoulders. "Haddock time." He took the picnic box and vinegar bottles from Dulcie with mock solemnity. "If I don't make it out... tell the others I gave my all, standing on my principles."

Dulcie gave a mock salute. "We will inform the palace, and have you stuffed for posterity."

Owen slipped through the back door and disappeared into the dim light of the shop's rear storeroom. Inside, with the caution of a man planting a fragile explosive or delivering a cursed artefact to its rightful tomb, he opened the door to the walk-in freezer. Gently sliding the fish inside, he placed it on top of the other identical cases already stacked there. Then he slipped the vinegar next to the other bottles on the shelf. Ten seconds later, he was outside again, beaming. "Box delivered. Nestled right in with the others. No one will ever know. The haddock has gone home."

They stood looking at each other, a wave of relief washing over them, as they started to laugh. Not loud belly-laughs, but the kind that come from your chest when you've been holding something in for too long. "This is mad," Dulcie said. "We've just broken into a fish shop. To return stolen goods."

"Not even *our* stolen goods," Owen said. "I'm the Robin Hood of seafood."

"I'm full of adrenaline and the thrill of justice." Dulcie hooked her arm through his. "Honestly, I feel like I should be wearing a cape and tights."

"Now that," said Owen, "is a very enchanting idea, and I think we should explore it further. But right now, let's get away from here and do whatever it is that superheroes do, to decompress." A few steps further, and they passed a small, deserted play park, tucked between rows of semi-detached houses. It had a climbing frame shaped like a pirate ship, a see-saw, and two worn swings that squeaked in the gentle breeze.

Dulcie paused at the gate. "Let's go in."

"This wasn't what I had in mind."

"Come on. I bet this is exactly what Superman does after a successful mission." They walked in and claimed the swings. Dulcie's boots kicked up the fine gravel underneath. Owen shuffled a little, trying to remember how to start the long-forgotten rhythm. "I'm not sure if this evening could get any more surreal," he said eventually.

"I know." Dulcie pushed herself back and forth. "I feel exhilarated. Like we just thumbed our noses at the World."

They swung in silence for a while, the breeze flicking their hair backwards and forwards. She glanced at Owen and saw him watching her, in that absorbing way people do when they're memorising something. "Thank you," she murmured, "for being so brave and undertaking a noble quest on behalf of a fair lady. You passed the trial with flying colours."

"It was a low bar, but I'm glad I cleared it."

The rusted chains creaked softly as she leaned toward him on the swing. He mirrored her movement, gripping the cold metal links to steady himself as they both drifted forward, their motion slowing to a jarring halt. Their lips met, brushing lightly at first, a delicate touch, as if they were testing the idea of it. But the softness deepened, giving way to something more urgent. The swings shifted beneath them, objecting with a sideways sway, like a pair of maiden aunts trying to keep them apart. Winding their arms around one another, they pressed closer, holding tight against the pull of the chains and the world beyond the empty park. His hand slid into her hair; her fingers curled into the fabric of his coat. The kiss grew bolder, breathless, their hearts thudding beneath layers of wool and evening air. He drew her into a full embrace, and she melted into it. "I don't know if there's something in the air tonight," Dulcie murmured, her cheek pressed against his chest, "but I think this anti-crime wave could be the start of something special."

"Agreed," Owen replied. "I haven't felt like this in a very long time. Since you arrived, my whole world has changed." He tenderly lifted a strand of hair from her face and carefully brushed it behind her ear. "

"So," Dulcie said, "what do you think the next exciting episode in our mission will be?"

"I don't know," said Owen, "but if it involves you, I'm in."

They rose from the swings and folded into a long, tender embrace, the kind that said everything words couldn't. Still wrapped in each other's arms, they turned and walked back toward Kay's flickering kingdom of candles and chaos, their shadows stretching out behind them under the watchful glow of the streetlights.

CHAPTER 36

Les carried the chocolate in a simple supermarket bag, attempting to appear like the kind of man who regularly delivers luxury confectionery to local stores on a Tuesday night. His stilted walk was unconvincing, and the bag swung wildly from his jittery hands as they approached the corner of Minet Road. Jamila walked alongside him, tall and determined, her face unreadable. She was dressed in a leather jacket that shimmered softly under the streetlight and jeans so tight that Les suspected they might cut off her circulation. As they neared the warmly lit windows of Bunce's Corner Shop, the air grew heavy with the smell of overripe bananas and newsprint, which always clung to the shopfront. They paused outside the door.

"Ready?" Jamila asked, inhaling deeply.

"Not remotely."

"Can I suggest changing your expression before we go in, Les?" She hissed. "To something like 'I'm here because I'm very fond of toffee,' rather than 'any minute I'll be caught red-handed.'"

"I can't help it. I've always been good at looking guilty. It's my fallback expression."

The bell above the shop door jingled with the same enthusiastic tone it always did. Stella Bunce looked up from behind the till. She was polishing a bag of dry-roasted peanuts with the edge of her sleeve. Her reading glasses were perched halfway down her nose, and her mouth was set in the welcome expression of someone always ready to stop and chat. "Well, look who it is. How are you both? I haven't seen you in here for a while."

Jamila swept forward, all bright eyes and confident energy. "Hello, Mrs. Bunce! Les here has just been telling me about your nephew in the Henley trials. How exciting! Is he still using that vintage boat? The one that nearly cracked in half last year?"

"Oh, that wooden deathtrap. Yes, he's still convinced it gives him an advantage. He claims it's as sleek as a 'water-splitting shark.' I said it's more likely to become a submarine."

Launching smoothly into a volley of rowing-related chit-chat, Jamila positioned herself in front of the counter, partially obscuring the view of the shop behind her. Les shuffled off down the aisle toward the confectionery section, the bag clutched tightly at his side. He edged towards the counter, ducking beneath shelves of cola bottles and mint chews, hoping his knees wouldn't crack like gunshots. Upon reaching the shelf labelled "Luxury & Imported Chocolate," he crouched down, trying to recall the exact location of the original items. He always thought this section was a bit pretentious for a corner shop selling disposable lighters and tinned spaghetti. Furthermore, tonight it resembled a minefield and, judging by the boxes on the floor, it seemed Les wasn't the only one in the middle of restocking the shelves that evening. Opening his bag, he pulled out the confectionery, trying to move quickly but quietly. Each little clink of cardboard seemed thunderous. He managed to slide the first two boxes of recovered contraband onto the shelf without incident and was halfway through placing the third box when a voice rang out across the shop.

"You alright back there, love? Looking for anything in particular?"

Les spun around far too quickly, and his foot caught a stack of Haribo boxes waiting to be unpacked for pick-and-mix. With a squawk, he went down like a felled oak, the remaining chocolates cascading out of his bag. There was a moment of surprised silence. Then Les popped up like a meerkat, arms stiff at his sides, cheeks flushed scarlet. "All good! Nothing to see here!"

"Is that so? You looked like you were auditioning for Bambi on Ice. Did you twist something?"

"Maybe just a little sprain," he said, wincing as he tested his foot. "It's nothing. Dignity in tatters. Ankle slightly less so."

Mrs. Bunce's gaze drifted to the shelf, where the boxes of chocolate sat just slightly askew. She frowned, walked towards him, and picked one up.

"This isn't the size I usually stock," she said slowly, turning it over in her hand. "And why are there more bars all over the floor?"

Les and Jamila exchanged a glance. The jig was up.

"We'll tell you. It's not what you think." Jamila lifted her hands. "Or rather, it's not *exactly* what you think."

"We're not shoplifters," Les added, brushing off his knees. "We're... sort of... shop-returners. We're trying to fix something."

Mrs. Bunce shook her head in slow amazement.

"Maccie found out who's been nicking stuff from you. Or rather, he guessed because there's no cold, hard proof." Les was desperate to avoid giving Kay's name to Mrs Bunce. "It's someone vulnerable, so we thought it would be best to put a stop to it and replace your losses quietly. No fuss."

"We thought it would be easier than explaining," Jamila added pleadingly. "You won't have any more trouble with them; it's all been sorted out."

Taking a moment to digest this information, Mrs Bunce snorted so sharply it startled the mint wrappers on the counter. "Well, I can't say I'm pleased about the situation, but I will say this. You two are clearly not criminals. Idiots, maybe, but not crooks."

"Does that mean we're okay?"

"You can't go about returning random items and think I won't notice." She said sternly. "However, I *do* appreciate the gesture, even though it is one of the most bizarre stunts I've ever heard of." She picked up the bars which Les had deposited on the shelves. "I'll accept the chocolates, but only as a personal gift. Frankly, I would have preferred a large bottle of Chanel No. 5 if I had the choice." She gave them both a stern look. "If you can assure me this is the end of the matter, then we'll say no more about it."

"Fair enough." Les could feel his face grow pinker and his ankle grow larger.

They left the shop a few moments later, Jamila holding the door for Les as he hobbled through it, trying not to look like a man who had clumsily slipped on a pile of jellied sweets. They walked a few steps in silence before Jamila said, "You were very stealthy until you fell flat. You bounced surprisingly well."

"You noticed that, did you? I practise in secret." Les winced. "Do you think it's possible to sprain your ego?"

"If so, you did it in style."

"Excellent. Glad I could provide entertainment whilst in the process of doing a good deed."

"I wish I'd caught it on film. I think it would have gone viral," Jamila teased. "Should we go back, maybe? I'll set up my camera phone, and you could try it again."

"As partners in crime go," muttered Les, unamused, "I'd trade you in for a different sidekick. I bet Dr Watson would be bandaging my leg by now, not mocking a man when he's down."

"Sherlock Holmes wouldn't have tripped."

"We'll never know, will we? But I do know that you'll have to link arms with me and let me balance on you a bit." Les wasn't one to miss an opportunity. "We're going to have to get cosy if I'm to walk back on this leg."

"Come on, Clumsy Clara," she said, not unkindly. "Let's go and make our report before Kay decides to write us into Act Two."

Jamila gave him her arm to lean on, and they

hobbled together into the night. Their escapade had been unexpectedly bonding, and Les was prepared to concede that every cloud has a silver lining. If his limp lasted long enough for someone to offer him a mention in despatches and a second helping of sausage casserole, he wasn't going to complain.

CHAPTER 37

All of the conspirators regrouped at their unofficial headquarters in Kay's lounge, feeling triumphant and self-satisfied, congratulating each other like the final scene of a heist movie. First, Dulcie and Owen, then Les and Jamila, had made their report and then slipped back into the night, full of the excitement of their shared experience, until only Maccie remained, acting as doorman and one-time host.

Sitting curled in her armchair, Kay clutched an empty sherry glass which still contained one last hopeful sip at the bottom. The candles around the room had burned low, dripping wax tears, their flames sagging sideways, exhausted by the evening's activities. She pulled a cashmere blanket across her knees. Despite the flames flickering in the fireplace, it was strange how much colder the room felt without an audience. Maccie re-entered and closed the door gently behind him. "That's the end of that," he said, brushing his hands together with a flourish. "Here's hoping tonight becomes an urban myth."

"I was on tenterhooks, sitting here waiting for everyone to come back. Honestly, Maccie, I think the deeds done tonight are the kindest anyone's ever done for me. Each of you came to my aid, not for reward, but out of old-fashioned compassion. Or perhaps," she added, lifting an eyebrow, "you simply couldn't bear to watch me unravel like a silken rope."

"They're good people. Salt of the earth. Even the ones who spout fairytales or spend their days hammering and crashing about in the backyard night and day."

"You know, I used to be accustomed to people going out of their way for me. When I was in the thick of it all, fans would treat me like royalty for the tiniest interaction. 'Oh, I saw Kay Kenneths at the Civic Centre and she was simply *charming*,' they'd say. It's quite a thrill to be boasted about."

"It must be strange, being famous. Everyone thinks they know you, and yet they don't know a thing about you at all."

"It was delightful. I always adored the attention. I didn't pay for a gin and tonic for decades. I never minded giving autographs. Indeed, it is heady stuff to know that, right across the country, people prized my signature as if it were treasure. But then, quite suddenly, it stopped. And no one prepares you for how to live with the silence that follows." There was a pause, and Kay's face tightened. "It's hard," she said finally. "Losing that kind of reverence. Not because of scandal or failure. Just... getting too old for the nips and tucks to be convincing."

"Nonsense. You're maturing. Like a ruby-red, vintage Malbec." He gave her a playful once-over. "You are still a fine figure of a woman. One in her prime, if I may say so."

"Do you mean that, or are you trifling with me, Maccie?"

He regarded her steadily for a moment. "I'm sorry, it's almost a reflex for me to ladle on the flattery. A bad habit. Got me into more trouble than I care to admit." He looked as shamefaced as a schoolboy sneaking tuck. "But just because you might not be the woman for *me*, doesn't mean you're not someone's perfect partner."

"What a silver-tongued charmer you are. Perhaps we should change the subject before I start planning a wedding." She flicked the tips of her fingernails with her thumb. "How did your own mission go tonight?"

"Most of it went smoothly."

"*Most?*"

"Well," he said, settling into the armchair opposite, "I went out like a shadowy postman, arms full of parcels, hat pulled low so no one could make out my face. The first few houses were simple. Drop the package, ring the bell, leg it. Reminded me of the game of Knock Down Ginger."

"I played that too!" Kay squealed, genuinely delighted. "My childhood friends and I would rattle door knockers and run away like wild things. I once tripped over a flowerpot and split my slacks in the fall. My mother nearly fainted when I came home, flashing my unmentionables to all and sundry."

"You? A *posh girl* like you?"

"I wasn't always posh, thank you very much. I grew up in a split-level maisonette, part of a concrete block. Those flats are long gone now, replaced by luxury apartments. Castlemain Court, I think it's called."

"Fancy," Maccie said with a grin. "Anyway. The bay tree was

easy. I'd stashed it behind the garage block earlier. Carried it over to Marjorie Donaldson's house and placed it beside her window boxes. It looked like something out of a garden design show."

Kay made an approving noise. "I hope she likes it."

"It was the windchime that nearly did me in."

"Go on," she said, eyes bright. "Spill."

"I crept through Mrs Pritchard's Garden gate. Still unlocked, by the way."

"Some people never learn." Kay huffed. "That's how I got in there in the first place."

"Then I pulled the windchime from my coat pocket, reached up, and hung it on the nail above the patio, exactly like you said. Job done. Or so I thought."

"And then?"

"The blasted woman appeared out of nowhere, like a ghost in a dressing gown. Hair like a snowstorm. Slippers shaped like hedgehogs.

"I can see her now!" Kay clutched her blanket with laughter.

"Standing right in front of me, she was. "What on *earth* do you think you are doing?" She hollered, right into my face, and I nearly swallowed my tongue!" Maccie shuddered at the memory. "But before I could think of a clever excuse, she took a better look at me and lit up like a slot machine jackpot. Said she recognised me from a talk I gave years ago on neighbourhood crime."

"You mean you were the star speaker at an event? I thought that was my role in this neighbourhood."

"It was quite a while ago. Back when I was still serving. Anyway, I spun a tale. Told her I was on an *unofficial* community initiative. Replacing things that had mysteriously gone missing. Privately funded. Anonymous donor."

"You didn't!" Kay squealed. "That was fast thinking. Must have been all those years working undercover, Maccie. Being on the side of the angels has made a devil out of you."

"Mrs Pritchard was fooled, and that's all that matters. She tapped her nose and promised to keep my secret. Honestly, she looked delighted to be part of some hush-hush civic plot." He leaned back, shaking his head in wonder. "If someone had told me twenty years ago that I'd end up sneaking around gardens in the dead of night, delivering bay trees and replacing stolen windchimes, I'd have laughed them right out of the station."

Kay smiled at him, warmth in her gaze. "And yet, here you are. My midnight magician."

I've used up my quota of smooth talking for the year," he muttered, rubbing his temples.

"Then you can rest up, Maccie," she said. "Because I promise that this will be the very last performance. I have turned my back on a life of crime, and I intend to take this one last bow and retire, without a single encore." She raised her arms high above her head before lowering them gracefully like a ballerina taking a curtain call. Then, she settled deeper into the armchair, her legs curled beneath her as the firelight cast shadows across her face. The room darkened as the flames died down, flickering as the final logs dropped to the bottom of the grate. Outside, the wind moved gently through the trees. Inside, the last candle sputtered and gave out with a sigh, its smoke curling in delicate wisps up into the stillness.

CHAPTER 38

"Seven miles," Dulcie said, squinting at her phone. "You promised me an adventure even better than the one last night, and then you only brought me seven miles from Brixton."

"Technically," Owen said, tugging her gently down a gravel path shaded by poplars, "I brought you about six-point-eight. Google Maps exaggerates." He shot her a sideways look and smiled. "Trust me."

They came to a clearing along the edge of the Regent's Canal. Trees arched over the towpath like spectators, their leaves trembling in the breeze. On the water, ducks drifted lazily past the painted hull of a narrowboat. Farther along, a scattering of tiny electric motorboats bobbed by a floating jetty, painted in candy colours—mint, peach, soft blue.

Dulcie stopped walking. "No," she said firmly. "Absolutely not."

"Don't you like my surprise?"

"The only thing I use a boat for is gravy," she said flatly.

"Come on. It's just a little electric putter. It barely goes faster than a mobility scooter. You're safer here than crossing Brixton Road. I dare you. In fact, I double dare you."

"Ooh, that is playing dirty." She regarded the little fleet with distaste. "All right, but no going too fast or making any waves."

"Noted." He gestured toward the boat with a grin. "Besides, we will spend most of the time on dry land. I've got a chilled bottle of Prosecco and a blanket to use on the other bank. What could possibly go wrong?"

For the first twenty minutes, nothing could.

After some impressive rocking as she boarded, which caused some even more impressive swearing and a brief panic about dropping her sunglasses, Dulcie was forced to agree that the boat trip was actually... rather lovely. They glided smoothly beneath leafy overhangs and cast-iron bridges, past old warehouses with vines curling along their edges. Moorhens darted out from the reeds, their chicks trailing behind like fuzzy punctuation marks. On the far bank, a heron stood frozen, tall and regal in the water's reflection. "This is ridiculously picturesque," she admitted, leaning back against the side of the boat.

"I'm aiming for a cinematic feel," Owen said, steering with one hand while passing her a plastic flute of Prosecco with the other. The sun shimmered on the water, casting everything in a golden glow. For a while, only the slap of the shifting water and the occasional rustle of waterfowl filled the air. Then, just as they approached a long stretch of overgrown bank with no one nearby, the boat decided it had gone far enough for one day and politely emitted an ominous cough. Following which, it stealthily stalled and allowed its engine to die. Owen frowned and tried the ignition a few times. Nothing happened.

"Is it out of battery? Have we run over a fish?" Dulcie asked, looking around as though a shoal of killer carp might erupt from the reeds in protest.

"Doubt it. Anyway, the motor runs on petrol. It seems to be deadlocked in some way, like a circuit-breaker scenario. I expect a knot of weeds has got caught in the propeller."

He reached for his phone and dialled the boat company's number. It rang out. "No answer," he said, frowning. "They said they'd be there until five, but maybe they're on lunch. I'll send them a message." He began texting furiously, both thumbs a blur.

"Do you really think it's weeds, or is it something more sinister?" Dulcie tried to calm her nerves with nonsense. "Is this the start of a slow-burn river horror, where we will be stranded and turn to cannibalism? I know it sounds far-fetched, but you were aiming for a vision suitable for the cinema."

Owen grinned and started unbuttoning his shirt. "Talking of which...let's turn this into an action movie."

"Wait! What on earth are you doing? I'm not starting any action, I'm not that kind of girl."

"I'm going in, over the side," he said, handing her his phone. "Film me swimming in the river and saving the day. I'll send the footage to the boat company. We might get a discount."

"You aren't serious?"

"No, of course not. Not about the discount anyway." He slipped off his jeans. "But I am going to dive in. I'll check the motor from underneath and pull us over to the bank."

"Don't do that! You'll get tangled." Dulcie gripped the sides of the boat, which had begun rocking as Owen stripped off his socks. "What if you drown? What if a pike takes your foot off?"

"I don't think either of those scenarios is very likely. Besides, there's nothing else for it. Unless we simply sit and drift downstream to goodness knows where?"

"I could ring Uncle Les."

What's he going to do, run out and rescue us with a giant fishing net? By the time he gets here, we will be halfway out to sea, waving to the tourists on the sunset cruises. Look, I'm very good at swimming," he said, standing in just his boxer shorts now, pale skin catching the sun. "And besides, you'll be there to save me if I need saving."

"Right! Because I'm *such* a strong swimmer, what with my 25-meter badge and everything. I don't think so!" But before she could talk him out of it, Owen pinched his nose, muttered something about going for glory, and rolled himself slowly over the side of the boat. Dulcie let out a little scream.

There was a heavy, watery splash, then a brief silence.

He stood up.

The water reached a point just above his knees.

"As rescue missions go, this is something of an anti-climax." He burst out laughing. "It's a lot shallower in this section than I thought." Still chuckling, he tugged the boat toward the bank, mooring it under the gentle sweep of a willow tree. The branches trailed into the water like loose green ribbons. Once it was secured, Owen climbed back in, dripping but triumphant. He picked up his clothes and threw them onto the bank before stepping back into the shallows and helping her to disembark.

They laid the blanket out on a small grassy patch a little above the waterline, far enough from the path to feel hidden. The willow shaded them from the sun, and the food was laid out in its shadow. Owen got partially re-dressed, and sat by her side, cold, content, and slightly damp.

"This whole thing," she said, gesturing vaguely at the picnic basket, the fizzing bottle of half-finished Prosecco, the grass-stained blanket beneath them. "It's lovely, but it's not exactly... standard dating etiquette, is it?"

"Well," he said, "we did set out for a pretty typical picnic, on a perfectly respectable, if somewhat ancient hired boat."

"Which then promptly conked out in the middle of nowhere." Dulcie pointed out.

"Whereupon I heroically waded through twelve inches of terrifying river shallows."

"To rescue us both from a fate worse than mild inconvenience?"

"Exactly so. Not enough credit is given for rescuing damsels in distress from sticky situations, in my opinion." Owen ran his hand through his wet hair. "Remind me to review my autumn-term lecture with you someday; it addresses that very injustice. A fair maiden, saved from the raging torrents." He waved his arm at the tranquil water in front of them. For a while, they watched the river flowing by, gentle ripples reflecting their mellow mood.

"I'm trying to say that we're not doing this in the normal order, are we?" Dulcie murmured.

"What would that order look like?"

She shrugged, pulling her knees up to her chest. "I don't know. Meet somewhere appropriately cheap and cheerful. Have a few dates involving tapas. Flirt over coffee, maybe a slow kiss in the rain."

"I can't give you tapas, or coffee, or rain, come to that. But I will kiss you slow, or fast or anyway you like." He reached for her hand. She laced her fingers through his, and he lay back on the blanket, pulling her with him.

The sun had dipped lower by the time they pulled apart, flushed and laughing, their limbs tangled like vines. The bulrushes around them, whispered in the late afternoon breeze, and the soft pop of Prosecco bubbles was long forgotten. Owen retrieved his shirt from somewhere behind the willow. Dulcie's hair was a wild halo. Her lips were pink from kissing, her cheeks warmer than the wine.

"Okay," she murmured, breathless, "I like this version of boating."

He gave a low laugh and trailed his fingers lightly along her arm. "We can add it to the list of things we're strangely good at together."

"Let me guess. We seem to be great at chatting, blanket snogging and wine tasting?"

"Shallow-water drama and synchronised eye-rolling," he said, pulling his damp trainers back on.

"You're funny."

"Funny 'haha' or funny 'peculiar'?"

"A bit of both. But I like it and I don't want you to stop."

Dulcie said.

Owen shifted, propped himself on an elbow, and looked at her with a gravity that made her chest tighten. "Me neither." They kissed again. It was deeper this time, less teasing, more intent. His hand slid to her waist, hers into his hair, and the need between them surged, full-bodied and immediate.

A distant dog barked. A cyclist zipped past on the nearby towpath. Somewhere, a toddler shouted, "Look, Mummy! A duck!"

They both groaned. "We really can't do this here," Owen muttered, rolling onto his back with a frustrated sigh. "Unless you're into exhibitionism, which I feel is a conversation we should've had earlier."

They lay together for a beat, catching their breath, arms entwined and hearts still a little wild.

"Okay," she said at last. "Where do we go, then? Your flat?"

Owen's heart soared. He hadn't dared to make the suggestion himself, but it was what he wanted more than anything. He hesitated. "There's... a complication."

"I suppose that you're talking about Tristan?"

We share the flat. I don't want to make things awkward or more challenging for him, but also—I don't want to keep us a secret. Not out of guilt."

"I understand. I live with Les, and let's say he doesn't always remember to knock. But Tristan is a grown man who probably already knows that we're an item. After all, it was him who tipped me the wink that you were single. Besides, what choice do we have, given that we can't avoid him forever?"

"You're right… Let's go back to mine." He nodded, eyes flicking up to hers.

"You sure?"

"I am if you are," he said, decisive now. "It's inevitable that Tristan sees we are together now. I'm not hiding it."

"All right. But if I have an unexpected eye-contact moment in the hallway with him while half-dressed, I'm blaming you."

"Noted. I'll shield you with a throw pillow if it comes to that. Not that I'm planning on letting you wander the corridors, or indeed, leaving you half-dressed."

"I'm looking forward to hearing the rest of your plans." She pulled him by the collar of his shirt and kissed him seductively on the lips.

"Should I remind you that we're still in public?" Owen asked, catching his breath.

"Which is a rotten shame," Dulcie murmured, resting her head on his chest.

"We could walk back to the boat yard. Let them know the boat conked out. Then… we head home."

She sat up slowly, smoothing her hair. "Finish what we started?"

"Hell yes."

As they walked hand-in-hand along the towpath toward the boat hire kiosk, Dulcie glanced up at Owen. "This has been a fantastic first date. Spending time with you is the best kind of fun. And this is a gorgeous spot, which I didn't even know existed in this part of the city." Their hands gripped a little tighter. "You do realise," she said, "that jumping into knee-deep water may be the most romantic thing anyone's ever done for me?"

"Wait until I ruin dinner later. Then you'll be completely smitten. I'm starting to think we might be the kind of couple who makes chaos look romantic."

She squeezed his hand. "Then let's go make a little more chaos."

CHAPTER 39

It was still early when Dulcie woke up. Not the frantic kind of early, where an alarm clock drills into your skull or a bin lorry rumbles past your window. This was the subtle kind, where the light filters in slowly, soft as a breath, and for a moment, you don't quite remember where you are. She stirred beneath the sheet, her skin warm against the cool cotton, still sensitive, still aware. She blinked up at the ceiling, not rushing to move. Then, turning her head, she looked across at Owen. Fast asleep, he was curled toward her, one arm flung across his pillow, hair rumpled and mouth slightly parted. There was something so peaceful and vulnerable about the way he slept. She let her gaze drift over the room. It was, undeniably, a man's room. The walls featured small folklore sketches thumbtacked in various spots. Not the whimsical fairy type, thank goodness, but cautionary tale images of goblins, golems, and giants. A worn brown leather armchair was positioned by the window, and above it, a plant on the windowsill was doing its best to flourish, or at least, trying to look like it was.

Last night had been really special. It hadn't been about timing or merely acting on some long-simmering desire. It was more instinctive than that. No nerves, no second-guessing. Just the steady realisation of something they'd both known for a while. She let her hand drift across the bed, fingers brushing against his. It had been undeniably emotional, wildly enjoyable, perfect in every way. From the moment Owen locked the door behind them and took her hand, everything seemed to unfold naturally, two people moving toward each other in time and space to reach a point of union. He stirred beside her. "Are you watching me sleep?" His voice was hoarse, his eyes still closed.

"No," she lied, smiling. "I'm studying the early morning light move across your woefully disorganised bookshelf."

"Sexy."

He opened one eye, looked at her, and smiled the kind of smile that made her heart lurch a little.

"Hi," he said.

"Hi." She leaned over and kissed his shoulder, then his collarbone. He pulled her gently against him, skin to skin, and they lay there for a long moment in the hush of new morning. Eventually, he sighed.

"We're going to have to face Tristan at some point."

"You had to bring him up, didn't you?" Dulcie groaned into his chest.

"Like ripping off a plaster." Owen gently kissed her head. "It might feel awkward at first, but it will pass quickly. Tristan is like a magpie; he'll soon be distracted by someone else with shiny hair."

"You flatter me. How nice to know I'll be so easily replaced in his affections."

"Make your mind up." He poked her playfully in the ribs. "I thought you wanted him to know that there is no hope, given that the better man has well and truly won you over."

"No regrets then?"

"What? Last night?" He tilted her chin so she met his gaze. "I've wanted last night to happen for a long time. No regrets. Just...an overwhelming desire for more mornings like this."

There was a knock at the door. They both froze. Another knock. Louder this time. Followed by a very familiar voice.

"Mate, are you awake?" Tristan called. "Have you seen the bike lock key? You said I could borrow it this morning to get over to Clapham Common.

Dulcie buried her face in the pillow.

Giving her a look of exaggerated pain, Owen rolled out of bed, pulling on a T-shirt and stepping into joggers. "I'm coming," he called out, voice casual. Then, under his breath to her: "Wish me luck."

He cracked open the door and stepped out. Dulcie listened. There was a pause. A thump of feet. A short, awkward silence. She cringed, pulling the covers over her head. A few minutes later, Owen returned, closing the door quietly behind him.

"Well, how did it go?"

"He took it really hard. He's heartbroken, broke down in sobs."

"Did he really?"

"No." He shrugged. "The reason he wants to borrow my

bike is that he's off to host a boozy corporate event, where he plans to seduce the fragrant CEO, then nip around the corner during the speeches to visit an old flame. I think it's fair to say he is over the worst." He crossed over to her in two long strides, cupped her face, and kissed her like it was the first time all over again.

"Wow, he really is a mile wide and an inch deep."

"Don't judge him too harshly; he's a good person at heart. As a matter of fact, he's heading over to Kays before starting his workday. She plans to store all her stage props and rearrange her rooms. Make a fresh start. I think she enjoys his company, and he knows it."

"You're telling me that he's off to do something out of the kindness of his heart? He certainly is a man of contrasts." Dulcie looked unconvinced.

"Enough about him." Owen rolled back onto the bed. "Let me show my appreciation for the woman who made the right choice, in the end. Because she is the best thing that's ever happened in the whole, wide, Road." Dulcie threw a pillow at his head.

After Owen's backhanded compliment and the lovemaking that followed, it took them a while to disentangle themselves from each other. They remained close, savouring a blissful afterglow. Words were unnecessary; everything had been communicated through their limbs, their touches, the whisper of their breaths. Eventually, Dulcie pulled the sheet around her and stood, stretching. She looked out of the window at the workshop below and felt a sense of homecoming. Queen of all she surveyed. "I feel like I've been rolled in velvet and left out in the sun."

Owen, already half-dressed and leaning against the doorframe, looked at her with such contentment she almost blushed. "I'm glad I could contribute."

"You know what I need now?"

"Food? Applause? More me?"

"A bath," she grinned over her shoulder. "Hot water and silence. And maybe one of those scented bombs that smells like a lemon tree."

"Would you settle for a splash of Super Matey? My mum always bought me one for Christmas, and she never got out of the habit."

"Sounds perfect." She disappeared into the bathroom, added a slug of blue bubble bath and watched the water swirl as it filled the tub. Steam began to fog the mirror, and she turned off the hot tap, leaving the cold to splash onto the crested foam. Untying the belt of Owen's dressing gown, she reached to pick up a sponge when her phone buzzed loudly on the bathroom shelf. She frowned, noting with surprise that it was a call from Maccie, and he answered with a smile. "Maccie, are you ringing to ask another favour, because…?"

Maccie's voice interrupted, urgent, taut, tighter than she'd ever heard it.

"Dulcie. You need to come now. It's Les."

"What's happened?"

"I popped by to drop off those gloves, from the… well, from our little adventure. Found him slumped in his chair. Foot's swollen up like a football. He wasn't breathing right. Said he didn't want to be a bother. Didn't want to be a bother, Dulcie. He looked grey."

Her throat tightened. "When did this happen?"

"A couple of hours ago. I've been ringing your phone, but I guess it was switched off, and I didn't know where you were."

"Where is he now?"

"I called an ambulance. They've taken him to King's College Hospital, and they're running tests now. I went with him, but you need to come."

"I'll be there. I'm on my way."

She ended the call with numb fingers. Her heart was pounding so loudly that she could barely hear her own thoughts.

"Owen!" she called, rushing out of the bathroom, her voice thick with panic.

He appeared instantly in the doorway, half-alarmed, half-expecting a prank. She looked up at him, eyes wide. "It's Les. He's in the hospital. Maccie found him—his foot was swollen, he's short of breath. They've taken him to King's."

Owen didn't hesitate. "Let's go." He grabbed his keys and shoes without another word. Dulcie threw on her coat, and they tore down the flat stairs. Owen didn't even stop to lock the door behind them. They were out on the street seconds later, running towards the taxi rank on the next street. The quiet morning was shattered by the slap of shoes on pavement and the sound of her heart thrumming faster than she could speak.

"Please be okay," Dulcie whispered to no one in particular.

Reaching over, Owen grabbed her hand mid-run, squeezing it tightly. "He will be. He's stubborn. He's got you to get back to."

But neither of them was comforted.
They just ran harder.

CHAPTER 40

Lying on a hospital trolley, Les was in a curtained cubicle when Dulcie and Owen arrived. His legs were slightly raised, and his chest was dotted with sticky pads connected to a heart rate monitor. His hair was tousled, his robe was open at the chest, and an oxygen tube was clipped to his nostrils. Despite his appearance, he managed to greet them in his usual off-hand manner. "Well, well, if it isn't the cavalry," he said. "I was beginning to think I'd been forgotten. Abandoned like an overripe pear."

Dulcie hurried to his side and grasped his hand gently. "Uncle Les. You scared me half to death."

"I scared myself. Do you know how undignified it is to be carted out of your home on a stretcher, one sock on and the other one off?"

"You look like you've made yourself at home, anyway." Owen squeezed Les's shoulder.

"I've been given a dose of blood thinner, a cup of tea, and a digestive biscuit," Les said with a flourish. "I give this hotel three stars."

Maccie shuffled in from the corner carrying a plastic chair "It's your turn now, you old rascal," he declared. "Time to be the malingerer."

"Malingering?" Les scoffed. "They think I've fractured a bone in my foot and that's sent everything haywire."

"Only you could damage himself falling over a box of jellied sweets."

"No one but me would have been trying to replace chocolates at Bunces whilst they were in the middle of a stocktake. All of which, I might remind you, was your idea in the first place, Maccie."

Around them, the A&E department pulsed with activity. Fluorescent lights buzzed overhead, and the air was thick with the mingled scents of antiseptic, sweat, and fatigue. A child cried somewhere behind the curtain that separated Les from the other patients.

What are they saying about your breathing, Uncle Les?"

"I'm not sure, something about the fracture causing a clot and the clot swimming about in places where it didn't ought to be."

The colour in Les's face was improving, his eyes alert and cheeky as ever, but Dulcie couldn't shake the image of him slumped in his chair, alone, breathless and silent, refusing to ask for help because he didn't want to be a bother.

"I should've known something was wrong," she fretted.

"Don't you go blaming yourself, sweetheart. I've made an art form out of playing down minor catastrophes. If there were an Olympic event for being 'absolutely fine, come what may,' I'd take the gold medal every time."

"But I should have realised you weren't well. I could tell your limp was getting worse, and when your foot ballooned. I should have made you see the doctor."

"You know I can't stand a fuss. I popped a packet of frozen peas on my leg and I thought it would be grand in a day or two. I'll know for next time." Les teased. "Look on the bright side, the nurses are delightful."

"I knew it," Maccie said triumphantly. "You're only here to chat up the staff. Shameless. And here's me knowing that you hate hospitals and thinking that you would be desperate to get free as soon as you were admitted. Looks like I brought a shovel to dig an escape tunnel under the ward for nothing."

"I'm not a big fan of places like this." Les agreed. "But there's no need to break me out of chokey just yet. As it happens, my nurse is terrific, but not my type. Here he is now:"

The curtain yanked aside, and in stepped Tyrese, a man in his late twenties, sharp-featured and frowning. "Oh, Les," he said, exasperated. "You've slid halfway to the floor again. What are you doing, trying to escape through the foot of the bed?" He helped Les adjust his position and carefully placed a thermometer in his ear. Then he looked at the beeping monitor and stood waiting as activity swirled around them. A paramedic swept past them, hastily transporting a new patient, while a nurse relayed updates through a headset. Phones rang, and the waiting room nearby hummed with murmurs, coughs, and distant voices. Tyrese took the thermometer out and shook it. "Not too bad, I'd prefer to see it lower."

"I like to live on the edge."

"Is that so?" asked Tyrese. "Well, the only place you are going to live for the next few days is here. You're being admitted for observation. We need to monitor you closely and decide the best course of treatment," he explained. "That means you will need some things from home. Pyjamas, slippers, phone charger, and any medications." His eyes swept across the group. "Can one of you bring those in for him?

"Yes, of course." Dulcie said, "Now that I've seen he's in good hands, I'll be happy to go back home and..." Her eyes widened; she clapped her hand over her mouth. "Oh my God," she whispered. "The bath."

Owen looked up sharply. "What?"

"I left it running." Dulcie stood up so quickly that her chair nearly tipped. "At your flat. The bubble bath. I was adding a bit of cold water when the phone rang, and I forgot all about it."

Owen's mouth fell open in horror. "That was... over an hour ago. He pulled out his phone with the urgency of a man calling emergency services. "Tristan. He might still be at Kay's house.

"Will he answer?" Dulcie asked, already pacing.

"He'd better."

"What are you saying?" Les was confused, trying to keep up with the conversation. "Have you left the taps on? Is my house filling with foam?" He pushed back into the pillows. "It's going to set me back, this. I can't even have an emergency in peace."

Everyone stared at Owen's phone, willing it to make a connection. At last, someone picked up. "Tristan, it's me. No time for that. Listen, I need you to run back to our flat and turn off the bathroom taps. Dulcie left the bath running. Yes. Just do it. Towels. Towels everywhere. Now, go! Thanks."

He hung up and sighed, pinching the bridge of his nose. "He's ready to save the day. We caught him just in time; he was still next door.

"Thank goodness for that!" Les wiped his brow. "I turn my back for one minute and my house nearly sails off down the street on a tide of water." He put one hand over his heart. "It's just as well Tristan was around. He's a terrific lad, the kind you can rely on. I've always said so."

The monitor next to his patient had started blipping madly, but now calmed again. Tyrese turned and regarded it for a moment. "I'll say something for this job: it may be underpaid and undervalued, but you never know what excitement the day will bring." He put two fingers on his wrist. "I had half a mind to check my own heart rate when you were trying to get through to your friend."

"We'd better get back and help Tristan do whatever we can," said Owen.

"Good. Go," said Tyrese. There are already too many of you here. I was about to tell you that this many visitors aren't allowed. He paused. "Don't tell me there's another one arrived?"

Jamila appeared around the curtain, holding a modest bunch of irises, her face a mask of concern. She took in the scene around the makeshift bed. "How's our hero?"

"Flirting with death and the nurse," Maccie announced.

"Not this one," Les mumbled, making room as Jamila leaned in to kiss his cheek.

Tyrese crossed his arms. "I'll have you know I'm very popular with the over-60's, as a rule."

"Uncle Les is doing okay, but I may have... accidentally set in motion a bath-related flood back at home. I'm so sorry," Dulcie said sheepishly.

"Ah," Jamila nodded. "No need to apologise to me. I'm in the top flat, so my feet will stay dry. Let's focus on what really matters here," she said, her voice trembling with the relief that comes when something might have gone terribly wrong but didn't. "Are you going to be okay, Les? How are you feeling now?"

"Could have been worse. Much worse." Said Les, milking the crowd for sympathy. "I felt the grim reaper standing behind me in the shadows for a while there."

"You're the most dramatic man I've cared for this month, and one of my patients is a Shakespearean actor," said Tyrese, pouring Les a drink from a fresh jug of water and rearranging his pillows again. "You keep slouching like that, and you'll undo everything I've done for you so far." He turned to the visitors. "Now, two of you need to leave, or I'll get my card punched by the doctor."

Dulcie took Owen by the hand, and they moved to the end of the bed. She badly wanted to stay and keep Les under her watchful eye. Nothing but a calamity would have torn her from his side, but fate had sparked a crisis of her own making, and there was nothing for it but to go home and face the music. "We'll be back this evening to see you on the ward," she said. "Behave yourself until then."

"If there's one thing I've learned in life," said Les, "it's that behaving yourself is highly overrated. Now get away with you. Go and bail out what's left of my house." He waved them away vigorously and slipped further down the bed.

CHAPTER 41

The sun was out, casting crisp shadows across the pavement, the kind of weather that didn't match the mood. As the taxi turned onto Minet Road, Dulcie leaned forward, straining to catch a glimpse of the house, as if the damage done might already be visible from the street.

"The door's wide open, Owen," she said quietly.

He followed her gaze. The front door was fully agape, like someone had left in a hurry or hadn't bothered to close it behind them going in.

"Can you see any water?" she asked.

"No. That's something, I guess. Honestly thought we'd pull up and see the front steps looking like Niagara Falls."

They paid off the taxi and hurried up to the door. As soon as they entered, a heavy smell enveloped them. Damp and muddy, the air was filled with the scent of soaked fabric and warped wood, accented by a faint floral note that could be disinfectant or floor cleaner. The hallway was a scene of functional chaos. Buckets and mixing bowls were scattered in a rough line down the corridor. Towels crisscrossed the floor like an enormous patchwork rug. Footsteps pattered upstairs, and the drip of wet materials being wrung out filled the air.

In the middle of it all, Tristan was holding a bath sheet, limp with water. He turned as they entered, relief on his exhausted face. "You're here," he said, and moved toward them like he wasn't sure whether to hug them or collapse.

"How bad is it?" Owen asked, carefully stepping over a cluster of bowls.

"It's all under control now, and probably not as bad as it looks, but when I arrived, water was pouring from the hall light. The bath was still running. Everything was wet – the floorboards, rugs, even the post on the mat. I panicked. I called everyone."

"What do you mean, everyone?"

"Our friends." Tristan said, "They all showed up."

From the stairwell, Iden emerged carrying a mop and a fluorescent towel. His shirt was damp, hair sticking to his forehead. "Second-floor landing is sorted. I think that's the worst of it."

Tom leaned over the handrail. "Someone owes me a pair of socks," he said, wringing them out, to the side of his bare feet. Altheya passed behind them with a large mixing bowl full of greyish water. Jen was kneeling in the front hall on a dry patch, carefully wringing out a tea towel with slow, focused movements.

Dulcie stood still. She scanned the hallway—every towel, every face, every improvised cleanup effort. "You called everyone?" she repeated.

"Everyone who might be free to spare us some time. I didn't know what else to do," Tristan said. "I thought it would take days. I figured... we'd need help."

Owen let out a slow breath and put his thumb in the air in a gesture to Tom. "Appreciate it, man."

"No problem. All hands to the deck."

Dulcie crouched beside Jen and placed a hand on her shoulder. "I don't know what to say."

"Then don't," Jen said without looking up. "Just grab a towel."

Owen began to assess the water damage. In the ground-floor flat, a section of the ceiling was visibly stained, with off-white plaster turning yellow and forming concentric rings that darkened inward. The stairwell wallpaper had peeled away in long, curling strips, exposing bare plaster. Some baseboards had swollen and bubbled, as if the house had developed a fever.

Up in his flat, the floorboards near the kitchen had buckled unevenly, causing the small table to lean to the right. A rug beside the sofa was completely soaked and looked heavy, dark, and waterlogged. A damp shadow was spreading up the side of the leather armchair by the window. Altheya had taken control of the most affected bedroom, which was Tristan's. She'd unplugged his lamp and tilted the bed frame into the corner, jamming it alongside a bedside table and two under-bed storage tubs. The duvet lay in a damp heap on the windowsill, drying in the sunlight coming through the open window. Clothes were gathered into a pile on a chair.

Tristan hovered, biting his lip. "That's the one room I didn't get to yet."

Out in the yard, Iden created a makeshift drying station in the garden, with towels hanging from fences, railings, and deck chairs. Tom had turned a standing fan to its maximum setting and stood next to it, like a lifeguard.

It wasn't a disaster, but it wasn't insignificant either. "We'll fix it," Owen said to Dulcie, pausing beside her as she dried the base of the radiator, brushing a damp curl from her forehead and putting his arm around her shoulders.

"It's such a mess," she said, close to tears. "I can't believe I could have been so stupid. When the phone call came, my mind was numb to everything except getting to the hospital. Now I've caused all this trouble, and everything looks so awful." She stood up and buried her face in his shoulder, feeling his arms close around her in a comforting hug.

"It's cosmetic damage mostly," he whispered to her. "The bath filled up quickly, but drained almost as fast down the overflow, so that slowed the amount of water spilling over the sides. If the pipe had backed up, we'd be looking at structural repairs." He went on quickly to reassure her. "This? We can manage to sort all of this."

"I hope so. Uncle Les said the insurance excess on water damage is astronomical. I don't want him worrying about this right now. He needs to concentrate on getting better."

Owen pulled her even closer, holding her tight. They remained pressed in an embrace for several minutes, until the urgency to rejoin the cleanup effort grew stronger than their need to stay locked together.

An hour later, the worst had passed. The remaining water was mopped up. Buckets emptied. Damp towels now clung to railings, fences, and the backs of mismatched chairs out in the garden. Dulcie's workshop had become an impromptu tea station. A row of mugs, each chipped or splattered with old paint, sat beside opened packets of biscuits and jars of tea bags.

"I don't even like tea," Iden said, sipping anyway. "But this herbal one is hitting the spot."

The garden looked like a surreal laundromat. Towels flapped in the breeze like faded flags. Jen lay flat on a sun-dried bath mat, arms stretched wide. "Did we just save a house?" she asked.

"I think we invented a new type of emergency service," said Altheya. "Flood Response: Friends Edition."

"Team Soggy," Tom said, dunking a biscuit.

Dulcie sank onto the step outside her workshop beside Owen. Her mug warmed both hands. She turned to him. "One thing is for sure, and that is I'm never leaving a bath running unattended again."

"You did promise me a romance full of chaos," he said, nudging her shoulder. "I guess this counts. It seems to me that we had better stick together, because the truth is, you've spoiled me for any other woman."

"In what way?"

"My gorgeous, funny, adorable Dulcie." He kissed her on the nose. "How could I return to normal dating after this? Who needs to watch movies or a soap opera when there's a chance to live in a real-life drama? Look back on the time we have spent together and tell me this: has any part of it been boring?"

"There was that chat at the bus stop…"

He pulled her onto his lap and gave her a bear hug, both of them laughing as the deckchair overbalanced and tipped them unceremoniously onto the floor.

CHAPTER 42

The next morning, Dulcie stood at the top of the stairs, a mug of tea cooling in her hands, and surveyed the damage properly in the grey light of day. It was as bad as she had remembered.

Damp had crept like invisible ivy along the walls, puckering the paint and leaving shadows where water had pooled. Down in the garden flat, the walls were streaked and stained. The air smelled of plaster dust and bubble bath. She turned to Owen, who was holding a clipboard and a pencil with all the grim focus of someone pretending he knew what "structural drying times" meant. "I think we will need the entire contents of a DIY shop to put this right." He set the clipboard down. "And a miracle."

On cue, a firm knock echoed up from the front door. Dulcie padded down the stairs barefoot and pulled the door open. Standing in the morning light, like a woman fresh from a black-and-white film reel, was Kay Kenneths, fully made-up at nine in the morning, wearing a navy trench coat, a crisp silk scarf, and an air of determination.

"Darling," she said, lifting the sunglasses she was wearing despite the overcast sky. "I heard."

Behind her, a rumble of movement came from a massive pantechnicon lorry. It bore the legend 'South East Theatricals' and, with its tailgate down, it took up the spaces usually reserved by five or six cars.

"What's going on, Kay?"

"Reparation." Kay stepped aside with a flourish. And there, lining up behind her like a very organised army, was a team of five men and one woman—all in dusty boiler suits, tool belts jingling, paint cans swinging, a dust sheet rolled under one arm, and a stepladder already halfway unfolded.

"Kay..." Owen appeared behind Dulcie, his eyes wide. "What is this? Who are all these people?"

She gave a modest shrug. "You could call it a well-timed coincidence. Or a very slight abuse of my remaining influence. The team are here to repair the damage for you," Kay explained. "Central's production of 'The Running Game' has gone dark. Which is theatre speak for 'closed early.' Bad reviews. Worse ticket sales. But every cloud, and all that. These wonderful souls were let go yesterday and were at a loose end. So I called in some favours."

The shortest of the men, a stocky fellow with a pencil behind his ear, joined them on the doorstep. "You must be the couple with the overflowing bath. Easy done. And easy to sort out, if you have the right tools and know-how, which we do." He pulled a pencil from behind his ear and licked the tip before making a mark in his small, red notebook. "We've got patching, papering and re-painting on the list. We'll need to work fast, but it's nothing we haven't done between matinee and evening shows before."

"Are all these people set designers?" Dulcie asked, dumbfounded.

"My dear," Kay said, smoothing her scarf, "They are some of the finest scenery builders in South London. Give them two hours and they can make a ballroom out of balsa wood. I can assure you that a little flood damage won't be a challenge to them."

Owen looked around at the crew, already unpacking brushes and laying down tarps. "This is... incredible, Kay."

"I may no longer be a leading lady, but I still have some influence. And after everything you all did for me—covering for me, not judging me, looking out for me—well. This is the very least I can do."

"This is too much." Dulcie stepped forward, suddenly overwhelmed.

"Not at all. I'm glad to have the opportunity to repay you. Les means a lot to me. So do you. And I can't bear the thought of him coming home from the hospital to a ruin. We'll have it sorted in the shake of a lamb's tail. Now step back and watch the magic happen."

The cluster of tradespeople filed past them, toolboxes and decorating supplies swinging at their sides. Paint-stained overalls, high-vis jackets, and the low hum of efficient chatter filled the air. One peeled off to inspect the curling wallpaper by the stairs; another ducked beneath the understairs cupboard with a flashlight. "We'll need dehumidifiers in both bedrooms," someone called. "That cornice is cracked—we'll patch and repaint." Another voice chimed in, "Skirting's warped here. Add that to the list." Jobs were claimed without fuss. They moved with rhythm and purpose, the house absorbing their energy like a film set.

One of the decorators called up from the hallway, "Do you want this jazz picture on the floor re-framed or float-mounted?"

"Framed," Dulcie said instinctively. "He likes a clean edge."

The decorator gave a thumbs-up and got to work.

Owen put an arm around Dulcie's shoulders as she looked around the flat, watching the quiet miracle unfold. "You okay?" he asked softly.

"I was so sure this was going to take weeks. That I'd ruined everything."

"You didn't ruin anything. There's nothing that can't be fixed, and we've got help now."

Kay turned on her heel, already issuing orders. "Someone bring me a colour chart. That kitchen wall is dying for a richer tone."

The team worked like magic. Within minutes, the garden flat echoed with the hum of power tools and the slip-slip-slop of paint hitting plaster. Ladders appeared from nowhere. Dust sheets unfurled with theatrical flair. Someone had a Bluetooth speaker blasting 70s funk, which no one questioned, least of all the man painting the skirting boards while occasionally breaking into song.

Upstairs, the hallway was already being transformed and the smell of fresh gloss mingled with the scent of coffee and paint thinner. Standing in the middle of it all, tea forgotten, arms loosely crossed, Dulcie watched the unfolding tableau like someone who had wandered into the closing scene of a feel-good film. Men in overalls danced past her with rollers and brushes. A woman in a tool belt was negotiating firmly with a wallpaper steamer. She turned to Kay, who stood near the window, sunglasses still on, giving silent, approving nods at the progress around her like a major inspecting her battalion.

"Thank you," Dulcie said, the words slipping out quietly but carrying weight. "I mean it, from the bottom of my heart."

Brushing the thanks aside, Kay waved her hand in the air. "Please. Save your gratitude. Just promise me you'll keep being kind to mature women with expensive tastes and illicit habits."

"I promise," she agreed. "They say that fate repays a kind deed, and I guess it must be true, but I didn't expect it to be this quick." She smiled. "It's going to look amazing when it's done. Let's not tell Uncle Les about all this before he gets home."

"Your wish is my command," said Kay, enjoying her role of fairy godmother.

"I can't wait to see the look on his face." Dulcie said, hugging herself with glee. Surrounded by clatter, bustle and activity, she allowed herself to believe that things might not just be repaired, they might actually be improved. Rewritten with better paint, brighter finishes, and restored by acquaintances who knew how to hold a roller and a secret at the same time.

CHAPTER 43

Three days later, Les returned home in a wheelchair he referred to as his "temporary chariot," pushed by Maccie, who looked both bored and bemused as Les regaled him with a passionate monologue on the decline of hospital puddings. "Back in my day, sponge cake had actual sponge. Texture, you know? Not bland, moist nothingness. Patients need feeding up, not filling with air." Les was in full flow. "Rice pudding with a sprinkle of scrunch on the top, now that's a dish that would put the nation back on its feet."

Tristan and Owen, who had been alerted to their arrival, raced into the street to help Maccie with the considerable task of pulling Les up the stone staircase, like an overstuffed emperor riding in a sedan. The front door was stretched wide by Dulcie, and Les entered his home backwards, giving instructions and clutching the arms of the chair, as if he feared being tipped out onto the pavement below.

As they pulled him into the hall, Les looked up and blinked.

For a moment, he thought he'd been delivered to the wrong house. He'd been expecting the worst. The reports Jamila had given him led him to believe that he was returning to a wreck. He was waiting to find a stained ceiling, bubbled skirting and peeling wallpaper. In their place were smooth, freshly painted surfaces in warm, inviting colours. Even the print of the jazz trumpeter had been re-framed and returned to its spot with loving precision.

"Surprise!" Dulcie stepped in front of him with a nervous smile. "Welcome home." Behind her, Owen gave a little wave. Jamila appeared beside them holding a homemade Victoria sponge. Maccie leaned on the doorframe, and Kay Kenneths stood tall at the back, resplendent in a tailored blazer and lipstick just a few shades shy of theatrical red.

Les took it all in. "Are you sure we've come to the right place?" he said slowly.

"Freshly revived," Owen said. "Walls, floors, light fittings… even the kettle got a polish."

"Thanks to Kay and her army of set builders," Dulcie added. "She called in a few favours." Kay stepped forward, chin lifted. "Darling, if I had known it would take near-death experience and a minor flood to refurbish the entire place, I would've staged an intervention months ago."

"You redecorated my whole house?"

"Parts of it anyway," Tristan said. "Our flat upstairs looks better than ever, and you saw how fancy the hallway is."

Straining to shift around in his wheelchair, Les took it all in, his eyes wide as he scrutinised the transformation. He turned his head slowly, his hands resting lightly on the wheels. "I can't believe it," he said. "I've never had anything like this done for me." His voice trembled. "It's beautiful." He listened to the excited chatter taking place around him, "It's all down to them," he thought. "If there's one thing I've learned in life, it's the people within a house who make it a home."

"Doesn't it look marvellous?" said Dulcie, unable to contain her excitement.

"It does. And you..." Les gestured at them all. "You did all this. For me?" His eyes welled with emotion. Not enough for him to admit it, of course, but enough that he coughed and looked away as if adjusting his collar. "I wasn't expecting anything like this," he said, his voice rough. "That's what makes it... bloody marvellous."

They pushed Les further into his home. New rugs had been laid down in the garden flat, and a soft sheen gleamed above the polished kitchen counters. All of the walls were clean, fresh and covered in pastel shades of paint. On the table sat a vase of irises from Jamila, a tin of his favourite biscuits from Maccie, and a handwritten note from Tyrese the nurse, tucked beside a jar of marmalade: "No flirting, no falls. No betting. We await your karaoke updates." Les covered his hand with his mouth, then sniffed once. "I suppose," he said, clearing his throat, "this means I can cancel my plans to get out the lime wash and step-stool again."

"Too right, step-stools are banned forever," said Dulcie. "I think your flat missed you. And so did we."

"I don't know what to say," said Les, brushing his hands over his knees. "You've gone to so much trouble." He came to a decision. "I want to thank you properly. With a dinner.

A real, sit-down one." He raised his hands in the air like the ringmaster at a circus. "I will cook a magnificent feast for you all."

The smiles froze on their faces.

"Great idea, Les," said Maccie. But you don't want to be overdoing it, and you'll never be able to manoeuvre yourself between the cooker and the fridge. Perhaps we should wait until you are back to combat fitness? Or maybe we could go out for a bite to eat somewhere?"

"Nonsense," Les said firmly. "Where else could we find a dining spot as freshly decorated as this? We need to celebrate the new look, and this is the perfect place. Maccie, you'll be my second-in-command, and I will orchestrate the courses. The rest of you can serve as my assistants and later as V.I.P. guests." He rubbed his hands together, delighted at the ingenuity of his plans.

Realising they couldn't persuade Les to change his mind, they gathered to finalise the finer details that would bring the ambitious scheme together. They decided that it would be best to rearrange the front room on the appointed night, fix the wings on the dining table, and bring mismatched chairs from their various homes to seat everyone. Preparing it as a team, readying for Les's triumphant return as head of the table made the event feel more meaningful, like a true homecoming, and they got caught up in ideas.

"I shall bring my silver candelabras," announced Kay. "They make any occasion feel like an event."

"Sounds like a black-tie event," said Maccie. "I don't have an evening jacket, but I think I could dig out a dickie bow, to show willing."

"Music is my forte, so how about I bring a playlist along?" Tristan asked. "And if you fancy something special, I can give you a tune on that old harmonica. The one you bring out at Christmas, Les."

"I'll make a shopping list of ingredients," Dulcie hissed quietly to Owen. "If I keep it simple, then even Uncle Les won't be able to go too far wrong."

Jamila whispered. "And I'll bring sandwiches as a backup."

"Wise," Owen muttered as they moved together into the kitchen to make further plans.

CHAPTER 44

As dinner parties go, it was set to be a riotous affair. The lights glowed soft amber, the smell of rosemary and lamb hung in the air, and Kay Kenneths, dressed in a satin blouse and a statement brooch, was already rearranging cutlery and criticising the trifle. "It's leaning to the left," she said, peering at it. "Emotionally, I relate. But visually, it's tragic."

Beside the drinks trolley, Maccie was already pouring himself a generous whiskey. "If it tastes good, I don't care if it's doing the conga." He had taken on the role of head chef and warned everyone that the food would be hearty and filling, but not necessarily pretty.

Tristan arrived, freshly showered and more subdued than usual, carrying a bottle of decent red wine and a humble bouquet of daffodils. "Something cheerful," he said awkwardly, handing the flowers to Dulcie. "You said that yellow is your favourite colour."

"Thanks," she said, genuinely touched, passing them to

Owen and pointing at the vases in the dresser.

"Are you two a proper item now?" Tristan asked.

"Yep, more together than ever." Dulcie beamed at him.

"Good." Tristan nodded, then added as an aside, "You were always much more of a match. As a pair, you look like a match made in heaven."

"That's gracious."

"Personal growth," Tristan said. "Great for the skin, terrible for my therapist."

She laughed and kissed him on the cheek. "Glad you came."

"I nearly didn't. Then I remembered I'm the only one who enjoys Maccie's roast lamb and Kay's stories."

"Rude," Kay called from the living room without looking up. Dulcie and Tristan joined her and Les in the front room. They sank onto the sagging sofa, enjoying the aroma of dinner drifting in from the kitchen. All four glanced hungrily toward the door, as if Maccie might come in with a tray of hors d'oeuvres. He did not.

Crossing her legs elegantly, Kay gestured at the walls. "I was just telling Les that transforming this place, with a little help from my friends, has been such a success that I'm considering a second career in interior design."

"Really? I work with clients who'd love to have someone like you on their team. In general, they have no taste and big budgets. Ideal combination. I'd be happy to introduce you," offered Tristan.

Dulcie nodded. "And I can help you find quirky furniture as conversation pieces. I'm not sure what that is exactly, but the magazines are always featuring articles on that sort of thing."

Kay sipped her wine and smiled. "Excellent. Between the two of you, I might stay busy enough to avoid scandal. Or at least delay it." She gave them a conspiratorial wink.

"Saints preserve us," muttered Les, who was already positioned at the head of the dining table.

Coming through! Take your places, everyone. Dinner is served," announced Maccie. He carried a large serving dish into the room, placed it in front of Les, flicked the tea towel over his shoulder, and began scuttling between the rooms, delivering a series of hot, covered bowls full of potatoes and other trimmings.

With perfect timing, Jamila arrived at the door of the flat, and Owen let her in. She was wearing a fitted wool dress and carrying two tubs of hummus—one made with beetroot, the other with lemon. Les looked up at her, and his cheeks turned a little pink.

"Well," he said, clearing his throat, "someone's made an effort."

"I heard there'd be sherry trifle," Jamila said, as she placed the hummus next to the candlesticks displayed proudly on the table before sliding into the seat beside him. "So, I thought my outfit had better be up to the occasion."

"Well worth the effort. That's a cracker of a frock, I must say, although you do look a bit warm."

"I'm glowing," she replied. "Women of a certain age bring heat. I'm hot stuff."

That earned a wheezy laugh from Maccie and a twinkle in Les's eye.

Owen whispered something in Dulcie's ear, and she bit back a smile as she watched the pair of them bicker fondly over cutlery and mint sauce. The meal began, and as expected, it was a chaotic blend of flavours, opinions, and stories. Les, fuelled by wine and survival, held court between courses, telling his version of how Maccie "heroically crashed into the room" during the medical incident, knocking over a side table and spilling its contents onto the floor.

"I didn't crash in," Maccie protested. "I knocked! You didn't answer because you were slumped in a chair doing your impression of a dying swan."

"Everything was under control. I was going to tell you to come in, like any civilised person, but I needed a moment to catch my breath."

"You were turning blue and only had one sock on," Dulcie added.

"I was unwell. But now I'm in fine fettle and I want to thank all of you for everything you've done. I want to propose a toast." They all raised their glasses. "Blood may be thicker than water, but to my mind, family is where the roots grow. I'm surrounded by all the important people in my life tonight, so here's to us: 'The bedrock of Minute Road.'" Misty-eyed, they cheered and clinked their glasses, which took a while because of all the reaching across the table and tangling of arms.

Conversation slipped into comfortable grooves, between bites of melt-in-the-mouth dinner and double helpings of dessert. Owen offered to top them up with more wine, Kay sang the first line of an old stage number before forgetting the rest, and Tristan told a story about accidentally sitting on a commuter's sandwich, which restored his position as court jester for the evening. All the while, Jamila and Les circled each other in conversation, playfully teasing, closer than before. When Jamila leaned in to wipe a spot of gravy from his chin with her napkin, the entire table noticed and pretended not to.

After dinner, people spread into the living room. Maccie and Kay argued over who had the better handwriting. Tristan played a sad, wandering tune on Les's old harmonica, and someone admitted that the much-maligned trifle had been something of a triumph.

Out in the backyard, which was strung with warm lights in honour of the party, Dulcie and Owen huddled together on the backdoor steps. The hum of the city felt far away, softened by the late hour and the steady flicker of lamp lights from the street behind the houses. Dulcie traced the rim of her wine glass with her finger, then glanced at Owen, who had the look of someone gearing up to say something risky. "These past few weeks have been crazy." He turned to face her. "You know, I think I fell for you as soon as you turned up on the doorstep. I've told you how much you mean to me, and I don't see that changing anytime soon. These madcap adventures we've had seem to have put us onto fast-forward." The words were hesitant, as if they might land too hard if spoken too fast. "I think we might be heading towards love."

"I think so, too," said Dulcie, her face beaming with happiness. "My feelings for you came out of left field and took over the park." She gripped him tighter. "But I need to stay down here as much as I can for now. I have to keep a close eye on Uncle Les. He's got one good leg and a thousand stories. He needs me to reach the kettle and monitor his biscuit intake. At least for now."

"Of course. There's no need to rush this; neither of us is going anywhere. We don't have to share a flat to share a life."

She reached up and brushed his chin with her fingers. "Don't ever pass me on the stairs, not without a kiss"

"Never." He pulled her into his arms.

The everyday city hum persisted just beyond the fence, but in this peaceful corner glowing with lights, something magical was happening. Inside, the gathering was winding down, the slow unravel that occurs when people are too comfortable to leave but too tired to keep up the chatter. Jamila was massaging Les's shoulders with the skill of a street healer, claiming she was aiding his circulation. He didn't seem to mind. Kay, meanwhile, had decided to critique Maccie's bow tie, tilting her head as if evaluating art, offering unsolicited comments on its symmetry, colour, and thread quality. Maccie looked alarmed but remained still while she tugged at the fabric around his neck. Tristan, half-slumped across the arm of the sofa like a decorative throw, raised his glass in another lazy toast before refilling it. Late as it was, the room still echoed with soft laughter, clinking glasses, and the dregs of a playlist. But the party was putting on slippers and stretching its legs.

Just before midnight, Missy-Mae, resident cat and ever-watchful observer, slipped soundlessly through the open window and claimed the room's highest perch. With a fluid leap from the dresser, she landed near the door, barely stirring the air. Her amber eyes swept across the scene: the clutter of human lives, half-eaten food, tangled stories.

Tail held high like a banner for feline emancipation, she circled the room's edge with deliberate, slinky steps. Then, as silently as she had come, Missy-Mae vanished into the night, stealthy, dignified, and wholly unimpressed.

Printed in Dunstable, United Kingdom

66283794R00190